THE RELUCTANT CANARY SINGS

by Faith A. Colburn

Prairie Wind Press

ISBN-13: 978-0-9972677-2-3
ISBN-10: 0-9972677-2-0
Library of Congress Control Number: 2017950144
PRAIRIE WIND PRESS, North Platte, Nebraska

DEDICATION

To my mother, a city girl who made a better farm wife than girls who grew up on farms. She never got to tell her story.

ACKNOWLEDGEMENTS

I want to thank my mother, Ella Mae "Bobbie Bowen," for the gift of her voice. Few moments in my childhood existed without music. She sang when she did the dishes, she sang when she swept the floor, and she sang all the hours she walked behind that miserable round baler, tripping a lever that released the bale. Dementia kept her from telling me much about her life BF (Before Faith), but I've taken the tidbits—about five facts—and made up the rest.

Thanks also to the several "layers" of beta readers (you know who you are) who read this book and helped me shape it through round after round of revisions. If not for you, I would still be floundering. You've made me a better writer.

TABLE OF CONTENTS

PROLOGUE

Along the north edge of Cleveland lies a beach that extends the length of the city. It's a blank slate where waves from Lake Erie sculpt elevation lines marked by broken shells and debris. The morning of February 23, 1937, high wind coming off the water spit spray and raised stinging curtains of sand. Just outside Euclid Beach Park, a ragged pile of clothing apparently washed up on the previous night's incoming tide lay fluttering madly. Drag marks and deep footprints marked the sand.

The rag pile hid the torso of an unidentified woman—the eighth human being murdered, dismembered, and left lying around Cleveland by The Butcher of Kingsbury Run, also known as The Torso Murderer. The killings had started with the so-called "Lady of the Lake" left along the shoreline in September 1934, and more than two years later, they showed no signs of stopping.

In December 1935, Mayor Harold Burton had recruited Eliot Ness of Chicago fame as Cleveland Safety Director, but month after month, The Butcher killed and escaped. Meanwhile, Cleveland's rival gangs had not stopped killing each other.

That day in 1937, during the second dip of a double-dip depression, auto manufacturers had closed their doors—at one time Cleveland factories produced 115 automobile makes—dock workers had no work, restaurants and bars had closed, the big department stores barely survived. The Holy Rosary Soup Kitchen in Little Italy provided a lot of hot meals but couldn't begin to take up the slack. Torn newspapers, cigarette butts, and dirt swirled into the faces of silent people hunched, heads down against the gale, standing in line, bellies growling, waiting and hoping something would remain when they got to the head of the line. A few cars crept along the street like dry, drifting leaves, drivers bent over steering wheels. Unkempt apartment buildings, backed by the New York and Erie tracks, lined the west side of the street and railroad cars rumbled through to some unknown, unimportant destination.

This is the city where Bobbi Bowen sang for her supper. Beginning during that second downturn, she scratched her way up a ladder of notes, seeking security that eluded her again and again.

PART I: CLEVELAND, OHIO

May 14, 1937

It all started with my friends trying to help me out. We were just kids, and we had no idea what dark, seedy places their help would take me. That spring day soon threw me into an adult world for which I only thought I was prepared.

I'd finished my shift making Humphrey's Popcorn Balls at Euclid Beach Park, and I strode through the amusement park looking for my friends and thinking about my mother's endless criticism of my "plowhand stride." The air felt sticky with the sweet aroma of popcorn balls and full of sound—the grinding of the roller coaster and the screams of riders, the roar of other rides' engines, the music of the merry-go-round, and voices—the raised voices of people trying to have fun.

Leaving the amusement park, I hurried off the bluff and down the ravine to the beach. I had three dollars in my pocket—my week's wages—and a lot of hope. Maybe if Dad got the WPA job he'd applied for, I could get some paints and a canvas—or at least some colored pencils—so I could mess around with color during the summer. I hoped I could fit an art class into my schedule in the fall.

It took a few moments to find Mary, Kate, and Helen among a Saturday crowd bent on washing away the scum of our grimy, industrial city. I spotted Kate's wide-brimmed hat, with its scarlet band, and honed in on it. As soon as I caught up with the others, I dragged my towel out of my bag, spread it on the sand, and peeled off my dress, leaving the swimsuit I'd worn underneath all day. I flopped on my towel next to Mary Teresa.

The moment I got settled, Mary waved a piece of newspaper at me. "Look at this."

"What?"

"A singing contest. Next Saturday night at the Pavilion. You could be a big band canary."

Well, I took the paper and read, just to be polite, you know. "Don't they put canaries in cages?" I asked as I scanned. "Too bad," I said once I'd read the ad.

"What's wrong?"

"You have to be eighteen."

Kate rolled her eyes. "So? You can pass for eighteen. How would they know?"

"I don't know. I'm only fifteen."

"It's a hundred dollar prize," Mary interrupted.

Well, that was moderately interesting, although I just knew Dad would get that job. Then again, I could get into the contest and if I won, gosh, a hundred bucks would come in handy. Maybe I really could get that canvas and some paints. Jeez, I couldn't make up my mind. I sang for myself and I liked it that way.

Anyway, Helen popped up from under the arm she'd had across her eyes. "It's a chance to sing with that new band playing at the Pavilion this summer."

I picked up the paper, smoothed it out, and read. "New tunes and old standards—top two winners get cash prizes, one hundred dollars and fifty dollars."

"But I'd have to *prove* I'm eighteen to get the cash," I argued.

I wadded the paper up and tossed it. You can never accuse my friends of lacking persistence, though. Helen grabbed it as the wind carried it past her and smoothed it out again.

"Maybe you won't. Lotsa people don't have birth certificates. You think your mom wouldn't tell 'em you're eighteen?"

"She probably would, but what if . . . ."

Helen frowned. "When did you become a Nervous Nelly? You've got all kinds of talent."

"You keep telling me that, but singing's something I do. Getting up in front of a bunch of people and doing it would be like having people watch me breathe. I want to be an artist."

"I know honey, but in times like these it's a way to get some money. And nobody's gonna fault you for helpin' out your family. Your dad's out of work, your mom's barely holdin' it together scrubbin' floors at night. Think what you could do with a hundred bucks."

Now they had me thinking like a grown up.

"Pay the rent for five months," I whispered, staring out at the waves. "God I'm sick of moving."

"See. You have to try it, Bobbi. The worst that can happen is you get beat—and I don't think you will."

Still not satisfied, I argued that I didn't know if I'd have the money to get *in* to the Pavilion next Saturday. And I'd have to pay an extra streetcar fare. If Dad didn't get that job, that quarter might be important. See how they do? By then they'd got me thinking the worst, not the best.

"Listen," Kate said, rolling over and arranging her shawl to protect her already pink skin. "I've got a quarter I can lend you. You put it in your shoe. And next Saturday you just don't go home after your shift. Bring along something to wear for the contest and save a nickel out of your week's pay so you can change in the bath house. We'll all be right there with you to cheer you on."

"I can't take your money. You're not any better off than I am."

"Actually, I am," she said, grinning. "My dad got a job Wednesday driving a garbage truck. There'll always be garbage, won't there?"

Well, we all piled on with hugs, but that only provided a moment's distraction. "Still," I said.

"Still what?"

"I can't take your money. It'll take a while for your family to catch up. How long's your dad been out of work and your mom with all the kids?"

"We'll be fine now. And it's just a quarter. When you win, you can give me fifty cents."

"And if I lose?"

"Then I've lost my bet. It's no big deal."

I turned toward the water, listening to the waves surging up on the sand and sizzling back into the lake. I looked up the beach at a bunch of guys playing sand volleyball and then back at my friends, all sitting around on their towels, smiling encouragement.

"I'm gonna go wash off the popcorn syrup," I said. "I need to think."

As I stood, the game broke up and two of the boys came running over, collapsing next to Mary and Kate like a pair of trained seals, spraying sand all over them.

"What's going on?" Ralph demanded.

"For crying out loud," Mary shouted, jumping up and shaking sand out of her towel. "What's the matter with you? You got sand all over us!"

Kate and Helen brushed off with disgusted glares. I grinned and started walking toward the water. *Ralph and Ed will keep them busy,* I thought—but I could hear them talking about *me* as I left.

I swam hard for the buoys at the edge of the swimming area where I could tread water away from everybody else. I wondered how I would ever finish high school if my dad couldn't get work. Even my little pittance of a job would only last the summer.

*Why does everybody think I ought to sing anyway? Sure I sing all the time. I don't want to make it **work**. It's mine and I don't want to sing on demand with people watching me all the time.*

I kept treading water, looking out at the horizon and thinking about the big lake. *No wonder people used to think the world was flat and that it ended in a waterfall. From here, it sure looks that way.*

I shifted from thinking "flat earth" to what might happen if I didn't do something about money. It appeared that, if Dad didn't get that job, my parents would be helpless. My friends had gotten me all worked up, but they'd also got me thinking I could do something to stop the slow-moving apocalypse. I thought about how my parents couldn't seem to earn enough to pay the rent—so we'd be out on the street probably. I tried not to imagine what living on the street might be like, but I'd seen enough street people to have a pretty good idea, and I did not want to be one. I thought about The Butcher and what great targets we'd be sleeping in doorways.

But a big band canary? Really? Me?

I remembered starlets who used to come into the restaurant when my dad managed Mowrey's. They'd retire to the restroom, pulling and tugging at their girdles or bras, or those corselette things.

I'd probably have to wear one of those itchy, rubber things, and high heels and stockings. That would just be miserable.

I couldn't seem to follow a train of thought. Obsessing again about having someone's eyes on me, I didn't even hear a splash before another swimmer grabbed me from behind. Reacting by rote, just like Jack had taught me, I took a huge gulp of air and submerged, grabbing the drowning swimmer's fingers with my left hand and ducking under his elbow as I shoved it over my head with my right. Within seconds, I had him from behind, underwater, feeling my way over his shoulder, reaching across his chest and under his arm. I lay over on my left side and headed for the beach, struggling for breath as the other swimmer dragged me under over and over. Sometime during my struggle for control, I recognized the supposedly drowning swimmer.

"Jack, if you keep fighting me, I swear I'll drown you!"

Of course, he didn't let up a bit. He kept thrashing around while I hung on, teeth gritted, until we reach the beach where I towed him up in the shallows and dumped him on his back.

"Jeez!" I said as I plopped down beside him, panting. "You don't have to sneak up on me."

Jack laughed, choked, and coughed.

"I suppose now you're gonna make me give you artificial respiration." I turned my head and peered at him.

 "No-o-o-o," he said between coughs.

We lay there for a while, like a pair of drowned seals, with the waves washing up underneath us. When Jack finally caught his breath, he rolled on his belly and propped himself on his elbows. "I believe you've passed the course, Bobbi. That was perfect."

I looked at the sky, resting, letting the waves wash up on me and my heart settle back to normal. We could do that, Jack and me— just be quiet together.

When I caught my breath, though, I turned my head toward Jack. "Long time, no see."

"I've been in Chicago."

"Doin' what?"

"Goin' to school."

"Really?" I rolled over to face him. "College?"

"Yeah. Just finished my freshman year."

"How was it?"

"Okay. Just general stuff."

We rested there in the sand and water, looking at each other. "You're a natural, Bobbi. You did great."

"Thanks, Jack. I could never afford lessons."

"You're in the water so much you could save some of these people who get in over their heads." He paused for a moment. "By the way, what were you singing on the way down from the popcorn stand?"

"What? Were you following me?"

"Nah, I was just coming out of the bath house when you came off the bluff."

"*Cream Puff*," I told him, "I was humming *Cream Puff*. It's a new Artie Shaw tune I heard the other day. Didn't know I was humming out loud . . . . Say! Why don't you join us? I'll introduce you."

"I don't think so, sweetie. I'm the wrong flavor."

"Because you're Italian? They're mostly Italian, too."

"Won't work," Jack said, "wrong flavor." He frowned. "What're you doing with a bunch of Italians? Aren't you Welch?"

"Irish and Welch. I just live in the neighborhood. Anyway, they won't care. Just join the crowd."

"I don't think so."

And then he did his disappearing act. He stood and walked off, leaving me to sigh and watch his trim, athletic back as he disappeared up over the edge of the little bluff. Oh yeah, he was a looker, even to me and I didn't usually notice boys. I stayed where I was for a while—at the far end of the beach from the girls— thinking about Jack. I didn't get why he wouldn't meet my friends. He didn't seem shy. Heck, he'd just walked up to me, out of the blue, and asked if I wanted to learn lifesaving. Then he'd started teaching me—but always as though it were a state secret.

I got up and started back toward the girls still thinking about my lifeguard lessons. We'd met by accident as far as I knew. Most people don't swim as early as I do—the lake's too cold. So I'd been out there pretty much by myself. All my girlfriends had been chicken. They even thought it was too cold for sunbathing. Anyway, when I'd got out to warm up, Jack had come over almost immediately. Said he'd been watching me. That seemed a little weird—some guy out there on the beach just watching me swim— but people *are* weird, you know? Before I could get bent out of shape about it, though, he'd wondered if I'd had lifeguard training. I thought he must be recruiting lifeguards for the Humphreys folks. I'd noticed they seemed a little thin.

When I admitted I was the only person I knew how to save, he asked if I'd like to learn.

"I can't afford lessons," I told him. "My father taught me to swim, but he doesn't know how to save anyone."

"*I* know," Jack said, "and I'd like to teach you."

So it seemed weird again. I couldn't figure out why this guy I'd never seen before would want to teach me.

"But why?"

"I've been watching you. You're a natural in the water."

"So?"

"Jeez!" You some kinda skeptic?"

"I guess. I just don't understand."

"How 'bout you don't worry about it?"

So we sat on the sand for a while. He seemed nice enough.

"Do I have to keep a schedule?"

"Nah, I'll just look for you when I come down and if you're around I can show you some stuff."

Now, a year later, walking down the beach, I still knew nothing about him. By the time I got to my friends, Ralph and Ed had dragged their stuff over and joined the girls. Ralph started in on me as soon as I sat down on my towel.

"You ought to, Bobbi. You ought to enter. You can win hands down. What's the hold up?"

"I'm supposed to be eighteen."

"Oh. You can just say you're eighteen."

"See?" said Helen.

"But, I'd have to get all dressed up and wear high heels and—stuff."

Kate cocked her head. "Stuff? What kinda stuff?"

"You know." I paused looking for a word. I didn't want to embarrass myself. "Underneath."

Kate laughed. "Like a girdle?"

I could feel my face heat up. I couldn't help it. "Yeah."

"So? What's wrong with that?"

I leaned over to the girls, shielding my mouth with my hand. "They're hot and rubbery and itchy."

The boys snickered.

"It's not funny."

Helen's voice came from under the arm she had slung over her eyes. "Maybe not, but what're you gonna do?"

"Maybe dad'll get that WPA job."

"WPA?"

Ralph turned to Helen. "It's one of those alphabet agencies Roosevelt thought up to give people jobs. Works Progress Administration."

"Yeah," I said. "Dad put in an application a couple of weeks ago."

Ralph took his arm from around Mary's shoulders. "But he might not get it and then the contest would be over. Hundreds of men are applying for those jobs."

"Jeez you guys, could we have a little more doom and gloom? I was feeling pretty good when I got off work."

"Bobbi. You're not shy and you're singing all the time," Ed said.

"Well, you know, I don't like people watching me. I really don't. I prefer to swim or play volleyball—or even stickball with the kids on the street."

Kate snorted. "You know the first thing she said when we gave her the flier?"

"I can hardly imagine," said Ralph.

"Don't they put canaries in cages?"

"Really?"

"Yup," said Mary with a disgusted glint in her eye.

Ed eyed me. I swear when he gave you the evil eye, you listened. "A chance the rest of us would give our eye teeth for . . . ."

"She's such a tomboy!" Mary threw up her hands; she's *very* Italian.

"You got it," said Helen.

Ed turned to me frowning. "Well, you'd better just do it. We're all hangin' on by our fingernails and toenails, but you could actually make it."

"That's what we told her," said Helen.

Sometimes those guys just made me feel like I was in the Spanish Inquisition. I wondered when they were going to drag me off and tie me to the rack, but Ralph picked up little piece of driftwood and began drawing in the sand.

"Listen, you won't be alone." He looked around at the group. "Let's think about how we can make sure she wins."

Ed lounged back on his elbows. "Freddy says the judges always pay a lot of attention to how the crowd responds."

Ralph looked at his buddy. "Freddy, who?"

"Freddy Carlone, fool."

"Oh and you know Freddy Carlone," Kate said.

"Well, *yeah*. He went to Central High too, just like us. A bunch of us used to noodle around in the music room after school—before he graduated."

"Sure."

"Well, we did."

"So?"

Ed grinned. "So we should all be there next Saturday and whistle and whoop when Bobbi sings. They'll love her. "

"See? You should do it, Bobbi," Helen said. "Ed and Ralph agree. You have to take the chance."

"Okay, okay, I'll try it." I said. "And I won't need Kate's quarter. I get an occasional tip and I've been hiding them so I could save *something*. Just in case I needed it, ya know? I've been trying to forget it's there so I won't spend it on a whim—and I kinda forgot about it. I just hope I don't get caught. But you know, if I would actually win it and get the job singing—I'm still only fifteen— Humphrey runs a 'family park' and I don't suppose he wants trouble with the law."

Helen moved her arm and squinted at me. "No law against it, Bobbi."

"You sure? I heard something on the radio about this child labor law. You have to be eighteen."

"Didn't pass. I was worried I'd lose my job at Sterling-Linder."

"But how will I finish high school?"

"It's only for the summer, Bobbi. Besides, you'll be a big star and you won't need to finish school."

"It's just a little contest, Helen, and I don't want to be a star. I want to draw."

"Okay, so just win the contest. Take the hundred bucks and sing with the orchestra this summer. You can go back to school in the fall. If your dad gets the job, you can let the second place winner take the job if you want and sing part time."

"Ya, you're right. Kinda cocky of me to think I'm gonna win it anyway."

Helen put her arm back over her eyes. "Oh, you'll win it. You just don't have to decide everything right now."

"You really think I have a chance?"

"Of course I do."

"I don't know. I think it's a long shot, but here I am planning what to do with the money and worrying about taking a job where I could get fired before I start. Pretty dumb, isn't it?"

Kate leaned against Ed. "Not so dumb. Just take it one thing at a time. You always want to run three innings ahead."

"Okay. Okay. Might be a kick for the summer."

"Then let's go sign you up before you change your mind."

So we all trooped over to the Pavilion to get me registered. Then we ambled through the cool, sycamore-lined streets of the park until we hopped on the next streetcar for home, chattering about new dance moves and summer jobs and what I could do with the money when I won the contest—but *that* wasn't any contest. I would pay the rent for as long as the money lasted. For the others, I think the contest took their minds off the dark, dingy apartments they were returning to—all of them cramped and crowded.

Back in my apartment building, I thought about the contest, trying to remember if the flier said anything about what the singers had to wear. I'd thought about telling my parents until I heard them fighting from three floors down. Even though I often heard yelling and thumping from other apartments, and I knew other parents fought, I couldn't stop the heat from crawling up my face. These were *my* parents. When I got to my floor, I cracked the door so I wouldn't get hit by a flying saucer—just in case Mom was throwing things again—and slipped inside.

"Come on you guys, cut it out," I said. "I could hear you all the way down in Mary Teresa's apartment."

I dumped my bathing suit and towel out of my beach bag and hung them on a bit of clothesline we had strung across the corner of the living room. I monitored the sudden silence, wondering how long it would take the fight to break out again. They'd taken it into their bedroom, but I could hear fierce whispers coming through the closed door. At least Mom could hold her own, for whatever that was worth. She wasn't like some of the little mousy women who never fight back. Dad wasn't a hitter, although he was big enough. Mom was the one who got physical, throwing things in frustration. Dad would duck and yell—and do as he damn pleased.

With nothing to do but wait them out, I checked on dinner. At least someone had turned it off so it wouldn't burn this time. My parents' ability to make something new out of pasta always amazed me. They'd both learned a lot from the chefs Dad had hired at Mowrey's when he still had a job managing the place. I turned the burners on and stirred the sauce. As I drained the spaghetti and turned it back into the pot with a little dab of lard, I thought about all the times my parents had separated. They were happier then.

I tried to ignore their rising voices. The screaming was about Dad's gambling. He'd lost a dollar at the track and Mom was beside herself.

"You know what that is?" she hissed. "That's steak and baked potatoes with a nice vegetable for all of us."

"I know. I know. But I usually bring home more than I left with."

"Fat lot of good that does us this week. Why don't you sell that watch you're so proud of?"

"You know I'm not selling the watch—and I win ninety percent of the time."

"So you say."

"Well I do."

He did, too. Once, he told me he didn't even look at the horses. Just figured the odds.

"Let me tell you a secret," he'd whispered to me. "I flunked out of school." I'd just stared at him in alarm. "You're real smart," he'd said. "You're gonna graduate and make me proud." Then he'd leaned over and whispered in my ear. "But I can do anything you want with numbers. You just watch."

I did watch and he hardly ever lost.

"Well, you didn't win today, did you?" Mom yelled."You know what we're having tonight? We're having spaghetti, just like last night and the night before."

"Look. I'm sorry I haven't got a job and I'm sorry I failed to make it up at the track. I'm sorry we have to eat noodles and potatoes all the time. I'm damned sorry for living. Alright?"

I shut my ears while I finished the meal.

"Mom, Dad! Soup's on!"

When they came out of the bedroom, they weren't saying much. I was humming again. That's what I do.

"For crying out loud, Bobbi," Mom said.

"I know. I'm sorry."

"Oh yes. I know. You can't help it. There's never a moment some melody isn't pouring through your head."

"Well, it does and I can't help it."

"Just leave her alone, Ella," Dad said. "She didn't do anything."

We all ate in silence, while they glowered at each other and I thought about the contest. Boy was I glad I'd signed up. I decided not to tell Mom and Dad, though. I didn't think Mom could take another disappointment and I didn't want to hear about it if I didn't win. I could just hear her grumbling. "Singin' all the time. Never a moment some song doesn't run through your head. Fat lot of good that's doin' us."

Nope. I decided to keep it to myself and see where the chips fell.

Of course, my friends knew. From the moment I signed up for that contest, they couldn't talk about anything else. Their excitement had me so wound up, I could barely concentrate. One afternoon, I wandered outside with Mary and Kate hoping for a break.

"Come on," I pleaded, "let's talk about something else. Anything else."

"You're going to be a star and sing with the big name bands."

"Alright already. Anything else."

Some of the guys were playing craps down on the street. Nobody had any money, of course, but they were playing for matchsticks. I noticed this new guy had quite a pile of them. I'm not a big gambler, you understand, but I liked to watch the guys goofing around and it was just good to think about something else. I asked Mary and Kate about the guy, but they didn't know who he was either.

He was a big, solid man, not long and lithe like Jack. Watching him, I couldn't help remembering Jack in the water, his sinuous body sliding through the waves like an otter. This was the kind of guy you could hide behind when the wind came barreling off Lake Erie. He was just wearing an undershirt and jeans. You know, I'd heard people talk about rippling muscles, but it was just a phrase to me—until I saw *him*. It seemed like he had bulges everywhere and they moved when he moved.

He looked older than Ralph and Ed and the Calibri twins. He was also going bald—in that sexy way some men have. You know the kind. They clip it short all around and let it shine. He walked the earth as though he had a full head of hair, standing tall, unembarrassed by the shine. And you hardly noticed because his eyes were so focused and engaged; his face interested and interesting.

After the game, he came over with Ralph and Ed. He said his name was Tony, Tony Falgione. Well, he certainly fit into Little

Italy. I didn't—Irish and Welch as I was. But good fit or not, I hadn't ever noticed him.

I looked up into warm, brown eyes with just a touch of a laugh in them.

"You live around here?" I asked.

"Nope. Over on Kingsbury Run."

"What brings you here?"

"My mom's folks live here. I brought her over for a visit—got kinda bored with all the old times and heard somebody out here fooling around so I came down."

Well, Ralph and Ed were making evening plans with the girls and it must have given Tony the idea. He wanted to know what I had planned.

"Aw, I was just goin' over to Euclid Beach, practice my strokes and stuff."

"Just come on with us," Mary interrupted helpfully.

I really didn't need the help, thank you. I'd been hoping maybe Jack would be out there—not that I'd ever seen him in the evening. I persisted.

"Well, I love to swim and . . . ."

"Come on, Bobbie. You planning to join the Olympic team or something?"

"Well, no. That was last summer but . . . ."

"Then come on. I'm sure Tony here would love to have an escort."

"Sure would. Where we going?"

"I'm not . . . ."

Mary put her arm around me. "Sure you are." She turned to Tony, "We're going dancing at the Pavilion. Bobbi entered that singing contest over there, you know."

"*Mary!*"

"Well you did."

Tony grinned down at me. "Then you'd better go dancing tonight. Once you win the contest, you'll be up there watching everybody else dance."

I wasn't too sure about dancing with him. Big as he was, I figured he'd be all over my feet. *And* I'd have to wear a dress—but I guessed I'd have to get used to it if I won that contest. I couldn't think of a graceful way out of the "date." I nodded. Tony smiled. It was the warmest smile I'd seen in a long time.

We agreed to meet on the street at seven, and we all went home to get ready. That was a big mistake. Next thing I knew, Mary was up in our apartment helping me pick out a dress. That done, she insisted I go down to her apartment with her so she could help me with my make-up. When I told her I didn't want to do all that stuff, she said I'd need to know how when I won the contest.

"Jeez Mary, that guy is *old*. All this fixin' up'll make him think I want to marry him or something."

"Maybe you will."

"Good grief, Mary. Is marriage all you think about?"

She stopped her lipstick application and took a good look at me. "Well, you may have to think about it too, or you'll be singing for your supper the rest of your life."

That was a little more reality than I wanted. The singing contest was days away and I hadn't won it yet. I had no idea how we would live if Dad didn't get that job—or if I didn't actually win the stupid contest.

"Let's go," I said. I did not want to think about it anymore.

Well, we danced and we danced. Tony didn't step on my feet once, either. He pulled me in a little tight on the slow numbers, but I guessed that was his style so I didn't make an issue out of it. I really didn't want to admit it, but I had a good time—and I didn't think about the darned contest, or our impending homelessness, *once*. I didn't even think about Jack. It was a wonderful break.

When we got back to the neighborhood, Tony wanted to know when he could see me again. I weaseled; reminded him I had that singing contest coming up and then I had my job and I might have to find another one, because my folks weren't doing very well in that department. We didn't have a telephone and he lived over east, so I hoped that would be the end of it—and it was, for several months anyway.

May 21, 1937

A week later, crammed into a little cubicle in the bathhouse, Mary Teresa helped me get ready for the contest. By then, the bank had cut Mom's hours. She couldn't even pay the rent anymore, let alone groceries. They said they'd had a sudden slow down and couldn't afford her every night. Dad hadn't heard anything about the WPA job, so my family could be out on the street by the time the government made its decision. I'd resigned myself to turning the thing I loved most—just for my private self—into a job. That's assuming I could win.

I fumbled with my clothes and tried to breathe normally. I'd never had any interest in clothes and now that I needed to look my best, I didn't even know how.

"It's okay, Bobbi, you're gonna win this," Mary assured me as she smoothed my skirt for the tenth time.

"I've got to," I said, "but so does everyone else who entered. Some of those gals have already been singing with bands. I recognize some names."

"But they're looking for a fresh face, Bobbi, new talent," Mary Teresa said, buttoning the side opening in my dress. "You've got your skirt all bunched up again."

"Why do you say that?" I asked as I scrubbed off my lipstick and started again.

"Well, if they want singers they already know, they don't have to have a contest."

"I guess that makes sense." I paused, looking into the mirror Mary held for me. "I'm scared, Mary Teresa. If I don't win this—at least come in second . . . ."

"I know, honey," Mary said, grabbing me and holding me, "but you will win this. I just know it and so does everybody else."

I'd never been a hugger, but that time, it felt good to have Mary's warmth, to know she was on my side, even though she hadn't convinced me.

I smiled at her. "If everybody knows it, why are all those other gals signed up to sing?"

"They don't know you."

As we left the bathhouse, I noticed the rhythm of the waves rolling in on the beach. The sound always soothed me. Mary gave me one more, quick, once-over.

"You look great, Bobbi."

"You don't think this dress looks a little too old?"

"Because you snitched it from your mom? I don't think so. You do need to look like an adult."

 "Oh. That's right." Next thing I knew, I was chattering like a chipmunk. I don't chatter, but I couldn't help myself. I kept running off at the mouth.

"I wonder if they'll call our names or how we'll know to go on stage. Oh no! I think I heard they're using the East Bandstand. I don't even know how to get up to the second floor. Where are the stairs? How do I get up there?"

"Bobbi, calm down. When we get to the Pavilion, we'll have plenty of time to find this stuff out."

We walked under rustling sycamores, Mary holding onto my arm.

"Maybe I'll just have to marry a pig farmer," I said.

Mary stopped short and stared at me.

"What? You always come up with the weirdest stuff! Where'd that come from?"

"Something from geography class. In the Appalachians, they're trying to get rid of the wild pigs and grow domestic ones on farms."

"You listen to that stuff?"

"Sometimes," I said. We turned and walked on to the Pavilion. When we got there, Mary stood outside the ticket counter with me, trying to calm me down. Our friends joined us there, and Helen glanced into my eyes. I think she could tell the state I was in, but she asked anyway.

"How ya doin'?"

"Okay."

"Then stop wringing your hands."

I dropped them to my sides.

The girls were dressed to the nines. With Kate's discount in the jewelry department at Halle Brothers and Helen in make-up in Sterling-Linder they could put on the dog pretty cheap. I didn't feel that dressy, but it was too late to do anything about it.

"They cut mom's hours—three nights a week now," I told them.

"You're gonna win and everything'll be just fine," said Kate. "Here's what we're gonna do." She started ticking people off on her fingers. "Ed and Ralph already know about the contest and they will be coming soon with their older brothers and sisters—and you know that's a flock. We got hold of Frannie and she's coming with Samantha and her boyfriend. Our parents will get here when they can. Hopefully, Bobbi, you'll be toward the end of the contestants. Dad knows this guy who used to go to Mowrey's. He said he'd bring as many of the old crowd as he can. He said your dad ran a great place and he really misses the good food and being able to relax with his friends."

I couldn't even say anything, so I stepped up to the ticket counter, hesitating only a moment before turning over my precious quarter.

"Wow! It'll be good to fill the hall," I managed to say finally, as I turned to go through.

"You're a little early. Are you contestants?" the ticket taker asked.

"She is," said Mary.

"Okay. Go under the East Bandstand and someone will tell you where to go and what to do. Good luck."

I said, "Thanks," and hustled toward the bandstand.

"Hey, wait for me," Mary panted. "My little short legs can't keep up."

"Oh, sorry. I just want to get this over with." I stopped until the others caught up. "You know, I sing because I love to, not because I have to. This is different and I don't like it."

"I know," Mary said, rubbing a hand up and down my back. I hadn't realized my muscles had knotted up until I felt her soothing touch. "You've got a lot of pressure on you, but I know you and I think the music will take you away."

We walked, our heel clicks echoing off the polished floor. I caught movement out of the corner of my eye. A startled glance revealed my own reflection in one of the many mirrors surrounding the hall.

"What if they have songs I don't know?"

Mary sighed. "Gosh, Bobbi, I think you know every song ever written."

"You really think I can ask for my own songs?"

Kate and Helen followed. "Everybody will be dancing and having a good time, but when you sing, we'll raise a little noise—you know, whistling and clapping and cheering."

Mary turned to Kate. "Sounds good, if they don't kick us out."

"Mary, you can find a dark cloud in a silver lining. I hope she hasn't been getting you more scared than you already were," said Kate, turning to me.

"She kept telling me I'm sure to win. I wish *I* were sure."

"Way to go, Mary. And, by the way, if they kick us out for being too noisy, we'll have made our point."

Ed and Ralph came through behind the ticket counter and joined us. Then, one by one, and in groups of two and three, the crowd started showing up and scattering around the enormous dance hall. I knew I could count on them to make a lot of noise, but I thought the sheer size of the place would swallow them up. I watched them take their places; then the girls and I headed for the East Bandstand

I still didn't know how to get up there and I fretted about that until Mary pointed to a woman headed our direction.

"Why don't you ask this lady. I think she's here to tell you want you want to know."

"That's right. You're a contestant?"

"I am," I said and I walked off with her, leaving my friends to find their places in the hall. She asked me a bunch of questions about myself and her calm chatting kind of settled me. When we reached the bandstand, the band had just finished tuning up. They started with an instrumental number and I found a chair among several other women. A couple of others arrived after me. I had to force myself to sit still without fidgeting. It was the hardest thing I'd ever done—harder even than sitting still in math class with a jazzy song running through my mind.

Then the contest started and, one by one, the others got up to sing—one fast number; one slow—as I kept my own mental tally sheet. I crossed off the first contestant. She didn't know how to use the mic and it distorted her voice. I didn't know how to prevent that, either. I watched the second singer. I liked her; the crowd did too. More important to me, I realized the first singer had gotten too close to the mic. That's what had caused the distortion. I made a mental note. I liked the third singer, too and the crowd showed its appreciation with a few whistles and clapping—my nerves went crazy. I listened carefully, noting anything that might help me. I tried to peek around from my seat behind the band. The fifth woman sounded lovely, but she moved like an automaton, so I scratched her off my list of possible winners.

The intense focus was driving me crazy, so between contestants, my mind flittered off to a time I spent with Dad. He and Mom were separated then and I was staying with him. I must have been eight or nine. We'd been wandering around the theater district. Dad had bought me a hot dog from a street vendor and I'd been concentrating on keeping the mustard off my clothes when I noticed a street artist. I already liked art and I'd watched, fascinated, as the guy drew Dad and me. I had the picture for a long time, but we moved so much that eventually it just disappeared. I hadn't forgotten it, though. The guy had looked so happy, sitting there on the street with his easel, watching the crowd and the noise and confusion, but just calm and quiet. I hoped, even then, that someday I could do something magical like that.

I dragged my mind back to the Pavilion and for an hour and a half, I sat quietly and listened—and watched. My attention paid off and I learned a couple of things from the others—smart things they did and things I hoped I'd remember to avoid. I got so busy with my assessments I almost didn't hear my name called. A little dazed from all the sitting and focusing and worrying, I stood and walked up to the mic.

"Do you have a couple of favorites, Miss Bowen?" the band leader asked.

"Oh. Yes. I haven't heard anybody do *Sing, Sing, Sing* or *Blue Moon*. Do you know them?"

"Sure do. What key?"

"Just like they're written."

"*Sing, Sing, Sing*, guys," he said, turning to the orchestra. "Just like it's written."

"Okay Bobbi. Whenever you're ready."

I composed myself as best I could, then I nodded and the band took off. Just like Mary said, I couldn't help myself. The music picked me up and carried me, and I was immediately swinging and stepping. After all, everybody's got to sing."

When I looked out at the crowd, I saw a mass of people in motion, jitterbugging, and I couldn't help smiling. As the band strung out the last notes of the song, the crowd erupted. I knew my crowd, strategically placed throughout the massive ballroom, started it, whistling and cheering and stomping, but it seemed bigger than that. It spread and grew into a roar I hadn't expected.

Startled, I stood and stared, wide-eyed, at all those people applauding and raising a fuss, as if they'd succumbed to mass hysteria. I caught my breath when I saw Jack right under the bandstand, whistling and clapping. I didn't see a girl with him, so I hoped he'd still be there when I got down onto the floor.

"Well," yelled the announcer, bringing me back to the contest, "that was Bobbi Bowen and it sounds like the crowd has voted, even if the judges haven't." The yelling and clapping started up again. "Okay, okay," he said, holding up his hands, as if to physically push the noise level down. "Miss Bowen has another number and I'm sure you want to hear it." The noise dropped to a murmur.

In the quiet following the uproar, I glanced down at Jack and he smiled back at me. The band started up with *Blue Moon,* and I sang it to Jack. This time the eruption had a quieter energy, but I felt the appreciation bone deep and bowed deeply. I didn't know if I was supposed to, none of the other contestants took a bow, but the crowd seemed to require it. So I bowed real quick and skipped off the stage—and waited—and waited, along with the others, all needing the money, all needing the job.

Sitting there behind the band, I started thinking—especially since I'd performed my numbers and had such a good response. Maybe I *could* win. Maybe they wouldn't worry about my age, and I could work all summer there at the Pavilion—maybe have enough money by the end of summer to go back to school and take some art classes. I really loved art—ever since the street artist. Watching him had been like being in the eye of a storm. By the time the announcer stepped back up to the mic, I felt more relaxed than I'd felt since Mom came home from work on Monday with the bad news.

"Would Miss Cecilia Napoli come up to the mic?" called the announcer.

So that's it. I was feeling like I had a good chance. I dropped my gaze to my hands in my lap. *Maybe second place. That's still fifty dollars and part time for the summer. It would keep us off the street.* I barely dared to breathe as Napoli got her check—for *second* place. *Oh. Second place.* As Napoli left the stage smiling, I sat, hands clasped, tight, in my lap. I still had a chance.

"And now. For the moment we've all been waiting for . . . ."

Why do they have to string these things out until you're ready to faint? I licked my lips, holding my breath, hoping I wouldn't pass out or something.

". . . would Miss Bobbi Bowen please come forward?"

I took in a huge gulp of air, jumped up and headed for the mic to thank the crowd and the Humphreys and the orchestra. I had already decided that I would sing all summer. Even if Dad got the job, I'd decided it would be good to have a little extra cash. And anyway who knew how long we'd have to wait for the government to decide. I finished out the night, dancing with my friends and wondering what had happened to Jack. Once down out of the bandstand, I scanned the crowd, trying to spot him again, but he'd disappeared.

"Who ya lookin' for?" Mary wanted to know.

I shook my head. "I just thought I saw somebody I know," I said, "but I don't see him now."

"Him? Who's him?" Kate demanded. The girls never could believe I had no interest in boys. "You holdin' out on us?"

I frowned. He'd disappeared like he always did. "Just nobody."

On the crowded streetcar, hanging from the straps, the girls teased me all the way home, trying to get a name. Kate and Helen walked with me and Mary from the streetcar stop to our building, giggling and demanding to know who I thought I saw.

Kate pointed at my face. "You're blushing, Bobbi. Something's up and you're not getting away with holdin' out on us."

Irritated, I yanked open the door. "It's nobody. Just nobody."

I stepped inside and the door slammed shut behind me. Mary started to say something, but I turned to her, frowning.

"Nobody. Alright?"

Mary could see the teasing had struck a nerve. She raised her hand. "Okay by me."

Once I left Mary off on her floor, I tripped up the stairs to sixth floor, singing.

But I began to hear the radio just before I reached the apartment door. It was reminding my parents, yet again, of the Torso Murderer. They didn't need a reminder. Mom was already paralyzed with fear—I couldn't help standing to listen.

For almost two years the killer had terrorized the city, beginning with two unidentified men's bodies found, decapitated, in September, 1935, near Jackass Hill on Kingsbury Run, in our end of town. Next, they found Florence Genevieve Polillo in pieces, January 26, 1936, in downtown Cleveland. They never found her head.

About five months later, the Butcher left another unidentified victim on Kingsbury Run. He'd been decapitated while he was still alive. The announcer droned on about the fifth victim, a man, found west of the city on July 22, hardly a month later. Authorities said the killer, apparently on the basis of blood spatter, dismembered him alive, too. They hadn't figured out who he was. Nobody ever identified the sixth victim, either. All they found was half a torso back on Kingsbury Run. They'd found him in September and his head had still not come to light. I didn't even want to hear about the last one from February. He dropped that one right next to Euclid Beach. I never quite understood why the radio had to give all the gory details. It seemed like people were scared enough without knowing about all the body parts.

I started to reach for the doorknob when I heard my parents' raised voices—Mom first. *Jeez! Not again.*

"I don't like this. Why did you let her stay out this late? That killer's still out there."

"She said she was staying at the park after work so she could go dancing at the Pavilion with her friends," Dad said.

"Well, she should be home by now."

"Calm down, Ella." Dad said as I stepped into the apartment.

"I'm right here, Mom," I interrupted. I looked around at them. "Well, *you're* looking pretty glum," I said, hoping to break the mood.

"Bobbi, there's a killer out there," Mom screeched. "Where have you been?"

"Mom, you're just getting paranoid about this!"

Well, that was the wrong thing to say. My grandmother had lived for decades in an asylum—paranoid schizophrenia, they said. Mom gasped and whimpered, dropping on the sofa. Her eyes were haunted. She'd been there when they'd come to take her mother away and I guess it was pretty awful. Seemed like she thought they'd come for her some day.

"Oh Mom," I said. "You're not a crazy like Grandma. You're just worrying too much. I'm taking care of myself. I was with my bunch."

Well, Mom buried her face in her hands, breathing slowly and deeply.

"Okay, but I don't like you out at night when I don't know where you are."

"But Dad knew where I was."

"I tried to tell her."

I glanced at Dad, nodding, then squatted in front of Mom and pried her hands away from her face.

"See Mom, I'm right here and I'm alright. And so are you." When I got no response but a frown, I went on. "*I've* got good news."

I reached into my pocket, stood, and flourished the one hundred dollar check, as a distraction. Maybe I could get Mom's mind on something else. Maybe the check would be enough to change the mood.

"Lookit right here what I've got. Ta da!"

Mom glared at me. It seemed like she'd been doing a lot of that lately.

"And what's got you so excited? There's a murderer out there and they found a woman right where you were playing around with your friends."

"A new body?" I asked, sitting on the floor facing my parents in their chairs.

"No," Dad said. "There hasn't been a new killing. The radio was just summarizing."

"But they haven't caught him."

"Ella . . . ."

"Oh Mom! This is important," I said with an attempt at a smile. "This is what I'm so excited about. This, my dear parents, is the rent. It is a winter coat for you, Mom, so you won't have to freeze like you did last winter."

"What are you babbling about? What rent? What coat? It's spring anyway."

"This right here piece of paper is a check for one hundred dollars on the U.S. National Bank—made out to me."

Well Mom grabbed the check. She wouldn't let any money slip away.

"What? My God, Paul. It is. It's a check for one hundred dollars. We've got to cash it tomorrow so the bank won't . . . Wait a minute. Where did you get this?"

"Well, I didn't *steal* it. There was this singing contest," I declared from my perch on the floor in the cramped room. "And I entered it. And I won it. I went on stage and I sang two songs."

I went on to tell the whole story, kind of glowing with the memory of all those people stomping and shouting and clapping.

"It was," I paused, looking at my parents in turn, "*grand* 'cause I was just sure I would win first or second and I'd have the money. So I took a bow. It seemed like the thing to do. And then I waited and waited. And waited—and then they handed me this check! Isn't it *won*derful? Just when we need it the most."

"Good thing, too. It's about time you pay your own way," Mom said.

I gasped. Mom had never been that harsh—but then we'd never been so completely broke, or without hope. I tried to chalk it up to her fear of starving, but it hurt anyway.

"For Crissake, Ella," Dad said.

"Well it is."

"We can go tomorrow and get cash and pay the rent and go shopping," I interrupted—trying not to cry while I made peace yet again. *Just once my parents could act like they're happy about what I've done. Just once.*

"We can stock up on groceries," I said.

"And maybe we can get some beefsteak," Mom chimed in, picking up on the possibilities my check gave us.

"Now wait a minute," Dad said. "You look at that check. Who's it made out to?"

 Mom squirmed. "Bobbi, of course."

"No. It's *our* money and I think we should spend it for rent and groceries—I wouldn't mind a little beefsteak myself. Just like you said."

"Bobbi, you're not going to support us. We're your parents. We're supposed to support you," Dad argued.

"You have. I'm fifteen now. I can help."

"You're not supposed to help us. We're supposed to help you."

I frowned, not wanting this to turn into another argument.

"Lots of things are supposed to be. Mowrey's is not supposed to be closed for one. Banks are supposed to be clean and sparkly and they're supposed to give back the money people put in them. The theaters are still supposed to be open and people are supposed to be wearing mink coats—not ratty old things that won't keep out the cold."

When I finished, Dad was sitting with his face buried in his hands, shoulders sagging. Maybe I'd poured it on too thick.

"Look Dad," I said, moving behind him. I ran my hand across his shoulders like Mary had done to sooth me. "This will just buy you some time to find work. Haven't you always taught me that we're all in this together? Well, this is my together part. And Mom," I said, turning to her, "You've always said women should take responsibility for themselves. Was that just words?"

"No, Bobbi. It wasn't—and I'm glad you were listening."

I didn't say anything more, thinking and continuing to rub a soothing hand across Dad's shoulders. I sure didn't want to start another fight, but we *had* to use my money—at least for a while.

"Okay. How about this?" I said. "I don't want to move out and live in a doorway, so I'm going to pay the rent here. I'm still going to need somebody to help me figure things out, so I need you to stay here. And you can pay me back when you get a job. Will you do that?"

"Alright," Dad said. I could tell he felt defeated.

"Mom?"

"How about a compromise?" Dad said, raising his head. "How about you and your mother open one of those new government-insured savings accounts with half of the money? You can use the rest for rent and groceries—and your mom's coat. I guess she does need one."

"Alright," I agreed, "This is a good time, because of all the sales—if they haven't put all the winter things away already. But I think we should use it all."

"No, Bobbi. You earned that money. You're going to have at least half."

"There's more, but I'm not sure I ought to tell you," I said, cringing inside.

Dad groaned. "You'd better tell us."

"Dad, Mom. I really loved it," I lied. "When I was on stage and everybody was whistling and clapping. I loved it when they danced to music I was making. And they all looked so *happy*. I want to do that. I want to be a singer."

"You have to finish high school."

"Well, yeah. But the money isn't all I won."

"What more?"

"The Pavilion has hired a new band for the summer, and I won a chance to sing all summer. I sang with them tonight and I like them."

"Bobbi . . ."

"Dad, if I take this, it will only last for the summer, and I can go back to school next fall."

"But you're only *fifteen*."

"I know, Dad, but the Humphreys run a family park, you know. No cussing. No drinking. No fighting. They close the park at midnight and I don't have to get up for school."

"But there's still a murderer out there and all but one of the bodies have turned up right around here. I don't want you out at night."

I sighed. *Can't anything be simple?* "I can get on the streetcar right at the park gates, Dad, along with a hundred other people. If I get off at the University Circle stop, you can meet me there and walk me home—at least until you find a job and then we'll figure something out. Maybe I can get a cab."

"That's expensive," Mom said.

"I know. I know. We'll figure something out. Anyway, we don't have to worry about it right now."

"Alright. Alright," Dad said, "if you think that's what you want to do. You've been singing since you made your first sound. Maybe you'll find out it's more fun to sing for yourself. That world isn't as glamorous as you think."

I already knew that. I crossed my fingers behind my back to neutralize my next lie. "Maybe not, but it's what I want."

I decided not to mention that I'd make fifteen dollars a week—enough for the three of us to live on—and Dad didn't ask. I just took his grudging assent and shut up.

When Mom and Dad wandered off to bed, I pulled down my own Murphy bed, still thinking about the whopping lie I'd just told. As I drifted off to sleep, I thought that maybe I hadn't told such a *big* lie. I *had* kind of enjoyed all the laughing and stomping after I sang—even though I knew my friends had set it up. And I was just letting my parents off the hook. Surely that wasn't a mortal sin— letting them off the hook *or* worrying about them. I only allowed a second to wonder if they'd do the same for me.

It's just that I sing what I'm feeling—not what someone else wants. Even Mom and Dad haven't figured that out. Aw nuts! I gotta do what I gotta do. It's only a couple of months and I'll be back in school.

I rolled over and snuggled down, letting exhaustion carry me into sleep with a vision of Jack standing under that bandstand, smiling up at me.

May 23, 1937

A couple of days later, I went back to the beach by myself, enjoying sun and water—maybe even hoping Jack would show up. As usual, I swam out to the buoys. It had become kind of a ritual without my even realizing it. Far out in the swimming area, I could still smell popcorn balls. Every shift I must have made a thousand of them, sticky syrup coating my hands. I didn't earn much—street car fare to get there, an occasional amusement park ride with my friends, dancing at the Pavilion, fall clothes for school. Sometimes, it had to go for groceries because my dad was out of work. At least with my new job, I wouldn't have to deal with sticky popcorn.

I considered my new job and what $15 a week would buy until Jack found me. We stayed by the buoys for a while, then we swam to the beach together. We sat together on our towels, drying off in the sun. He'd parked next to me, since I'd come alone.

"So what do you do when you're not here swimming?"

"Oh, I do a lot of the cooking and cleaning while Mom scours the streets for jobs. Dad's still waiting on the WPA job. He gets something once in a while—for a day or even a week or we'd be out on the street—but he's looking too. They're both gone all day; come home dead beat, feet sore from walking. How about you?"

"Aw, my family has all kinds of jobs for me to do."

"Like what kind of jobs?"

"Deliverin' stuff an' goin' around with my dad an' my uncle talkin' to people. Just business—makin' deals."

"You must be rich."

Jack grinned. "We do alright. It's just business."

"What kind of business are you in?"

His face got a hard look, mouth closed into a tight line and eyes narrowed. I wondered why the question bothered him. I thought maybe they'd gone broke like everybody else.

"Nothin' particular. This 'n that. Wherever they can make some money. Say, let's go practice some more." He jumped up and ran into the waves.

Well, that was strange.

After a hard workout, we lay panting on the beach, me on my back studying the colors in the clouds. "I wish I could go to college," I said.

He rolled over to face me, head propped on an elbow. "What would you take—music?"

"Actually, I'd like to paint."

"But you're a *good* singer."

"I keep hearing that, but it's not what I want to do."

"I guess we're both trapped—but you *are* good. You won that contest."

"Oh yeah. I saw you at the Pavilion. Where'd you go, anyway?"

"I had to be somewhere, but I wanted to hear the new singers. Congratulations on your win. I didn't know you saw me."

"You were *right* under the bandstand. You smiled at me."

"Well, yeah, but I didn't think you could see me. I thought the stage lights would blind you. I hear you singing all the time out here anyway."

"Where? How could you hear me sing out here?"

"How could I not? You're always singing."

"But we're usually in the water."

"Sometimes I see—and hear—when you come down to the beach."

Frowning, I rolled up on my elbow. This guy really was kind of strange. "Do you follow me?"

Jack studied the sand a moment. "More like just look for you—and I can always hear you coming."

"So why don't you say somethin' instead of catching up with me in the water?"

Jack looked into my eyes, as if defying me to make something of it. "Because I like to watch you walk and I love to watch that long, smooth, stroke of yours."

"I do love the water."

"You're like a porpoise."

"A porpoise! When did you ever see a porpoise?"

Jack lay on his back with his hands behind his head. "Oh, we used to go over to Atlantic City before the stock market crashed 'n we'd go out on the boats 'n fish."

"You *must* have been rich!"

He grinned. "We did alright."

"Did you lose it all?"

Jack shrugged and closed his eyes. I decided to change the subject.

"What're you taking?"

He sat up and stared at me like I'd wandered into Wonderland. "Takin'?"

"In college."

"Oh, my mind had wandered off. I haven't majored yet. Just general stuff."

"So what're you gonna take?"

"My dad wants me to major in business."

"And?"

"And what?"

"What do *you* want to take?"

"Me?" He made a dismissive "pft" sound.

"Yeah you. You must want something different."

He flopped onto his back, staring into the sky. "You know," he said, "My mom insisted, when I was a kid, that I get piano lessons." He glanced over at me like he was checking for a reaction. "She's not a very, um, forceful woman. But she kept nagging at dad."

"He didn't want to spend the money?"

"Money! Nah. He just thought it was the most useless thing—to teach a boy to play the piano. 'Do you want him to grow up queer?' he'd say."

"Queer!"

"That's what he thought. 'Teach girls to play music, but leave my son out of it,' he'd say."

"How'd she get around him?"

"She just kept bringin' it up in her quiet way."

"So you got your lessons."

"With a lot of grumblin' and moanin.' That is, until I got so I could play ragtime 'n he wanted me to play at his parties."

"What about the girls?"

"They weren't as," he paused, looking at the clouds, "interested as me 'n, well, there was a lot of drinkin' 'n he didn't want 'em there."

"So *you* want to major in music?"

Color rose in Jack's neck.

"You're blushing!" I said, laughing at him.

He rolled back up on his elbow, giving me a sheepish grin. "I want to be a concert pianist," he confessed, reddening even more. "Kind of a wimpy profession for a man, huh?"

"Of course not. I think it's a wonderful ambition! I've noticed those long, slender fingers of yours and thought maybe you could play piano."

"You have?"

"Sure. I know you can do it. I'll bet you'll be *great!*"

"I don't think my father will allow it."

I sighed. "Parents can sure mess up your life, can't they?"

"Uh huh. What about yours?"

"Oh, they're struggling all the time to make a livin' an' they fight over money, yellin' an' screamin.' Sometimes Mom throws somethin' at him."

"An' then he wallops her."

"Oh no. Then he just walks out, slams the door practically off the hinges an' does what he damn pleases."

"*That* wouldn't happen at my house."

"Your parents must be really," I stopped and searched for a word, "civilized."

Jack frowned, thinking a moment. "I don't know about that. My dad is just the boss. No question."

"Doesn't your mom have a say?"

"Not very often and not about anything big."

"Huh," I said, lying back down on the sand with my hands behind my head. I studied the clouds for a while, thinking about men and women and how they treat each other.

"I wonder why men and women have to be on this," I took a moment searching, again, for the right word, "seesaw all the time."

"Seesaw?"

"Well yeah, like always strugglin' to run things."

"But men run things."

"Mostly, yeah. But women have their ways of resisting."

"Like what?"

I laughed. "And give up my trade secrets?"

We didn't say much for a while. I wanted to gather up my loose thoughts, jumping around in my head like they had for a while. I'd been watching my parents and trying to figure out why they couldn't get along. They were both smart people, but they always seemed like they were fighting for control. Mom especially— especially about money. I kept looking at the clouds.

"I mean, why can't men and women be partners? Why can't they share responsibilities and make decisions together?" I lapsed into silence, staring at the clouds. "Look at that one," I said, pointing. "It looks like a rabbit." I glanced back at Jack. "Why can't men and women be equals?"

"But they're not!" Jack said. "Men are stronger."

"Physically yes. So if a woman gets uppity, he can smack her around and get his way, but women have to take it and go on." I hesitated. "We bear the children and take care of the children an' do what's best for the children even when it means gettin' smacked down for it."

I stopped, still gathering my thoughts, thinking out loud. "An' they go on, even when the man decides he don't want to be a husband an' providin' for his kids is just too much trouble—an' he leaves it all to the woman. So she picks it up and makes do." I stopped again, glancing over at Jack, who said nothing. "How much courage and strength do you think that takes? How much courage do you think it takes to risk a beatin' to keep insistin' your daughter needs new shoes when your husband wants to spend the same money for beer?"

"Or piano lessons," Jack murmured.

"What do you mean?"

"Nothin.' Not important."

We lay there without saying a word for a few minutes.

"Say Bobbi, I gotta go," Jack said.

He rolled onto his stomach, reached over, and kissed me on the mouth. Well, that was a shock! Startled, I jerked away, then leaned up into the kiss—and Jack was gone, loping up the beach and disappearing over the bluffs.

Who is this guy?

June 2, 1937

A few days later, I again walked onto the raised east stage in the Pavilion Ballroom—without the girdle and spike heels I feared I'd have to wear. It turned out the Pavilion was more informal than the nightclubs. I looked down at the crowd, and sang. Again, I got a great response, even without planted enthusiasts. Cecilia and I worked out a schedule so I could have a couple of evenings off. As lead singer, I worked five nights and Cec took Sundays and Thursdays.

Summer had started off great. Suddenly I had a few dollars saved, and I earned enough to pay the groceries and the rent—and I still had afternoons for swimming and clowning with my friends. What could be better?

Sure I had a job with a decent income, I realized my voice might be the ticket to security. For the first time in months I could quit worrying about where I was going to live and what I was going to eat—even the Torso Murderer seemed less threatening. I simply hadn't realized how much I'd worried about getting kicked out on the street, until I didn't have to—at least for a while. I thought if things didn't straighten out so Dad and Mom could get decent jobs, singing might turn into a profession—whether I wanted it to or not. I couldn't get over how much I liked having some control on my life. I thought if Dad couldn't get a job by the end of summer, I might be stuck supporting the family indefinitely. I dismissed the possibility that I wouldn't be able to get a job either. I wouldn't let anything burst my bubble. *But* if my mother had taught me anything, she'd taught me not to "count my chickens before they're hatched."

I got to thinking voice lessons might help me compete with more experienced singers, if it came to that. I knew I'd be up against a lot of them. I'd seen a bunch at the contest, so I signed up at a studio I'd been walking past for years—wondering why anyone would have to *learn* to sing. One day I trudged up the steep steps to the third floor studio, thinking about a remark one of the other contestants had made.

"Of course you won this one," the woman had said, "You're fresh meat."

"Fresh meat?"

"Yeah. Men like 'em young. Wait 'til you're twenty-five. You'll have to depend on talent and technique."

I'd hoped the remark had come out of sour grapes, but I was beginning to like having a little insurance. When I reached the landing, I heard Enrico Caruso's tenor filling the stairwell.

Oh no, maybe I don't want to work with her. I hope she's not a classical snob.

I found the studio door open and the singing instructor standing next to her Gramophone, eyes closed, hands clasped as if in prayer, swaying slightly with the rhythm of *Vesti la Giubba*. I waited for the record to end, then stepped in and introduced myself. I inquired about lessons and we made an appointment for the following Monday.

When I came back, I found her—Greta von Barron was her name—listening to Caruso again and I hoped I hadn't made a mistake.

"Excuse me," I said after the last vibrations of Caruso's voice flattened out and von Barron stirred. "Excuse me," I said, taking a step into the room and reminding her of our appointment.

Von Barron lifted the phonograph needle and flipped the switch. "I've been looking forward to it," she said. "I've listened to your demo recording and you have a very nice voice."

I smiled, glancing at the sheet music she had standing on the baby grand piano. All classical. I shuddered inwardly.

"You also use it reasonably well without a lot of affectations. Have you had lessons before?"

I shook my head and shifted my focus back on the voice teacher. "Actually no."

"Then your instincts are quite good, but I think I can teach you some things to improve your technique."

"Thanks. That's why I'm here."

After some initial getting acquainted and settling in, I stood to von Barron's right next to the piano as she prepared to accompany me.

"Okay," Greta said. "Do you normally warm up?"

"Well, no," I said.

She sighed. "A lot of young people don't, and those young voices haven't been abused, so you can get by without it. It becomes more and more important as you use your voice and push its limits. I want you to start warming up any time you're going to sing, even if it's just a few minutes in the dressing room by yourself." She swept her skirt out of the way and sat at the piano. "We'll start at C and I want you to sing 'mee-hee wah-hah mee' like this going up and down the scale in thirds. That will warm up your voice while I assess your range."

As I sang, Greta got a great big smile on her face. I comfortably reached a high A and Greta pushed on for the A sharp."

"I can't get it."

"I think we can get you there; maybe you can get another step. We'll see. Now let's go down."

Again I sang the nonsense syllables, reaching down to a low E. When I got to the D sharp, I faltered.

"So Bobbi," Greta said. "You've got two octaves, plus five half-steps. That's a *very* good range."

"It is?"

Greta smiled. "Believe me, it is. Now did you bring something to work on?"

I handed over my sheet music, *Blue Moon.* "I bought this yesterday. This is my theme song," I said. "I thought we could work on this."

"Alright. What key?"

"I do this just like it's written, in A flat.

"Good. There's nothing more important than the first number when you begin your first set. I want you to just sing it through as you usually do." She accompanied as I sang the song through once without stopping. "Alright, Bobbi, here's what I want you to change. In the first line, when you get to the word alone, I want you to sing ah-lohn and open up those vowels. Here's a pencil so you can mark it to remind yourself. When you get to the "dream in my heart," you're going to sing hahrt and you're going to hold the ah until the second beat of the measure before you close with the rt. Be sure to sing an open ah, not a pirate's ar-r-r-r. Pronounce the end of the phrase like this, 'lahv ahv mahee ohn, using that same open ah sound. Those open vowel sounds will help you stay on pitch, especially when you hold a note."

"This is pop music," I protested. "I don't think nightclubbers want to hear opera."

"Believe me, Bobbi, this is not opera," Greta said. "But good singing is good singing whether it's Puccini or Rogers and Hart."

Well, I couldn't argue with that, so I just listened and tried to learn everything I could.

"I want you to make another recording in a couple of weeks and I think you will not only hear a difference, but you'll also see it still sounds like pop music only cleaner and more expressive. Be sure you sound those consonants so you're spitting on the piano, especially when you sound the plosives like 't' 'b,' and 'p.' Those crisp consonants turn the lyrics from mush into something your audience can actually understand."

I sang for another ten minutes or so as Greta accompanied and mouthed the words with me, continuing to interrupt from time to time for a correction in my pronunciation.

"If you don't emphasize those consonants," she said, "they don't come out in a concert hall—or a nightclub. Think of all the other sounds you compete with."

After another run-through she reminded me to keep rehearsing correct vowel sounds and really spitting out those consonants."

"Okay Bobbi," she said then, "You've already got good posture, but I want you to straighten up. Push the crown of your head up as though someone's pulling the hair on the top of your head. Let your shoulder blades drop down your back. Now breathe."

"I *am* breathing," I said, without thinking.

Greta smiled. "Of course you are. But I want you to breathe differently. I want you to pull your breath from the bottom of your abdomen. Really push it out."

"But I'll look fat."

"No you really won't, and you're going to be singing so beautifully everybody's going to be looking at your face anyway. But here's what's going to happen. You're going to take a deep breath from the very bottom of your torso, and you're going to have enough breath to hold out the whole phrase. Now sing the first line again as you have been singing it here."

I heard that word torso and my mind went blank for a moment.

"Bobbi?"

"Oh. What did you say?"

She gave me a quizzical look. "Sing that first line again like you normally do."

I sang the line, broken into four phrases.

"Now take a deep breath and sing the whole phrase."

I sang, then stopped and stared. "Wow!" I said. I'd managed the entire line without a breath—and I wasn't panting for air.

"See," said Greta. "This song is about longing, about waiting and hoping for a once-in-a-blue-moon love. It needs to be smooth and deep. It needs you to hang on to that phrase like you're hanging on to that hope. It needs to build up to a peak of longing and needing that blue moon."

I nodded. "I guess I felt that, especially the blue moon part, but I never really thought of it that way."

"Your music needs to be really intentional. That's what rehearsal is for. You've got a lovely voice and an instinctive grasp on how to use it. But what you do now is what will make it great. Before you go, I want you to stand quietly and think through everything we've covered today."

"Okay," I said, pulling myself up straight and closing my eyes.

sang through that phrase again, in my throat. When I finished, Greta stood facing me.

"Bobbi, I noticed some movement in your throat while you were standing there. Were you singing it through in your mind—and your throat?"

"I guess I was."

"That's good. It means you can rehearse anywhere."

"This has been fun," I said. "I didn't think it would be."

"It was, wasn't it? I think it's always fun to learn how to do better what you really love to do," Greta said "By the way, do you read music? I didn't see you looking at the sheet."

"Not really," I said.

"Alright. Hmmm. Do you remember those greater than and lesser than signs in math? The little sideways vs? We have them in music too. So before we meet next time, look for them in the songs you want to work on. They'll be longer than the math signs. And think about singing more loudly when the v opens to the right and more quietly when it opens to the left. Next time we'll talk about the letters and symbols too."

"Okay," I said. "And thank you. This has really been fun."

It was, too. Even though I still wanted my music for myself, it was really nice to make it sound better.

"You've made a lot of progress today, Bobbi. Just practice what you've learned and we'll build on it next time."

June 7, 1937

With summer off to a roaring start, I headed for the beach every time I could. I had no afternoon shifts making those darned popcorn balls, so I had plenty of time. One afternoon the sun burned in a bald sky. Sparkling water nearly blinded me as I swam out by the buoys. I thought about how much better I felt knowing we had enough money to live. The Rocket Cars snatched my attention, though, as the ride started up, gears grinding. While I watched them swing out over the lake, I remembered how the ride had once snapped its chains, and dumped a carload of people into the water. *I guess you can't ever count on anything.*

Somehow, the image of those scared people falling and falling, unable to save themselves, made me think of my parents' angry red faces. When they fought, I felt kind of like *I* was on a tether that might snap. They'd already separated several times and I knew they only stayed together because they couldn't afford two households. When they separated, I got passed back and forth like the baton in a relay race. I guess I'd already learned that it hurts to care—even before I started kindergarten. My relationship with my parents seemed like a living arrangement born of necessity, not a family anybody cared to continue any longer than necessary.

I'd already made myself sad when Jack swam up behind me. "Hey, Sugar, what are you thinking about out here treading water all by yourself?"

"Aw nothin.' This 'n that." I didn't want to be a wet blanket, you know?

"Looked pretty serious."

"I was thinking how good it feels to have a little money of my own coming in."

"Hmm," he said as he submerged and pulled me under.

We swam that way, ducking and splashing each other, for a while then walked up on the beach and flopped on our towels. As we lay there soaking up the sun, I wondered about Jack's mysterious appearances and disappearances. I still wondered why he'd been so intent on teaching me lifesaving.

"Am I the only person you've taught to save lives?"

He didn't answer for a while and I began to wonder if he'd heard me.

"You're the only girl," he said at last.

"Why is that?"

"You're the only girl I know who's such a strong swimmer."

"Really?" I thought about all my friends and realized not one of them swam like I did. They were too busy thinking about boys and clothes and make-up and stuff. "Have you taught a lot of guys?"

He glanced over at me from under the arm he had slung across his face. "A few."

"Why?"

"Why what?"

"Why all the lifeguard training?"

"What's with you and all the whys and wherefores?"

I rolled over on my elbow to face him.

"I just don't know anybody who worries so much about people drowning. Did you ever see anybody drown?"

He flinched like I'd struck him. I thought he would get up and leave right then.

"I don't like to talk about it," he said finally.

I was about to let it go, but it looked to me like he *needed* to talk about it. I frowned. "Something happened?"

"I guess I'm making up for my little brother," he said after another long pause.

"What do you mean?"

"Aw . . . it's . . . I don't like to talk about it."

"So you said." I couldn't decide whether I should quiz him. One more question, I decided. "What happened to your little brother?"

"He drowned," Jack wouldn't look at me, "and it was all my fault."

I gasped. "Couldn't have been," I said before I had a chance to think.

In the silence that followed, Jack closed his eyes. His face sort of melted as he fought for control.

"Joey and I were playing around my uncle's swimming pool." He opened one eye and looked at me, then closed it again. "We were about six and four." He inhaled a deep breath and sighed into our silence. "Uncle Al and Dad had stepped inside the house. We could hear them arguing." When he opened his eyes, he still wouldn't look at me. He gazed out at the water, squinting into the glare. "All of a sudden Uncle Al started *screaming* at my dad. Don't even know what he was saying." He stopped and faced me. "Joey jerked around, looked into the house, turned, and ran right straight into the deep end of the pool. I don't know what he was thinking. I guess he was just scared."

I nodded, eyes riveted on Jack's face.

"I yelled for my father, but he couldn't hear over Uncle Al, so I jumped in and tried to drag Joey out, but he was on the bottom and I ran out of air."

"Oh my God," I said.

"By the time I got Dad's attention, Joey was dead."

"But you were just a little kid. You weren't responsible."

"I was the one out there with him. I was the only one who saw him."

If I'd been standing, I'd have stomped my foot. It's bad enough feeling like you're a big inconvenience, I knew about that, but this was just beyond the pale.

"The adults are supposed to know better than to leave two babies out by the swimming pool without anyone to watch them!"

I was almost shouting, and people were looking at me, but I didn't care—didn't care who heard me. It seemed like I'd taken a cork out of my own anger—anger I hadn't even known I felt. Jack stared at me until I got hold of myself.

"It's not your fault, Jack," I said. "It was your father's responsibility, not yours."

I scooted over and put my arms around him, lay my head on his chest. I heard him sob, and then he kept swallowing hard. I stayed that way until he seemed quiet. I lifted my head and looked into his eyes.

"Are you alright?"

"Yeah. I think so. I've never talked to anybody about Joey since it happened. My family acts like he never existed, but I still see him playing on the deck with the sun shining on his hair. Did I mention he was a blond?"

I just listened.

"Mom's Austrian—Anyway, Joey and me were only about 18 months apart—tail enders—everybody else is quite a bit older. We played together all the time," He paused and swallowed hard again, "and then he was gone."

That's when he did his disappearing act, but at least this time I knew why he'd jumped up and left. I couldn't imagine what he was feeling, but my emotions were pretty raw, too. I still didn't know if he had a girlfriend, but I felt really close to him after all he'd told me. I hoped it helped him, even a little bit, to talk about it.

June 15, 1937

When I was well into my summer schedule, Dad finally got the WPA job. He was helping build the lakeshore highway linking east and west Cleveland. He really wasn't in shape for heavy, pick-and-shovel work. Managing restaurants hadn't required such physical stamina. He would get a regular paycheck though, and when you can get a job, you take it. We'd need that paycheck when I went back to school in the fall.

At home one afternoon, Mom and I prepared a special birthday supper for Dad. He was forty. After six weeks of prosperity, we thought we could go all out—at least I thought we could. I was beginning to thaw, to actually believe we had a future.

Mom worked on beef slices with rosemary while I made an amaretto cheesecake. Right in the middle of a rare, comfortable afternoon between Mom and me, the radio announcer broke in with a bulletin. I'd begun to hate those bulletins. This time the police had pulled a man's decapitated body from the Cuyahoga River near Cleveland Flats.

Mom stopped chopping rosemary. "My God! That's just around the corner. What if he got your father this morning on the way to work? It was pretty dark."

"Mom! Sh-h-h-h! Listen." The announcer nattered on until I heard what I wanted. "See? They say he's been in the river for two or three days. And now, I'm turning this thing off."

"No. I want to hear."

"Well, I don't. Dad's okay and there's nothing we can do about that poor man. The police are working on it."

"But there was that colored woman last month."

"Yeah, I know. Nothin' we can do for her either."

I flicked the radio off and went back to crushing almonds for the cheesecake crust, popping one into my mouth so I could enjoy the sweet, nutty flavor. I made them as fine as I could—almost almond flour.

"Do you think this is enough?"

Mom glanced at my pile, hesitating. "I think so."

I grabbed a saucepan and dropped in a bit of butter, which I melted slowly, before pouring it in a bowl with the almonds. After mixing the butter and almonds into a kind of thick paste, I scraped the mixture into the bottom of a springform pan and molded it to the sides and bottom.

"I'm sure glad we were allowed to keep some of the utensils from Mowrey's," I remarked.

"I'm not sure we were *allowed*," Mom said, without looking up.

I squeezed by Mom and reached in the icebox for eggs and sour cream. I added them to the cream cheese that had been sitting out on the counter since Dad left for work. As I measured out a heaping tablespoon of almond extract, I hummed *Tar Paper Stomp*.

"Whoa, Bobbi. That's supposed to be a tablespoonful. You probably poured another tablespoon over the side."

I glanced at Mom, noticing she looked almost happy. The lines around her mouth seemed softer than usual.

I grinned as I licked the spoon, enjoying the burn of alcohol on my tongue and the sweet, warm almond flavor behind it.

"That's my heaping tablespoon. We want to taste the almonds, don't we?"

"Well go easy. We can't afford . . . ."

"Sure we can. You're working. Dad's working. I'm working. Sure we can."

As Mom went back to chopping the rosemary, I inhaled the sharp, spicy aroma of fresh herbs filling the kitchen.

"You never know when things will change."

I returned to my song, ignoring her perpetual worry.

"Did you put the mushrooms to soak?"

"Dried onions and dried mushrooms right here in this bowl, sucking up water. And the spinach is boiling. So is the rice. They'll all be ready to drain soon."

Mom glanced at me out the corner of her eye. "I been hearing Mary and Ralph are getting pretty serious."

"Looks that way."

"Think they'll get married?"

"Wouldn't be surprised. Eventually."

She kept probing, and I realized that, for once, I didn't feel like flinching away from her questions. In fact, her comments hadn't seemed so sharp lately.

"How about Kate and Ed?"

"Dunno. They seem to pair off sometimes."

"How about Helen? Has she got a boyfriend?"

I looked up from the cheesecake. "We're in high school, Mom. What're you gettin' at?"

"I just never hear *you* mention a boy."

An image of Jack lying on that beach, telling me about his baby brother, flashed into my mind.

"That's because there isn't any boy," I said. "What's your hurry?"

I got a fresh burst of scent as Mom rubbed the beef with the rosemary. "No hurry. Just wondering. I'd like you to have someone to take care of you."

"There's just nobody interesting," I stated with all the certainty I could muster.

We prepared recipes we'd learned from our Italian neighbors and Mowrey's chefs, and I imagined Jack's warm body against my own in the cold water. I shrugged mentally. No point even thinking about it. He must have a girlfriend—probably somebody his age. He'd never ask me out.

I made rice into risotto with dried mushrooms and oregano. I'd thrown a little rosemary and chopped spinach into the mix. While Mom stuffed artichokes with pesto sauce, I sneaked a taste with the tip of a spoon, delighting in the warm flavor of sweet basil combined with garlic and olive oil.

"What a feast," I exclaimed as I sliced into a gorgeous purple eggplant. "Look at all these colors."

I cut some eggplant wedges and laid them out on the counter to sweat under a layer of salt.

"You know, your dad's lucky to have his birthday in the middle of summer. All the vegetables are fresh."

Immersed in the complex aromas of cooking, I just nodded and sang. For once, Mom seemed to like it.

We were still standing side by side at the counter, chopping, slicing, and tearing vegetables for a fennel salad, when someone pounded on the door. Mom wiped her hands on her apron as she scurried over to answer. She cracked the door and two burly men pushed past her, carrying a stretcher that held my dad.

"Where do you want us to put him, ma'am?"

"Oh my God," Mom exclaimed, wringing her hands and staring into Dad's white, sweating face.

I pointed over Mom's head to their bedroom door.

"In there! Put him on the bed." I knew he must be hurt, but Mom blocked my view. "What's happened?"

As they passed me, I saw the bone coming through dad's trousers leg and a wet clot of blood soaking his pants.

Recovering herself, Mom hurried into the bedroom, threw back the covers, and pressed herself into the closet doorframe. The men lifted Dad over the footboard and, barely wedging themselves between the bed and the dresser, lowered the stretcher on the bed.

"Wasn't paying enough attention to the next guy; stepped right in front of a pick on the swing," the taller man said. "Guy saw him, but couldn't stop the momentum. Just managed to turn a little so he didn't catch the point."

Mom peered at me over the men carrying Dad—where I stood in the doorway unable to crowd into the tiny bedroom.

"Bobbi, call the doctor."

I couldn't move. I just stood, watching. Mom turned toward the men.

"Now wait a minute." She turned, worked her way into the closet, and rummaged around inside. She pulled out a sleeve ironing board. "I'm going to slide this under his leg and wrap it so it doesn't move when you take the stretcher out."

She maneuvered herself between the two men and slipped the board under Dad's leg. He howled, "God damn it. Hurry up!"

Mom'd found a couple of rags and tied the leg to the board—above and below the break. I didn't know she knew how to do stuff like that.

"Okay, you roll him off the stretcher. I'll move the leg. Paul . . . ."

"I know, Ella. This is gonna hurt. Just do it. Ow-w-w-w!" He yelled, then subsided back into moaning as Mom pulled the covers over him, carefully avoiding his injured leg. "Thank you men for bringing me home." He spoke through clenched teeth.

As the men headed for the door, Mom stopped them. "Thank you so much. Can I pay you something for the time you lost?"

"Nah," said the tall one, ducking his head.

"We were about done for the day," said the other. "You just take care of this guy. Could have been any one of us."

"Yeah. I don't suppose we'll see him back on the job."

Catching a whiff of something burning, I rushed into the kitchen and turned off the oven. Then as the men stalked out of the apartment, carrying the stretcher, I scrambled for my purse and then for the pay phone down on the street. Running down the stairs, past the stretcher bearers, I wondered how much of our special meal was ruined.

When I got back to the apartment, I bent over, hands on my thighs, catching my breath, and told Mom Dr. MacKay would arrive in about twenty minutes.

"He said to keep Dad warm. He said you could save a little time if you cut open the leg of his pants, so he can get to the break. He said if you have any ice left in the icebox, you should wrap it in a towel and hold it on the wound to keep down the swelling, but only for about ten minutes at a time."

"Okay. You get the ice." Mom scurried back into the bedroom.

We fluttered around for the next half-hour, trying to make Dad comfortable. Mom found her sewing shears in her basket under the bed and cut his pants all the way to the hip, carefully maneuvering them around the exposed bone. My frantic chopping with the ice pick reduced a fist-sized block into chips. I wrapped it up in a dish towel and took it to Mom to arrange on the torn flesh around Dad's bone end.

"Let's grab the blanket off your bed," Mom said. We flopped down the Murphy bed with a bang and snatched the blanket. By then, he was shivering.

In a few minutes, Mom let the doctor into the apartment. MacKay looked like he'd been through the wringer, clothes rumpled, hair standing up on end. His eyes looked tired, but sharp. I wouldn't have wanted to try putting one over on him.

"Where's my patient?"

Mom led him to the bedroom and I crowded in behind him. That was the first time I'd seen the leg with the pants cut away. My stomach lurched, but I got hold of myself, following the doc's every move with my eyes. He reached between the rails of the footboard, removed Dad's sock, and grasped his foot in the webbing between his two largest toes.

I demanded to know what he was doing. Glancing over his shoulder at me, he said he was checking his dorsalis pulse.

"And?"

"It's nice and strong. Apparently his major arteries are intact, but I wish they'd taken him to the hospital."

"Does he need to be in the hospital?" Mom asked.

"It would be better but stabilizing that leg in order to move him again might do more harm than good. I think we'll have to set it here."

"Paul, this will hurt like hell. You'll think getting hit with that pick was a picnic."

Dad rolled his eyes. "Didn't think it could get much worse."

"Oh, it can," MacKay said as he loaded a syringe. "I'm giving you some morphine to take the edge off and while it takes effect, I'm going to explain to Ella and Bobbi here how they're gonna help me. Alright?"

"Sounds peachy." Again, Dad spoke between gritted teeth.

MacKay administered the injection, then stepped back into the living room and sat. "Now, here's what has to happen. I have to pull that bone back into place, but if I start yanking, it could rip some nerves or a blood vessel or tear a muscle, so it never functions again. Do you understand?"

Mom nodded. "So how can we help?"

He looked at me and held my eyes. "I have to guide the bone back into place so it doesn't do any more damage. I need you to do the pulling. You look pretty athletic and I think you'll have the strength this takes. I need you to pull on your father's leg. I'll guide you. You'll need to turn his foot a little bit and vary the pressure when I tell you."

I stared at him

"This will not be pleasant. Your dad will very likely yell and holler in pain. Can you do that?"

 "Will it save his leg?"

"I hope so."

What else could I do? It was my Dad. I nodded.

"Ella." He looked at Mom. "I'll need you to crawl onto the head of the bed and work your way under Paul's shoulders so you can get a firm grip under his arms. Basically, you and Bobbi will stretch him—gently—between you."

"Oh my God." Mom brought her hand to her mouth.

"Now Bobbi, I don't have any way to pin the break, so once the bone's where it needs to be, we're going to splint it and then run a rope over the footboard and tie some kind of weight on it. We don't want too much weight because we don't want to pull it apart. I'll need you to hold on while I do that too. This will take some time."

He turned back to Mom. "Afterwards, I have to finish cleaning and disinfecting the wound and take some stitches, from the inside out. None of that will be pleasant either. Hopefully, the morphine will help him stay still so he doesn't do any more damage. Once we get the bone in place, I'll have a better idea of whether he's severed any major nerves or blood vessels."

"What if he has?" Mom wanted to know.

"We'll have to get him to a hospital. I'm not qualified to do that kind of repair."

"How will we pay for that? Paul's only been working for six weeks, and now we won't have his paycheck."

"Ella, I think a lot of people are paying what they can when they can. But we're not to that point yet. Let's see what we can do for him. Are you ready for this?"

My eyes locked on the doctor's face. "I guess so."

Mom's mouth was a thin line. "Yes."

"Alright, let's go get that bone set." Dr. MacKay stood, stoop-shouldered and stepped back into the bedroom. "I imagine you heard most of that, Paul?"

He nodded.

"Has the morphine taken the edge off yet?"

"It's a strange thing, doc. Seems to hurt as much as before, but I got a divorce from it and it's way over there."

"I'm sorry, but we're gonna bring it back."

"So I hear. This will be tough on Bobbi."

"I'll be alright, Dad."

As Mom took her place, raising his head and shoulders, the harsh ceiling light glinted on a tear sliding down Dad's temple. "She *will* be alright, Paul," Mom whispered as she settled under him, grasping him under the arms.

I nodded, catching his eyes and holding them. "You can yell all you want, Dad. I won't let go of you."

Brave words, they were.

"Alright," said MacKay, filling his lungs. Slowly, he worked his fingers under the shattered end of Dad's femur. "This is good," he said, "There are no loose fragments on this exposed bone. Let's hope it's the same inside." The sound of grinding teeth filled the room.

"Now Bobbi, get a firm grip on your father's foot. You'll have to hold on a long time."

I reached through the bars in the wrought-iron footboard and closed my hands around his heel and arch. It was awkward reaching through there, but I got a grip I thought I could hold. I felt Dad's foot sweating and MacKay must have noticed, too.

"Hold on, Bobbi. Put his sock back on to absorb the sweat." He waited. "Now are you ready?"

I nodded.

"I want you to pull, very steadily, straight and level with the mattress. Got it?"

So I pulled, bracing myself against the footboard, and MacKay guided as the bone made its way back inside the flesh of my dad's thigh. Inch by inch it moved as sweat beaded up and poured off Dad's face and into Mom's lap. A big dark spot kept growing under his head. The hollow grinding of his teeth seemed to echo off the walls.

"Now Bobbi, keep that tension just like it is and twist the foot counterclockwise—slowly."

I made a tiny, tentative adjustment.

"That's good, Bobbi. Just gradually keep twisting."

Dad moaned, a low, rumbling sound that seemed to fill *my* bones with the vibrations of sound. Dad nodded, just barely, and I kept twisting and sweating.

"Okay, Bobbi, that's it. Now pull back just a little more."

I pulled, still looking directly into Daddy's eyes, my own tears spilling down my cheeks. Sweat dribbled down my spine and ribs, but the bone end disappeared back inside flesh with a kind of squishing sound and the doctor's fingers followed.

"Ah-h-h-h-h!" groaned Dad between his teeth.

"That's it!" said MacKay.

I kind of jumped and almost lost my grip.

"Now hold it right there." MacKay gathered splints and wraps.

"I'm afraid I'll slip. My hands are wet and Dad's sock feels like it's coming off."

Hw kept wrapping, stabilizing. "Just a bit more, Bobbi. I know you're worn out but I'm almost done." He paused a moment. "Okay. Now very slowly release some of the pressure. Even with the splint, we'll have to keep some traction on it until it starts to knit, so hang on there while I set it up."

Wiping my tears against my shoulder, I held on and the doctor maneuvered around my hands to rig a sling on Dad's foot. He lifted the splinted leg while I held the pressure, and hung a weight over the end of the iron bedstead.

"Now Bobbi, you can slowly let go."

Gradually I released the pressure then slumped to the floor, knees to my chest, face buried in my knees, still listening in case the doctor needed me.

"Now Ella, I have to clean out this wound, disinfect it and wrap it. I can use some help and I think his weight will provide enough resistance now, so you can climb out of there.

"Paul, you haven't fainted yet. How are you doing? Still divorced?"

Dad's bleached-out face looked older than I'd ever imagined—and exhausted. He gave me a weak smile.

"No, doc," he said. "We just had a wedding while you poked around in there."

"I am sorry, but I had to do that and I'm going to have to hurt you some more, but I promise the worst is over. I've got to pour alcohol in this. We just can't risk an infection."

"Just do it."

"Okay Ella. This will be messy, so if you want, you can stand by and sop it up."

Mom had grabbed a basin from the kitchen, and she maneuvered it under the raised leg, then took some rags and sopped while MacKay irrigated the torn flesh. He cleaned out all the dirt, bone fragments, damaged skin and torn tissues, then stitched the wound closed.

"Considering the damage that bone could have done when it came through, his leg seems to be in pretty good shape." He packed up his equipment. "See, the lower leg is nice and pink." He pulled off Dad's sock and again checked his pulse. "He's got a good, strong pulse in his foot. The bone wasn't fragmented."

Mom and I followed MacKay into the living room on weak knees. Mom sagged into the chair by the window, staring at the bricks on the other side of the alley, and I dropped to the floor, continuing to listen to the doctor's instructions.

"We won't know about nerve damage until he's had a chance to heal, but for right now he seems to have sensation in his foot, so that's a good sign. He will probably have a limp for the rest of his life. There was enough muscle damage to cause some restriction.

"Oh," he said as he started out the door. "I'll send my nurse over right away to teach you how to take care of him until he can get up and take care of himself."

"When will that be?"

"We'll probably give it a couple of weeks to start knitting and make sure he doesn't have any infection. Then we'll cast it and I hope he can get around on crutches. But he's not to put *any* pressure on that leg until it heals. I'm going to say he'll be walking on crutches for a year at least. That was a bad break."

When Mom closed the door, I took a deep breath and sighed, wishing the muscles in my arms would stop quivering. The back of my neck seemed to have a vice clamped on it, and my stomach felt like a battle front.

Mom glanced in my direction. "You alright?"

"Just exhausted, Mom." I groaned. "I thought I was gonna lose my grip and hurt his leg even worse." I rolled my shoulders to release some of the tension, but it didn't help. "How about you?"

"I just don't know what we're gonna do now."

I leaned my head back and stared at the ceiling as if I could see my high school diploma floating around up there on its way out the open window. I tried to clear the painful constriction in my throat.

"We'll be alright for the rest of the summer," I croaked, clearing my throat again.

"But I don't know after that."

"I can't think about it now, Mom." Facing toward the window, I curled up around my burning stomach and closed my eyes. "Maybe later."

July 27, 1937

For the first couple of weeks as Dad's leg healed, Dr. MacKay made daily visits to check for infection. I served as nurse so Mom could keep looking for another job. Dad's face flamed each time I had to help with the bedpan, and mine felt pretty darned hot, too. He never said anything, but his face went rigid, lips drawn tight. At night, I turned a couple of shifts over to Cec so I could stay home and Mom could go to the job she did have. On my work nights, I walked myself home from the streetcar stop, keeping up a brisk pace until I was inside the building. It was hard to forget that Kingsbury Run wasn't far away and the Butcher liked to drop his victims in the area—but nobody had thought of my walk home—Mom's either—and I would not to bring it up.

When Dad got up and started using the crutches MacKay had dropped off, it took him a few days to regain his strength and the stairs kept him at home, champing at the bit, for another week. When he managed to navigate them, he resumed meeting me at the streetcar stop. Most nights he grumbled about having to beg Mom for a nickel for a cup of coffee or a dollar to bet on the horses.

"Mom's just scared, Dad. My check pays the rent and groceries and she has to pay the doctor bill. She wants to save something for the end of summer when I go back to school."

He would stump along in silence, stabbing his crutches into the pavement with each jarring step. "But I can help. I always come out a few hundred ahead—every year. It's not luck. You know that. It's math—the odds."

"I know, but Mom's worried about *this* week. She can't look a year ahead. She sees a couple of dollars lost now and it scares her to death."

Every night, we had the same conversation.

One Thursday evening, I cut loose and went dancing at the Pavilion with my friends. It only cost a quarter and that wouldn't change my future.

Mary and Kate, monopolized by Ralph and Ed, headed for the waxed and polished honey oak floor while Helen and I stood along the edge—but only for a moment until some guy I'd never seen before swept Helen away. I made myself a little dizzy watching their reflection move in the mirrored pillars holding up the balcony level. Flashes of color from spotlights on mirror balls spinning on the ceiling added to the mind-numbing effect. As I followed my friends with my eyes, I thought I saw Jack once, standing at the far side of the dance floor, but decided it was just my wishful imagination—until he stood right in front of me, holding out his hand, asking if I'd like to dance.

Surprised, I gave him a fast smile and stepped onto the floor, swinging into a fast boogie woogie, before he could change his mind. As I stomped and spun with him, swinging under his arm, I couldn't help noting what a smooth lead he gave me. We came together and pushed apart, clapping as we separated. Jack looked completely at ease, carried away by the music and his body in motion. He grinned.

At the end of the number, he held onto my hand and we remained standing, waiting for the next song. When the band started *Sweet Leilani*, he drew me close and stepped into the slow sway of the tropical melody. He must have come right from the barbershop, because his fresh smell was heavenly. Bay rum has kind of gone out of style, but the smell still takes me back to that night.

"Where you been, anyway?"

"Did you miss me?"

"Huh," he said.

"Dad broke his leg—bad—and I've been taking care of him—and working here, of course. He's on crutches now so we're both free—kind of."

We danced in silence for a while.

Out of the blue, he whispered into my ear. "Wouldn't it be nice to live in the islands?"

"Mmmhmm." I leaned into the strong arm around my waist.

"We could lie around on the beach—swim in the surf—and it would never be cold."

"You don't think you'd get bored?"

"I could stand it. Couldn't you?"

"Maybe I could too, especially if you were there to rescue me if I got out too deep."

"You could sing whatever you want, whenever you want, and learn to hula dance, and wear one of those grass skirts."

I leaned back to look into his eyes. He grinned at me.

"I think that would *itch*!"

"And wear coconuts."

"*You're* nuts. Besides where would you have your concerts?"

"There will be plenty of hotels before long. Just you wait."

"Maybe your family could invest in one."

His mouth tightened. "I think I'd rather play piano than run a hotel."

"But the Hawaiian crowd won't want classical."

"That's true. I could play and you could sing—jazz maybe."

"I thought . . . ."

"Aw, it's just a dream anyway."

I snuggled a little closer. "I like to dream."

"Me too," said Jack bowing his head so he could whisper in my ear. "I do too, but I hate the disappointment when they don't come true."

"Surely some of them do."

His breath fluttered on my neck. "Some," he said, "I'm here with you in my arms."

A sweet chill ran up my back. "You're givin' me goosebumps, Jack. Did you really dream of dancin' with me?"

"I dream of a whole lot more than that, Angel. But I don't see how . . . ."

"Like what?"

"Like what . . . what?"

"Like what do you dream about me?"

"Wouldn't you like to know?"

"I dream about you too."

"You do?"

"Sure. I've dreamed about this, too."

He had a grin in his voice. "Is that so?"

I nodded, nearly jumping out of my skin when the band plowed into *One O'Clock Jump*.

We danced every number, oblivious to my friends watching us, until the band closed with a slow ballad.

"You free next Thursday?"

"Sure, I have Mondays and Thursdays off, but you knew that didn't you?"

"How about I meet you at the Mayfield Street Soda Fountain. We'll make a day of it, then have dinner and go to Danceland."

We agreed on a time and danced the rest of the number in silence, with me hoping he'd see me home.

"Well," he said at the end of the number. "I'll see you next week." And he walked away.

Damn, I wonder why he's so shy.

Before I could think any more about it, my friends caught up with me.

"Who was that?" Mary demanded.

"What?"

"Whadaya mean, what? Who was that guy you danced with all night?"

"Oh him," I teased. "His name's Jack. He just came over and asked me to dance."

"And?"

"And what?"

"You were with him all *night!*"

"Yeah Bobbi," said Kate. "I *thought* you were holdin' out on us."

I stifled a grin. "He came over and asked me."

Helen stood, hands on her hips. "And you've never seen him before in your life."

"What makes you think I have?"

"We saw the way you looked at each other."

"Oh, I've seen him at the beach a few times. He likes to swim early and late in the season, when it's cold—like me."

We walked out into the warm summer night under rustling sycamores. "We think you've met him more than a few times at the beach." Kate nudged me with a shoulder.

"Yeah," said Helen. "We think you've got somethin' goin' that you're keeping from us."

"Oh, you guys. I never dreamed I'd see him anywhere but at the beach."

"Sure Bobbi," said Kate. "When're you gonna see him again?"

"Next week!" I squealed. "Dinner and dancing."

Ralph, always suspicious—like me, I guess—wanted to know why he didn't come over and say hello.

"I don't know," I said, frowning. "Seems like he's really shy."

"Shy hell," said Ed. "He don't *look* shy."

"I don't know," I repeated as we trooped onto the streetcar. "Maybe he will next time."

"Just be careful, Bobbi," Ed said. "There's something not quite right about that guy."

"I'll be fine." But of course those guys brought back my little niggling doubt about Jack and it kept gnawing.

July 28, 1937

Next morning, Mom and Dad's muffled bickering barely penetrated the bedroom door for once. I woke up stretching, feeling the luxurious loosening of muscles tight from all our exercise the night before; then rolled out of bed and tucked in the sheets and blankets. Smiling, I slipped into some clothes, plopped my nightgown under my pillow, and folded the bed against the wall with a thud.

"For cryin' out loud, Bobbi," Mom yelled, "Take it easy."

Still smiling, I yelled back, "Sure thing, Mom."

In the kitchen, I poured a bowl of cornflakes. When I reached for the milk, I found an empty bottle—or nearly so.

"Fudge," I muttered, wondering why somebody would put an empty milk bottle in the icebox.

Grabbing my purse I headed for the door. "I'm going to Mileti's to get milk," I yelled. "You need anything?"

After a moment of silence, Mom came out of the bedroom tying the belt on her bathrobe.

"Yeah, hold on. We'll make a list."

I sat at the table and counted my cash while Mom checked the cupboards. We'd watched the sales and had them pretty well stocked by then.

"Don't make it too long, I only have two dollars and thirty-seven cents. I don't get paid 'til Monday."

Mom found her purse and added a dollar.

"Alright," she said. "Get a quart of milk and five pounds of flour. See if you can find some fruit." She thought for a minute. "Beans."

"What kind of beans?"

"Navy beans. I'll set them to soak as soon as you get home." She paused, thinking. "Kidney beans too. And stop at the butcher shop 'n get us a chicken."

"How about some ham?"

Mom grimaced. "That's so expensive."

"Maybe just a hock for the bean soup."

"Maybe." She opened the icebox. "They'll deliver ice tomorrow," she said. "There's still some left. Get a half-pound of cheddar cheese."

"Anything else?"

"Don't think so."

She folded the list, and I stuffed it in my purse just as Dad came out of the bedroom, swinging his cast and banging into things with his crutches.

"Mornin' Pop."

He looked me over. "You're sure chipper this morning."

"No point in bein' anything else."

"What's got into her?" he asked as I started out the door. I glanced back at Mom who just shrugged.

Skipping down the stairs humming, I wondered what they'd say if they knew I was actually going out with a boy. Mom was in a big hurry to see it, but I didn't know about Dad.

Out on the street, I kicked a can back to a neighborhood kid playing with several other little boys. I played with them a little while, and then headed for Mayfield Road in the heart of Little

Italy. Passing the soda shop, I stopped to look in the window, remembering that I would meet Jack there in just a week—six-and-a-half days by then. I picked out a booth in the corner. We'll sit there, I decided, and he'll take my hands.

Oh phooey. Maybe he won't.

I turned and walked down the block to Mileti's, inhaling deeply as I passed the bakery. I loved the sweet aroma of fresh pastries wafting out onto the street. At Mileti's, I grabbed a shopping basket and wandered to the dry goods aisle, noting the colorful labels on some of the containers—Clabber Girl baking powder with its bright red lettering and cornstarch in blue and yellow. I found the flour and chose a sack from Houghly Mills with a floral pattern, figuring Mom could make something for the house from the cotton sack—or give it to one of the neighbors to make something for their babies.

I added a pound of dry beans to the basket and moved on to look at fresh fruit. I chose half-a-dozen ripe peaches, and then, dazzled by the colors and smells of the produce, picked up a fat red tomato, sniffed it and added it to the basket, along with an aromatic bunch of basil. As I walked through the aisles toward the dairy counter, I sniffed my palm, taking in the strong aroma of sweet basil and tomato. I nudged the fresh produce aside and added a quart bottle of milk and a half-pound block of cheddar cheese.

Singing to myself, I stepped up to the check-out counter. As Angela Mileti rang up my groceries, my mind wandered to dancing with Jack. Absently stroking my forearm, I remembered his warm breath on my neck when he bent down to hear me.

"That'll be eighty-four cents," Angela said, smiling.

"Oh," I said, bringing myself back to reality. I reached into my purse and pulled out a handful of change, selecting three quarters and a dime.

"You must have been thinking about something pretty nice," Mrs. Mileti said, handing back a penny.

I grinned. "I was, I went out dancing with my friends last night. We had a good time."

Angela's knowing smile told me the woman suspected more and my grin got bigger as I left the store, turning in next door to look for a chicken. Stepping up to the meat counter, I studied the chickens.

"I want that one," I told Bruno, pointing, when I'd made my choice. "Third from the back."

"Thatsa nice fat chicken, Bobbi." Bruno grinned, and reached for the bird. "You're looking happy this morning." He tore off a sheet of butcher paper and wrapped my purchase.

"It's a nice morning."

Bruno glanced out the window at the blazing street and shrugged.

"Is there anything else?"

"How much is the ham?"

"Sixty cents a pound."

"Slice me up a half pound, please. Oh, and you got a ham hock?"

"Gonna get hot," he said.

He sliced the meat and wrapped it, along with a ham hock.

"Guess so," I said, turning to look as another customer walked in, ringing the bell.

He tied up my packages. "You wanna put these in the box with your groceries?"

"Yes please." I took my packages off the counter and fit them into my grocery box. I counted out ninety cents and took the two pennies Bruno handed back.

"You have a nice day," he said, "and try not to get too hot."

I smiled and waved as I pulled the door shut with another tinkle.

At the bakery, good things sent tendrils of sweet scent swirling down the street, wrapping themselves around passers-by and slipping silently into our noses.

Ahhh," I whispered as I turned into the shop, drawn by those creeping tendrils. Setting my box on a table, I stepped up to the counter.

"I think I smell cream puffs."

"Just took them out of the oven," said Rosa. "I'm filling them now."

"How much?"

"Five cents . . . can I wrap one up for you?"

"Oh, Rosa, I'll eat it right here. This place smells heavenly."

Rosa picked up a warm cream puff in a sheet of tissue and laid it on a plate.

"I'll tell you a secret," she said. "That's why I opened this place."

"What a great reason." I smiled, handed Rosa my nickel, and took the pastry.

Sitting next to my box of groceries, I savored my purchase, holding each nibble in my mouth to get the most possible enjoyment from every vanilla morsel. When it was all gone, I picked up my box and walked home, lugging the groceries up the stairs to my family's apartment. I'd only made it up two flights, though, when Mary Teresa came tearing down the stairs like she had The Butcher on her heels. She met me on the landing.

"Whoa." I tried to grab her arm, but she was moving too fast.

Instead, she yelled up the stairs at me. "Mom's hurt. I gotta get doc!"

"What happened?"

Her only answer was the slamming door at the bottom of the stairs. I ran up the rest of the steps and leaned my box against the doorjamb to fish out my key. Once inside, I dropped the box on the table and yelled at Mom.

"Mom, I gotta go back down to Mary's apartment. Something awful must have happened."

Mom stepped out of the bedroom. "What's goin' on?"

"Don't know. Met Mary runnin' downstairs like a scalded tomcat."

"Want me to come?"

"I'll just go 'n see what's goin' on."

Running back down the stairs, I heard Mary's little sister wailing. Inside the apartment, two of the kids stood around their mother, who was lying on the sofa, trembling. They stopped crying when I squatted down on the floor and put my arms around them.

"What happened?"

The panting woman struggled to speak through chattering teeth. "C-c-c-canning. L-lid c-c-c-came off."

I looked at Tommy and Sylvie. "Th-th-they w-were in h-here."

"Where you burned?"

The woman gestured from her chest down to her thighs. I noticed her hand was badly blistered as well.

"Sylvie, Tommy, go get some blankets and bring 'em here. Can you do that?"

They both nodded and left the room together, holding hands. When they were gone, I turned to Mary's mom.

"Mrs. Calibri, I think you're in shock. I want to get you warm, so I'm gonna cover you up."

The woman nodded her understanding, shivering so violently I
worried she'd slip off the edge of the couch. I noticed the muscles in
her neck had all corded into quivering strings. When the children
returned dragging a couple of blankets, I bundled them around the
scalded woman, propping them away from her burned torso as
much as I could. It all seemed routine after Dad's accident.

"Tommy, you've been to my apartment sometimes. Can you find
your way?"

He gave me a solemn nod.

"Okay. The number's six three two. Can you go up there and knock
on the door. Tell my mom we need her here?"

He nodded again and ran out of the apartment, pumping his little
legs as fast as they would go. The thumps of his feet, tearing up
the stairs, resounded through the door he'd left swinging.

I looked into the little girl's wide eyes. "Sylvie, where's your
daddy?"

Sylvie's lower lip trembled.

"It's okay Sylvie. Don't you know?"

Sylvie shook her head.

Mrs. Calibri tried to raise her head. "He-he-he-he's g-g-got a j-j-j-
job t-today."

"That's good. I guess we'll just have to wait for him to get home
when he's done."

Tommy came back into the apartment in just a few moments,
towing Mom by the hand.

Mom squatted down in front of the worried little boy. "Thank you
Tommy. You did a good job. Now do you think you could take
Sylvie and find something to play while we help your mommy?"

"Will she be all better?"

"I'm sure she will." She watched Tommy take his little sister's hand and lead her into the next room.

"Mom, she scalded herself. See her hand? She apparently got scalding water down her front from chest to thighs. Mary's gone for the doctor, but I thought she'd like to have another woman here to help her."

Mom knelt beside our neighbor. "What can I do?"

"C-c-c-can you s-s-stay and h-h-help d-doc?"

As Mom and I stood watching our patient, whispering about what we could do for the family, Mrs. Calibri explained.

"Th-that s-seal was b-bad. C-couldn't aff-ord a new one."

Soon, Mary returned, saying the doctor was right behind her. I suggested Mary and I could take the little ones upstairs and see if we could find something for everyone to eat. Little kids just don't need to see their parents hurt like that. Truth be known, I'd probably had enough for the summer myself.

Mom turned to me before I got out of there. "I put some beans to soak, but you better put the rest of them in. You know how to hurry 'em up."

"Yeah, boil 'em a couple of minutes and let 'em set for a couple of hours.

"Right—and that ham hock's in the icebox."

As her body warmed, Mrs. Calibri's trembling became less violent. "M-mary, I made those s-soda biscuits yesterday. We had s-some left. I figured on 'em for t-tonight."

As we walked up the stairs, each holding a child's hand, I asked about Mary's other brothers.

"Dino's out in the street playing kickball with a bunch of other wild kids. Nick and Rico went over to a friend's apartment. I told Dino he could stay outside for a while. The twins'll wander home when they get hungry."

In our kitchen, the two of us talked about Mrs. Calibri's accident as we worked together on a meal for both families. Frustrated, I turned to Mary.

"It's always about money, isn't it?"

"What do you mean?"

"Your mom said she knew the seal on that canner was bad, but she didn't have the money to get a new one."

"Oh, yeah. I know. And now she's . . . ."

Mary started to cry.

"She'll be okay. I know she will."

I slipped a comforting arm around her shoulders. It seemed like we'd been doing a lot of that for each other lately.

"Oh, I hope so, but she'll have terrible scars. And her hand."

"That worries me, too, but you know, Mary, people heal from awful stuff. Look at my dad."

"How's he doin'?"

"He'll be on crutches for months yet, but doc says he'll just have a bit of a limp. So see? You should have seen it when they brought him home. It was awful."

We spent the rest of the day listening to the radio, comforting Mary's siblings and hoping her mother would recover.

August 3, 1937

The following Wednesday night, rain made the street car stop dark and gloomy. Since I'd become especially aware of the Torso Murderer, I couldn't ignore his presence when I was alone, like before. Waiting for Dad that night was just excruciating and I kept glancing over my shoulder at the deserted streets, thinking I heard something—a whisper of sound I couldn't place. Both my parents had been out in the drizzle, looking for work, and must have been tired. Maybe he fell asleep. Wherever he was, he wasn't waiting for me at the streetcar stop. When I was just about to walk myself the few blocks home, he came charging across the street, pounding along on his crutches. "Let's get outa this rain."

He turned and started back toward the apartment with me racing along to keep up. At home, he maneuvered into the bedroom, banging his crutches against furniture in the cramped living room.

"G'night," he said as he shoved the door shut with a crutch.

"Goodnight."

I stripped out of my damp clothes as soon as the door closed, pulling down the Murphy bed dragging out my nightgown, slipping it over my head and crawling in. My parents were murmuring together as I snuggled under dry sheets, dropping off to sleep and dreaming of an apartment with its own bathroom. How sweet it would have been to soak in a nice, warm tub, to settle down after four hours of singing. But you can't soak with twenty other people waiting for the bathroom.

It's hard to know how long my parents murmured before the murmuring erupted into shouting.

Not again.

"Look, Ella," Dad yelled, "I hardly ever lose. Ninety percent of the time I win. It's the only way I have to bring anything in."

"Your luck will run out and we'll all starve," Mom yelled back. "You're just too fond of those ponies."

"Ella, I don't even look at the horses. I bet the odds."

"Oh that's great! A guy who flunked out of school bets the odds."

Light flashed under the bedroom door and I turned on the one by my bed as well. No one would sleep much that night. Someone rustled noisily behind the closed door.

"Why don't you sell that precious watch of yours instead of risking what little money we have on the horses?"

"I get 'em right almost all the time!" Dad yelled. "And I'm not selling my dad's watch. Someday, Bobbi's son will have it."

Mom said nothing as the rustling and thumping continued. Maybe the yelling was over. But Dad—stung by the reminder of his failure, I suppose—hadn't finished.

Into a silent moment, he shouted, "You're just as bad as that crazy mother of yours."

Then the rustling resumed. Mom said nothing. My parents sure know how to hurt each other. But then, after a few long moments Mom's low voice came through the door.

"You don't know nothing about it."

Dad slammed out of the bedroom looking ashamed—at least I hoped he was ashamed. What he'd just said was brutal and unfair. Mom was already scared enough of waking up some morning in an asylum.

Dad glanced at me, and I caught his gaze for a moment and held it, giving him a nasty look. Then he turned and slammed out of the apartment, thumping along on his crutches. I wondered briefly where he'd go that time of night in the rain, but at that moment I really didn't care.

When Mom came out a few minutes later, her normally olive skin gleamed white in the glow from the streetlight around the corner from our tiny window. She had a wild look in her eyes.

"You're not crazy, Mom."

Mom sat in the chair by the window, gazing out at the blank wall across the alley.

"I don't *think* I am," she said, "but sometimes, when we can't make enough money, I feel like I'll blow up like my mom did."

 Hugging my knees to my chest, I tried to give her some reassurance.

"You're just scared, Mom, not crazy."

"Isn't it the same thing? Paranoid, they called her. Isn't that being scared of everything?"

"But you're not scared of *everything* and you don't see things that aren't."

"I'm not sure *she* did, either." Mom fidgeted with the folds of her nightgown. "That's an awful place. I'm sorry I ever took you there to see her."

"It *is* horrible, but what do you mean you're not sure she did?"

"I was never sure if she imagined things or if Father just wanted to get rid of her—of her nagging."

I couldn't help staring, noticing a cold draft running up my spine. "What are you telling me?"

"Bobbi, they fought and they fought and they fought. My mother was not one to let him have his way just because he was a man— because he was bigger and stronger." She got quiet then, but in a moment she seemed to rouse herself. "Guess I got that from her." She glanced at me and back out the window. "I never remember her talking about anything that wasn't real."

"But wouldn't the doctors know?"

I was a little surprised at myself that I didn't question my grandfather's willingness to send his own wife off to be imprisoned and tortured. That's what the asylum had felt like to me—full of silence pregnant with fear and screams that echoed down long halls. I'd never even met my grandfather, yet I willingly accepted the possibility. I wondered if that was only coming from my mom— or somewhere in me.

"Bobbi, it seems to me that they all figure any woman who doesn't agree with her husband—or *any* man for that matter—must be crazy." Mom continued to stare at the bricks, her voice expressionless.

"You don't think she was crazy?"

"I don't know, Bobbi. Sometimes—a lot of times—she," Mom glanced at me and back out the window, "she'd just blow up, yelling and screaming about stuff that normally didn't bother her. That's what made it so hard. You could never count on anything." Mom fidgeted with her nightgown again. "The little kids would hide and shiver in fear."

"What did you do?"

"Kind of ducked my head and did whatever she wanted, if I could figure out what that was—and wait for her to wear herself out."

"Was she always like that?"

Mom frowned. "Seems like it started when I was about, I don't know, maybe ten—eleven—after she had Mildred. We all worried she'd hurt Millie when she'd get mad, so I'd try to grab the baby and keep her quiet."

"What about your dad? Couldn't he keep her calm?"

"Like I said, they fought and fought." Mom glanced over her shoulder at me and back out the window. "He'd tell her to calm down. He might try to get hold of her hands 'cause she'd be striking at him—and she'd be screaming. She'd get wild sometimes with anger, always about his women—kickin' and spittin'."

"*Were* there other women?"

"I don't know, Bobbi. I was just a kid. He was gone a lot."

"Is that when they put her in the asylum?"

"No. Not then. She had three more babies and the blowups happened more and more often and father couldn't control her at all—nobody could." Mom's fidgeting got more agitated. "And then we were all scattered out everywhere." She turned to me. "You don't need to hear this, Bobbi."

"No, Mom, no wonder you get scared. I'm glad you told me."

We both stared out the window at the wet bricks across the way, listening to the thunder. "What about your dad? What did he do after?"

"After he had her locked up?"

"Yeah."

"Well he farmed all us kids out with relatives. And he was there all by himself." She shook her head, clucking her tongue. "I don't know—did she just wear him out? Did he drive her crazy? He just gave up on everything; didn't even try to get the kids back." She sighed. "I stayed with my friend, Evelyn. I was sixteen and her parents let me stay until I married your father."

"What about your brothers and sisters?"

"They all went—no two together." Mom looked around at me, her eyes indistinct, like flat, muddy ponds. "We never saw each other again. I've tried to find them."

"That's why . . . ."

"That's why we never see my family—except Moreen. She's the only one I ever found."

"And she never found the others?"

"The family disowned us, Moreen and me."

"*Why?*"

"We were Irish Catholics."

"So?"

"She and I married Protestants."

"They *disowned* you?!"

"That's what they did back then."

I couldn't say anything. Just sat there and thought about my mom's miserable life.

"And your dad was an orphan."

I stared at my mom. What? Why hadn't I known this? How could I not know this? I remembered the yelling about the watch.

"Wait a minute. What about the watch?"

"The sisters gave it to him when he left. Said they found it in the box with him."

"Box?"

"Yeah. An apple box. On the steps."

"That's awful. What happened to his parents?"

"Nobody knows. There was a big diphtheria epidemic about that time. Maybe his parents died, and some neighbor took him to the orphanage. Or maybe his mama died having him. I don't know."

"Wouldn't somebody keep track?"

"Apparently not. He says that watch is the only proof he has that he came from real people. Otherwise, he says, he'd have to think he hatched out of a dragon's egg—I think they treated him pretty rough."

I sat, stunned, trying to imagine not having parents. Mine could frustrate the hell out of me and, when they separated, they passed me around like a baseball with two men on base, but I always knew one or the other of them would take care of me. It seemed like neither of my parents even had that comfort. No wonder Mom got married so young.

"Then there were just the two of you."

"And then you came along."

Mom turned back to the window. "Just the two of us," Her voice trailed off and she stared at the bricks across the alley. "just tryin' to be normal. An' *we* don't know what that's like or how to make a family. How would *we* know?"

She seemed to be talking to herself, so I listened.

"An' so mad. Him just a little baby boy an' no parents. Nobody to love him. Just tellin' him to keep his mouth shut an' do what he's told. An' me—listenin' to 'em fight. An' her screaming and clawin' at him about his women an' him hittin' her and tryin' to shut her up. No wonder she went crazy—or maybe it was him went crazy."

A flash of lightning illuminated the bricks across the way and nearly blinded both of us. Blinking, we waited for the thunder.

"I always swore I'd never be like them—your dad and I made a kind of pact—but sometimes I feel like I'm gonna explode, like my skin's stretching and stretching—and I'm gonna blow up and splatter all over." Mom looked back at me again. "I'm sorry. I try to be calm. I get so scared I'm like her."

"You're not, Mom. I'm scared too. It's hard to be poor."

When the thunder came, it was a low, guttering growl. We sat watching lightning flashes on the wall as the storm retreated, rolling and growling away like a dragon seeking its egg.

August 4, 1937

On Thursday, Mom left to pound the pavement, still looking for work. Dad took off for a day job he had lined up, shuffling papers somewhere, he'd said, and I was still wondering if my grandfather really could have done what Mom suspected. As I got ready for my date I paused to think about what kind of man could do that to the woman he's promised to love, honor, and cherish as long as they both shall live. I remembered Dad's comment about dragon's eggs and the drawings of dragons along the edges of old maps we'd looked at together in the museum—dragons drawn along the edges where the water fell off the world. I shook my head as if to shake the thought out of it and went back to selecting a dress.

I changed a couple of times before I chose a plain navy shirtwaist with a wide, white belt that showed off my waist. I primped a few minutes in front of Mom's dresser mirror, as if I knew how to primp. Then I shrugged, grabbed my purse and started out the door a little ahead of time, turning back to leave a note for Mom.

"Mom, I've got a date. May be late. Don't worry about me, he's big and strong."

That'll give her something to think about. She's always asking if I'm seeing someone—and she won't have to worry the Torso Murderer will get me.

I skipped down the stairs, arriving at the Mayfield Street Soda Fountain a little before two. I found Jack already pacing outside on the street. "You came."

"Of course, why wouldn't I?"

"No reason. Just—I don't know. You want a soda?"

"Sounds great!"

We stepped inside and found the very booth I'd picked out the week before. We slid in across from each other and ordered strawberry sodas. Jack took my hand across the table and my fingers tingled with the warmth of his grip.

"How would you like to spend the afternoon looking at art?" Jack asked, hurrying on, "We could go over to the art museum—that exhibit of paintings by Cleveland artists is there now."

"What a great idea!"

"And we can go over to the Expo. There's the gallery there."

"Do you think we can get to both in one day and have time to look around?"

"I've got a car, Sweetie. We can go anywhere we want."

I giggled.

"What?"

"My mom's always worrying about me at night because she thinks the Torso Murderer will grab me off the street. But I won't be *on* the street."

He grinned. "Just getting in and out, 'n I'll protect you."

"I told her you were big and strong."

"I'm not sure that'll be reassuring, Bobbi. She doesn't know me."

I hesitated, thinking. "You mean she'll think . . . ."

"That I'm the threat."

"Hmm. I hadn't thought of that—she's pretty focused on the Butcher, though."

"Everybody is, Bobbi. But *I* could be the Butcher, you know." Jack took a sip of his soda and I gasped. "I could be Dr. Jekyll." He screwed up his face, crossing his eyes and sticking out his tongue.

I laughed.

Jack got a really serious look. The corners of his mouth drooped and he frowned. "Usually when somebody gets killed, there's some reason for it—a jealous husband, somebody's gonna make some money off it, somebody's been betrayed," he said. He'd really sobered up and I could see he worried too. "This is just random. What's the point of lopping off body parts? Why would you behead people?" He paused. "There's no point to it, no reason."

Unsettled by Jack's uneasy remarks, I wondered if I shouldn't have been a little more specific in my note. But then, I remembered I didn't have much more to tell Mom. I'm going out with Jack Mosso that nobody knows but me. That probably wouldn't help.

"Could we talk about something else? I'm feeling pretty safe right now."

"You *are* safe," Jack said, "as long as you're with me."

As we left the soda shop, though, Jack made one more puzzling remark. "If your dad finds a job, Bobbi, who's gonna take you home from the streetcar stop?"

I kept walking, noticing Jack's light touch on my elbow. I frowned. "How did you know my dad meets me at the streetcar stop?"

Jack stopped by the passenger door of an eggshell yellow Packard convertible, opening it with a flourish and handing me in.

"Just seems logical," he said. "Your mom's worried about the Torso Murderer—as she should be—and your dad's out of work. Who else's gonna meet you at the streetcar stop?"

"I guess that's true," I said, not entirely convinced.

At the gallery, I headed right for the Tahitian Landscapes by Paul Gauguin. Didn't even think about my date for a moment. "My dad used to bring me here when I was a kid," I said over my shoulder. "Look at these colors!" I glanced at him and Jack smiled.

"And over here—look at this one. Here's Van Gogh painting Sunflowers. Don't you think it's fun that Gauguin painted a picture of Van Gogh painting a picture?"

Jack chuckled. "It's even more fun watching you looking at Gauguin painting a picture of Van Gogh painting a picture," he remarked.

I blushed. "Oh no," I stammered. "I just took off running like a racehorse without even asking what you want to see. I'm sorry."

"No need. I really meant it. I'm having fun just watching you."

Subdued and embarrassed, I shut up, concentrating on colors and brush strokes as we walked through the gallery, sometimes pushing against the ropes to get closer to something that interested me.

"I think they look better from a little farther away," Jack suggested once.

"I know. But I want to see how they do it; I want to see the brush strokes." I looked down at the floor. "You must think I'm just an overbearing . . ."

"I think you're sweet."

We wandered into the Public Works Hall and stopped just inside the entryway, staring at the paintings.

"These are really dark," I said. "Grim."

"Well," said Jack consulting the brochure he'd picked up in the entryway, "These are by out-of-work artists who managed to get jobs with the federal art project. Who knows what they had to do to survive until they got the job?"

I nodded, still absorbing the contrast—especially with the Gauguins.

"They only hired sixty-nine of them, so there must be hundreds of their friends still out there."

I shivered, thinking about what might happen to my own little family. Squaring my shoulders, I stepped farther into the space, concentrating more closely on how the artists created the sense of miasma with nothing but color—or lack of it. I noted the preponderance of grays and browns and blacks and, low and off center in the most poignant of the paintings, a tiny, pink flower of some kind—dianthus maybe—that created a heart-wrenching contrast. I wondered if I could create that kind of contrast. I wandered around the space, thinking about the mood in that room. Maybe I could create that with my voice, but—that's not what people want, just what I felt sometimes.

"What're you thinking about?" Jack asked.

I turned to him. "Look at this one." I pointed out the one with the little flower. "That flower—you'd think it would make the painting cheerier, but . . ."

"But just makes everything around it so much more drab."

"Yeah," I said, glancing back at him. "How'd you know what I was gonna say?"

"When you stop and study something, it brings me into it, too."

"What're you doin'? Just watching me?"

Jack shrugged. "Yeah, I guess so."

"Why?"

"You're so much fun to watch."

"Fun?"

Jack stuffed his hands in his pockets. "Yeah, you're so *alive*. You study everything as if you can figure out what it all means."

"Oh," I said. "I'm not sure it means anything—factories shut down, people out of work, theaters and nightclubs closed, everyone walking around in drab old clothes with their heads down and their shoulders sagging. You know, I thought everything had gotten better. Some of the boarded up stores opened. I just knew—well, never mind. You can see it right there," I gestured at the painting. "What could *that* mean?"

"I don't know, Bobbi, but I'm pretty sure you do. I think you struggle with that darkness yourself."

I stared at him, eyes narrowed.

"You do too, Jack," I said finally. "It's different, but you've got the dark in you too." I looked back at the painting. "Let's get out of here. Look at something brighter."

"Okay, you want to go to the Expo?"

"Maybe we could just walk on the pier? Feed the seagulls—unless you really want to go to the gallery."

"Bobbi, I just suggested the galleries because I thought you'd enjoy them. I'm happy with whatever you want."

I turned fully to stare at him. "Really?"

"Sure," he said, smiling. "Let's go feed the gulls." He turned to leave the gallery.

I stood watching him for a moment. I hadn't felt like that since I was a little kid and Dad had brought me here. Then I ran a couple of steps to catch up.

"I'm really having a wonderful time," I said, taking his arm. "I hope you are too."

"I am," he said, grinning down at me.

So we took a stroll on the pier, arm in arm, tossing an occasional handful of popcorn to the gulls and watching waves roll in. Once in a while, I noticed a sly glance and smile from passersby and that brought a smile to my lips too. I couldn't help walking a little taller. It seemed the people we met thought we made an attractive couple—me and Jack. I sure felt lovely.

"How'd you happen to get interested in art, Bobbi?" he asked as we strolled along the promenade. I told him about my parents' multiple separations and visiting the galleries with Dad. It seemed like that's the only thing he knew to do with me.

Jack remained silent for a while after I'd finished and I drifted into a memory of Dad and me at the gallery, looking at the very same pictures I'd led Jack to that afternoon. He'd held my hand, engulfing it in his safe, warm grasp, as we walked up the broad steps to the imposing portico—The Cleveland Museum of Art. I'd been enormously impressed.

"Daddy, it's so big."

"That's because there are so many big, beautiful ideas in there."

I'd looked up into his smiling eyes. It was great being with my dad.

"What kind of big, beautiful ideas?"

"Oh, ideas about life and love and pretty little girls like you."

I'd grinned and stepped inside with Dad, thinking I must be the prettiest girl in the world to get that kind of smile.

"Let's go over this way, sweetheart," he'd said, leading me off to the right. "There's a temporary exhibit of Van Gogh paintings over here."

"What's temporary, Daddy?"

"It's just here for a little while."

I'd started pulling on Dad's hand. "Then we better hurry up, Daddy, before it's gone."

He'd grinned at me. "Maybe so." He broke into a fast shuffle with me.

"Exquisite," he'd whispered as we stepped into the special exhibit hall. He'd stood motionless as I stared at the sweeps of deep blue in a painting.

"What's ex . . .qui . . ." I stumbled over the word. Dad didn't even laugh at me.

"That means special," he said and pointed to the same painting I'd been gazing at. "That's called 'Starry Night,'" he'd said. "See how the night sky sweeps and swirls around the stars?"

"Stars?"

"All those little spots in there? Those are stars. And see, there's a little touch of pink in that one and a tinge of green over here. I saw stars like that when I was on the ship."

"In the Navy."

"That's right, sweetie. When I was in the Navy."

"Let me see, Daddy." I reached up to him and he picked me up and swung me onto his shoulders, then stepped up to the velvet ropes.

I gazed at the painting. "Daddy, I never saw stars like that."

He squeezed my ankles where he held me steady.

"Maybe someday I'll have a couple of days off and I'll take you out on the lake."

I clapped my hands, thinking how lovely that would be and how wonderful it would be to make a picture that Daddy would think was so great.

Jack put his arm around my shoulders, bringing me back to the present with a start.

"So you had your dad to yourself those times in the gallery?"

"Yeah. I guess that was it. I actually felt he liked being with me those times."

"Not the other times?"

I hesitated. I hadn't thought about it that way. Hadn't allowed that kind of thoughts.

"No. I guess not."

"So that's where your dark comes from."

"From visiting the gallery with my dad?"

"No from all the separations. So you lived with your dad?"

"No. they traded me back and forth."

"Because neither of them could bear to give you up?"

I stared at him. "I never thought of it that way."

"How'd you think about it?"

"Like I was too much trouble and neither wanted me all the time."

Jack didn't say any more and neither did I. The sun rested on the waves by the time we'd walked from one end of the pier to the other.

"I'm gettin' hungry," Jack said. "How about you?"

I was too, so we headed downtown. Inside the hotel restaurant, I glanced around at white tablecloths with vases of cut flowers—fresh flowers—glittering glassware and carefully-folded cloth napkins. When we got to our table, Jack held a chair for me.

"Wow," I said, "you sure have better manners than the guys I know."

He laughed. "I'm the youngest and my dad kinda forgets about me, so Mom gets to 'civilize' me."

"Sorry about your dad."

"I'm not. If he forgets long enough, maybe I can . . . ."

"Become a concert pianist!" I finished for him.

People were staring at me, so I grinned and ducked my head.

"You remember that? That was just a dream."

"It's still a good dream, Jack. You should do it." I took his hands. "Look at those hands," I said, "they were made for the piano."

"Yeah, well, I'm workin' on it. If Dad has his way . . . ."

"I hope he'll forget about you then," I interrupted just as our beverages arrived.

I chattered over dinner about the paintings we'd seen, trying to sort mood and meaning from technique. When I noticed Jack hadn't said much, just listened and smiled, I stopped, embarrassed again.

"I just keep runnin' on. What do *you* think?"

He studied me for a moment, frowning, and I froze. *Oh, I'm boring him to death!*

"I wonder if you don't miss the forest for the trees," he said.

"What do you mean?"

"Well," he shoved his plate aside and took both my hands. "You're so focused on technique—can you lean back and just enjoy?"

"Oh," I said.

"I had to learn to do that with music. When you're learning to play, you have to pay attention to every note—every notation in the music."

I watched his eyes, the warmth in them, the way they seemed to look so deep into mine that he knew everything about me already.

"Pretty soon, you can't hear the music. You hear that A flat or the run down the scale or something about the dynamics."

"Oh. I see. You're right."

He grinned. "Of course I am," he said. "Let's go dancing before this gets too philosophical."

He signaled for the check and in moments we were back in the Packard, heading for Danceland. Once inside, we headed immediately for the floor, jitterbugging to the *King Porter Stomp*. As we had the previous week, we stayed on the floor and danced all night, taking breaks only to dance the slow numbers, like *Stardust*.

Sometime around midnight, I thought about Mom.

"I suppose, we'd better start heading home," I said. "Mom's always nervous when I'm out at night."

"Especially since she doesn't know who you're with."

"Yes."

"Okay," he said, taking my hand and starting for the entrance. "Maybe we can do this again before I leave for school."

"I'd like that," I said to his back as we walked out.

He took me directly to my apartment building. I hadn't been thinking about the fact he never asked for directions.

"Hey," I said as he pulled up in front. "How'd you know where I live?"

"Followed you once."

"Oh. Why would you do that?"

"So I'd know where you live."

I gave my head a little shake. "Why not just ask me?"

"Didn't know if you'd tell me."

"Hmmm," I said to myself as he walked around to open my door. When I stepped out of the car, he looked over his shoulder into the alley across the street.

"What's wrong?"

"Thought I heard somethin' over there."

I shivered and looked over his shoulder into the darkness.

"I don't see anything."

"I'm sure it's alright."

He walked me to the door and we stepped inside where he turned to me and wrapped his left arm around my waist, cradling my head in his right hand. He leaned in for a kiss.

"Mmm," I said, pressing against him. When I tipped my head back to look up at him, he kissed down my jawline and into the curve of my neck. I thought I might faint as I clung to him, running light fingers down his spine—until someone stumbled through the door, humming raggedly and nearly running into us. He came to an abrupt stop, swaying.

"Whoa," he said. "Whachoo doin' here?"

We both stared at him.

He stared back, weaving. "Guess I'll go on to bed," he said as he shuffled to the stairs and started plodding upward.

"Guess we better say goodnight."

"I s'pose," Jack murmured. "Maybe I'll catch up with you at the beach or some night at the Pavilion."

"I'll look for you." I turned and started following the drunk up the stairs. I stopped three steps up, though, still tingling. "Good night. I had a wonderful time. Take care of yourself."

"You'll never know," he said, as he turned and pushed out the door.

"Know what?" But he was gone already.

August 5, 1937

Mom got up early the next morning. I felt her watching me sleep—trying to sleep.

"Okay Mom," I said without opening my eyes, "I'm awake."

"I didn't mean to wake you."

"You ever tried to sleep when someone's watching you?"

"When you were little."

"I guess turnabout's fair play. You want to know about last night."

I stated a fact. Mom sat in the chair by the window and nodded. I sat up, hugging my knees, knowing I was about to be grilled.

"We went to the art gallery and then over to the pier, walking. We fed the gulls."

"What's his *name?*"

"Oh. Jack Mosso."

"That doesn't sound like one of your gang."

"No. He's a new guy."

"Where'd he come from?"

"Oh. Right here in Cleveland. He went to Central, too, you know. Graduated now. He's just new to the crowd."

Mom frowned. "What's his family do?"

"They're in business."

"What kinda business?"

"I don't know, Mom," I said, grinning. "Jack says, 'this an' that. Wherever they think they can make a buck.'"

"Down an' outers, then."

"No." My grin grew to Cheshire cat size. "He's goin' to college."

"College! Why didn't you say so." Mom was smiling then, too.

"I thought you wanted to know about my evening."

"Okay. You said you went to the gallery and then what?"

"We went to the Statler for dinner."

"That's way over on . . ."

"Yup. He took me in his car. A Packard convertible with the top down."

"Bobbi! He must be rich!"

"I think they do okay."

"Which dining room?"

"The Pompeian Room."

"Okay!" Mom said. "I guess okay." She frowned, narrowing her eyes. "But I don't know that name. Sounds Italian."

"Most of my friends are, Mom. We live in Little Italy."

Mom rubbed her hands on her thighs. "Bobbi, he's probably Catholic. His family might . . . ."

"Disown him?" I finished for her. "I've been thinking about Grandma since last night, Mom, but we're not getting married."

"But you might. You could fall in love and *want* to get married."

"*Mom!* It's just a date! You been hinting you want me to go out. Now I have."

"Just be careful. I told you what happened to me."

I got up and sat in the chair facing Mom. "You know," I said, "I really like this guy." I ran my hands through my hair, making it stand up in tufts. "*We* don't ever go to church, so I don't care."

"No, but . . . ."

"If it ever got that serious—I'd convert."

"That might not be good enough."

"Mom, I'll cross that bridge when—if—I come to it. You're just looking for trouble."

"No Bobbi, I've just got more than my share of it."

"Oh I know, Mom, but I'm more worried right now about how we'll get along at the end of the summer when they close the Pavilion. Has Dad found anything at all?"

"No. There's not enough work for able-bodied men. I don't know where he'll get something he can do with that leg."

"Hmm," I said. "I think I'll get some breakfast. Nothing I can do about it now."

I stood and started dressing while Mom went into the bedroom to get ready for the rest of the day.

"When will you see that young man again?"

"Don't know, Ma. He said he'd try to catch up with me before he goes off to college, but I guess his family keeps him pretty busy in the summer. Without a telephone, he has to find me."

"Well, he knows where you live."

"I guess so," I said. "Maybe I'll never hear from him again."

Later in the day my parents had gone to look for work and I was putting away the groceries I'd bought after they left, when a knock interrupted me. I put the grocery box on the table and opened the door.

"Hi," said Jack, grabbing me and kissing me before I could even move out of the doorway.

"Um . . . hi."

"What cha doin'?"

"Puttin' the groceries away," I turned back to the kitchen. "C'mon in."

"Need any help?"

"Nope." I put a quart of milk in the icebox. I caught him looking around the apartment when I turned back to him, glad Mom and I had straightened up in the morning.

"Done."

"C'mon then. Let's go."

"Where we goin'?"

"How 'bout the botanical gardens? I want to show you something."

Once inside the gates, Jack took my hand and strode toward the center of the gardens, stopping in front of a low knoll with a marble fountain—a little girl pouring water from a jug onto the flowers at her feet.

"My grandfather made that."

"It's beautiful, Jack. So, your family are sculptors?" I couldn't stop gazing at that little girl.

"More like stonemasons. Dad wasn't as good with stone as Grandpa. He runs the business end and hires stonemasons."

"The LakeView Marble Works?"

"No. Grandpa worked there. Learned how to carve. Then he opened his own shop."

"So I'll bet I could see some of his work at Holy Rosary, too."

"Nah, my family's from northern Italy. We're actually Protestants."

A sly grin spread across my face.

"What?"

"Nothing. Any more of his statues here?"

As we strolled around the grounds, hand in hand, among splashes of color in flower beds and reflecting pools that reminded me of Claude Monet's water lilies, he pointed out a couple of other statues.

"Are there any others here in Cleveland?" I asked as we left the gardens.

"Sure, but I don't know if you want to see them."

"Why not?"

"Most of his work's in the LakeView Cemetery."

"So? When I was a kid, I climbed almost every tree in the cemetery."

"What for?"

"Birds. To look at birds' nests. It was close to home, so I could walk over there."

"Let's go then."

Nearly deserted, the cemetery offered cool respite from the heat on the streets under a canopy of white oaks, elms and sycamores. Walking between rows of mausoleums, Jack pointed to one facing a quiet lake, with an elaborate front depicting a young woman, dancing.

"That's unusual," I said.

"It's what the family wanted, I guess."

Further in, under an old white willow tree, I stopped before a weathered figure in a lichen-covered robe with its hood pulled over its eyes. She stood alone, head bowed, holding an urn.

"This one looks so *lonely.*"

Jack took my hand without commenting and we walked in shade between silent stones. He pointed out an occasional statue or grave marker.

 "When I was in high school, I helped Granddad set a lot of the newer stones," he said as we walked to the 123rd Street gates, "when Dad and Uncle Al didn't have me running errands for them."

He stopped next to one of the pillars that lined the gates.

"Did your family carve these too?"

"No," said Jack, frowning. With his toe, he nudged a pile of cigarette butts next to the stone. "It looks like somebody's been standing around here waiting for something."

I glanced at the ground. "Long wait."

"Yeah." He walked around studying crushed grass and tire tracks, "it's not like you usually meet your friends at the cemetery."

"No-o-o-o," I said. "What's the matter?"

"Ah, nothing. Just odd."

He pulled me behind the pillar, out of sight of the street, and took me into his arms, kissing me. When he released me, I remained leaning against him, arms around his neck, looking into his eyes.

"Your family has all kinds of talent, Jack," I told him. "I think you should keep working on your music."

"You know," he said, grinning, "between you and my mom, I couldn't get out of it if I wanted to."

"Is your dad giving in?"

"Mmm. I don't know. He hasn't said much lately. Speaking of my father, he and Uncle Al have something for me to do this evening, so I have to go before long."

When we realized the time, we scurried back to my apartment building where Jack left me at the door with a quick kiss and a promise to see me again before he left for Chicago.

I watched him drive away in the yellow Packard with the breeze ruffling his black hair, then turned and sprinted up the stairs, singing.

PART II: CLEVELAND, OHIO

August 25, 1937

We managed a few more Thursday dates before Jack shoved off for Chicago. Once he'd gone, I divided my thoughts between the time we'd spent together and my family's increasingly desperate situation. As the season at the Pavilion got shorter, those thoughts got more and more intrusive. Mom started talking to me one morning when I was thinking about Jack—while I ate my breakfast—and, to be honest, I was not listening. I sort of heard her talking, even took in the words without paying any attention to them. I just kept munching my corn flakes, staring at the box, until Mom raised her voice.

"Bobbi?"

"Huh?"

"Where you at, anyway?"

"Just thinking. Wha'd you say?"

"Your voice, Bobbi. It's a real asset."

I smiled. "Mom, you've been hanging around banks too much. An asset?"

"Well yeah. You can make money with it."

"Yeah I know, Ma. I been supportin' us all summer."

Mom flushed. "I know, Bobbi. There's just nothin' else out there. How much longer you got at the Pavilion?"

"Couple of weeks. Don't you think one of you'll find something before we run out of money? We've got that hundred Dad won at the track. That gives us a little cushion."

"No, Bobbi. Your father and I have both been walking the streets all summer. There's nothing."

"The clubs open at seven or eight o'clock and don't close until three or four in the morning, Mom. Even if I could get hired, I couldn't go to school. When would I sleep?"

"I don't know, Bobbi. I don't know what we're gonna do."

"I don't know either, Ma." I put my bowl in the sink and grabbed my swim bag. I'd been trying real hard not to think about the end of summer. "I'm goin' swimmin' with the girls. I probably won't have many more chances," I said, and stepped out the door before Mom could say anything more. I don't suppose that was very fair of me but, you know, I was only fifteen and I was already tired of being an adult.

Hurrying down the stairs, I tried to avoid thinking about it, but I knew that time was getting short. Soon, I'd be out of a job—just like we'd planned when I won the contest. Except things had changed and we would run out of money a couple of months after that. I'd made enough money during the summer to support all of us and we'd saved some of it, but it wouldn't last long. I tried really hard to shake it out of my head that afternoon so I could enjoy my friends. But the thought hung there in the air around me.

I was thinking about it when I met the girls at the streetcar stop. They must have noticed that I hadn't said a word since we stepped on the car because Mary Teresa stopped gossiping and asked about our job situation.

"Nothing yet," I told her, looking around in a little bit of a daze.

"What're you gonna do?"

"Well, my mom's been askin' me how long the job at the Pavilion's gonna last, an' if there are any other singing jobs I could take after school."

"My gosh, Bobbi," said Kate, "when would you sleep?"

"I know, Kate. In the daytime. I couldn't finish high school—let alone college."

"College?" said Helen. "Were you thinking about college?"

"Dumb, isn't it? We don't even have money for rent."

"Not dumb at all," Kate said. "Just . . . ."

"Impossible," I finished for her. "I'm gonna have to go pound the streets and see if I can find something."

"We're sorry," Helen said.

"You know, as much as I want to finish school and as much as I dread working the nightclub circuit, I really do like having some control over my life. I guess I'll be running around from club to club for the next couple of weeks."

"Maybe I can help with that," Mary said. She always looked out for me. She pulled out a newspaper ad listing an audition for a female vocalist at the LakeView Jazz Club. "That's not even very far away."

I shivered. This was getting too close. I'd thought about it, but the idea had always been an abstraction. I'd walked by the LakeView Jazz Club lots of times on my way to somewhere else. Jack and I had even considered going there one night, but I'd remembered how scary Mowrey's had felt sometimes when the people came out of the back room—that scary secret back room.

"Interesting how there are always jobs for nightclub singers," I muttered. "Don't ya wonder what they do with them?"

The others remained quiet for a few minutes. "Maybe they get married and quit," Mary suggested.

"And give up a good job?"

"Women do that," Kate said, "and you can meet some high rollers in those places."

"Ugh," I said.

"Rich people need love too," said Helen.

Mary handed me the ad without another word and we stepped off the streetcar when it lurched to a stop. My friends were all looking out at the amusement park—wondering why their friend wasn't excited about the chance to be a star, probably. They all knew I wanted to finish high school, but they just didn't get why. They seemed to be tongue-tied, maybe looking for something comforting to say as I tried to imagine myself in a nightclub, all glammed up, with people drinking and dancing—prohibition was over after all. The secret back rooms had come out in the open along with the people who scared me when I was little.

"I think I'm going to swim for a while," I said, as soon as we got settled on the beach. I tucked the piece of newspaper in my bag. "After this, I may not get much chance."

I stripped out of my shirt and shorts and walked into the waves, hoping maybe Jack would turn up, but knowing he'd probably left town already. When the water reached my waist, I set out for the buoys with long, smooth strokes—away from the crowd. Far out in the deep, I treaded water and looked at the curve of the far horizon. Then I held my place and looked and tried not to think of Dad's dragon's eggs or my grandmother's asylum—or falling off the edge of the world.

Back when Dad managed Mowrey's, I'd been around drunks a time or two. They came out of that hidden room where people could drink and gamble. No babysitting services when I was little, and no grandparents, so Mom and Dad had to make do. I went to work with my parents and played on the floor in a far corner of the kitchen with the cook's little boy—napping on a cot when it got late. But sometimes, someone would come stumbling out of that back room, yelling and knocking things over and I would cower against Dad's broad chest, peeking over his shoulder.

Well, no shoulders to peek over anymore. Swimming back with slow, tired strokes, I'd left high school and my wild dream of college out there in the lake. I knew I'd be alright because I had to be. And that was it. My friends had some consoling things to say by the time I reached them.

"Bobbi," said Helen, "a lot of people don't get to finish high school and they do just fine."

"Yeah," said Mary Teresa, "You can sing without a diploma. If you can land this job, and we all think you can, it will be a step. Some more experience to get you where you want to go."

"I'm not sure I know where I want to go. I'm just sick and tired of worrying about where I'm going to live. Do you know we've moved fifteen times in the past six years? Fifteen times! And each time we've left owing rent." And each apartment had been crummier than the one before it.

"You'll be singing with Artie Shaw or Bennie Goodman one of these days," Helen told me. "Think about the men, the cocktails, the fur coats—diamond jewelry."

"I don't care about any of that stuff. I just wish they'd keep the Pavilion open all year. I wouldn't have to get all super dressed up, wouldn't have to be there all night, wouldn't have to quit school."

"Look Bobbi, we're all gonna to get married and have babies and get fat and we'll never get out of here," Mary said. "But when we go out with our husbands and you're up there belting out some song we can dance to, we can say, 'Hey, I know her!'"

"Yeah, someday my husband and I will be at Danceland, jitterbuging to some big name orchestra and there you'll be, singing with that band," said Kate.

"And when I'm ironing shirts and I hear your voice on the radio, I'll just dance with the shirt and smile," Helen said.

"Look, you guys. I know you're rooting for me and I know what I have to do. For now, I'd better round up something to wear to an audition. A nightclub is different from the Pavilion."

"Oh Bobbi, I didn't think of that," said Kate.

"It could be worse. Mom's still got some of the gowns from when Dad managed Mowrey's and she was the hostess. I think they'll fit. Trouble is; all the accessories are gone."

"Well, let's go shopping," said Mary. "We can help you find some things. You've got a little something left from that fifty bucks, don't you?"

"Yes, I stopped the singing lessons when Dad broke his leg."

So the girls made a date with me for the following evening—to look at dresses after Mom left for work and Dad left for the track, or the bar, or wherever he went those days.

August 26, 1937

Next evening, Mary arrived first, grabbing Mom's threadbare chair. Kate followed and commandeered Dad's spot. When Helen came, she sat on the arm. With my friends lined up like three magpies I dug Mom's three gowns out of the closet. My first choice was an emerald green silk that draped from my right shoulder to my left toe.

"Wow, Bobbi!" Kate gushed, "You look twenty-five and sizzling! You've got the shoes. That's good. I wouldn't add too much to that. Long gloves. White. Maybe a gold chain around your neck, but maybe just earrings."

"I'll need stockings."

"Yeah. Oh. Oh. I know just the thing. I've been eyeing this necklace and there are hoop earrings that would complement that dress. They're big hoops, but your neck is long enough to carry them off."

"Makeup, too," Helen added. "You've been doing great at the Pavilion, but in a nightclub, you'll need to be a little sultry. More eye liner. A little darker with the eye shadow—you know, in the crease of your lid. I'd get something greenish, or smoky—smoky eyes. Brighter lipstick."

As I grimaced and scribbled down their suggestions, Mary was ready to go on.

"What about that red one? Try that on."

The girls critiqued the second dress, making suggestions about accessories and makeup. We'd been listening to the radio, snapping fingers in time and dancing a step or two in the crowded apartment. I wore a shimmering midnight blue gown and held a shoe in my hand when the announcer broke in with a bulletin. I'd begun to dread those and sure enough, The Torso Murderer had claimed another victim. A body had turned up under the Lorain-Carnegie Bridge. She'd apparently been buried there months before. This was the tenth murder, all victims dismembered.

I dropped the shoe I was about to put on and flopped on the arm of Mary's chair.

"Why can't they catch this guy?" I wailed, bravado flagging.

Mary turned thoughtful, tapping a finger on her lips.

"You gotta tell your dad," she said. "Have him take you and bring you home. I know you don't want to, but you can't be out alone when the lounge closes. Even just the twelve blocks."

"He'll have a conniption fit. He didn't want me to sing at the Pavilion. Besides, he's old. He can't come get me at three or four in the morning and still go look for work all day."

"Things have changed, Bobbi. Your dad has to know. There isn't any choice. This is too dangerous," said Helen. "You can't do this without him."

"Of course I can," I said, standing up and pacing. "I just have to watch out for anyone out on the streets at three or four in the morning. There aren't many that time of night. And I'll have to keep my distance."

"Are you crazy?" Kate demanded. "This guy does horrible things to people."

"He has to catch me first."

"Bobbi, honey, you're fast," Helen said, "but you don't know who this guy is. He may be an Olympic runner like Jessie Owens for all you know."

"And he's definitely stronger," Kate said. "You can't go. I don't know what you're gonna do about your dad, but you can't do this without him."

"No, I guess not. But Dad won't let me do it, and I'm scared we'll be out on the street. That's not safe either."

"Your mom and dad will think of something," Mary said.

"I wish I could believe that."

We murmured together for a bit, but the fun had gone from our project, and in a few moments the girls all headed for their apartments, assuring me that the audition was out of the question—unless I got my father to help. It was the least he could do, they told me.

"For what it's worth," Kate said as she pulled the door closed behind her. "I liked the green one best. It brings out the Irish in your eyes."

Thinking about the poor, colored man who'd been dumped under the bridge in the same area where they found the ninth victim, I took off Mom's clothes and carefully returned everything to the closet and the dresser. I wondered if this was really the same killer, though. The announcer didn't say anything about missing body parts like the one last week—and all the others.

My parents didn't know that sometimes when I said I was going to visit Mary, I went out walking alone, just to get away from their bickering. I stood with a hangar in my hand, thinking of the Torso Murderer wandering *my* streets not too far away from Jackass Hill and over by the river—and at Euclid Beach. I hung up the last dress and turned up the radio, wondering if I'd have to lock myself up every night at dark now. But I knew I couldn't.

No, damn it. I pulled myself up to my full five foot six and squared my shoulders. *There's less danger walking home than living on those streets.*

As I paced the apartment, I played out how I could escape if attacked. I scrounged for something heavy I could put in my bag and found a book that I'd forgotten to return on the last day of school. That would do some damage if I swung it at an assailant's head. I *would* audition at LakeView—and I wouldn't tell my parents until it was done and I had a couple of paychecks to show them.

I might have to go to several interviews, but I'll do it. Mom's ready. She's all but begged me. Maybe the money will sway Dad. I only have to wait until Monday to get on with it.

I chose the green and the matching ankle-strap shoes, then wrote myself a little list for the next day's shopping—still thinking about how to be safe.

In the morning after breakfast, as my parents began their morning rant, I said I needed to get some things for my evening performance at the Pavilion. They barely acknowledged me.

I left the apartment and scurried down the stairs. Outside, I noticed the cloudless sky and hurried to my first stop before the pavement got too hot. I'd had an idea overnight, and I stopped first at the pawn shop, two blocks away. I found a little gun that would just fit my hand. Burt, the pawnbroker, called it a woman's gun—a derringer. But would it stop someone if he wanted to catch me? That's what I wanted to know.

"What do you want that for?" Burt asked.

"They still haven't caught the Torso Murderer, and I'm coming home after dark from the Pavilion, Burt."

"Ya, but there are a lot of people getting on and off the streetcar with you. I thought your dad was meeting you when you got off the car."

"Well, he is, Burt, but sometimes he gets held up, and I have to wait there for a while. Besides, with his leg, I'm not sure he could protect either one of us."

That wasn't a lie.

"Your dad should be using the gun."

"With his crutches?"

Burt sighed. "I've done a lot of business with your family, Bobbi, and I'm not in favor of this. Do you even know how to use it?"

"I was hoping you would give me a demonstration."

"Huh," Burt said, eyeing me. "What *is* going on with your dad these days?"

"Oh, you know. The crutches make him slow. He can't find any jobs—at least until that leg heals. He's not very happy."

Boy was that an understatement.

Thinking about Dad kind of scared me. It reminded me of his shorter temper and the way he kept forgetting things—things he was supposed to pick up for supper, meeting me at the streetcar stop. Sometimes he even forgot his wallet when he left the apartment and had to come back for it. When he was home, he sometimes just sat in his chair for hours and stared at the wall across the alley. Sometimes his behavior unnerved me. I hoped he'd be alright.

"Huh," Burt said, taking the gun from me. "This is how you open the action to load it," he said. "See. It's loaded.

"Shoulda checked that," he muttered. "You close it like that and here's the safety. Don't flip that safety off unless you're ready to shoot or you'll shoot yourself in the toe."

I gave him a half smile.

He insisted that I play with the gun for a while as he watched. "That's it," he said. "I'd get a box of ammunition and practice, if I were you."

"Where?"

"I probably have something that will fit that."

"No. Where would I practice?"

"I don't know," he said.

"I don't either. I guess I'll just take my chances. Thanks for the lesson," I said as I pulled out my wallet and paid the bill.

Back on the street, I consulted my list and headed for Sterling-Linders' makeup counter. I was looking at green eye shadow when Helen bustled up.

"What are you doing?" she hissed. "You can't be thinking about that LakeView Jazz Club job. Have you talked to your dad?"

Without answering, I set my purse on the glass top of the counter, peered around to see if we had company, and brought the gun out just far enough for Helen to see.

"I'll be just fine," I whispered, nudging the gun back in place.

Helen's eyes widened for a moment, then she smiled. "You're always Bobbi, aren't you? You just don't give up. Do you know how to shoot that thing—without shooting off your foot?"

"Burt over at the pawn shop showed me how."

"Well, let's get you some stage makeup."

"I know I really need that stuff, but I hate spending the money."

"I know, Bobbi, but like you said, a nightclub's different from the Pavilion."

"I suppose."

"You're just lucky your mom still has those dresses, and they fit you."

Helen gave me a makeup demonstration, and I bought the items I didn't already have.

"Where are you off to now?" Helen asked as she rang up the purchases.

"Halle Brothers to look at the jewelry Kate suggested and to buy some long gloves. More money out the window. I'd better get a job out of this."

"I don't think Kate's working yet," Helen said.

"That's alright. I know where to look and I want to get done before it gets any hotter."

By the time I arrived at the department store, the thermometer already read seventy-five degrees without even a breeze. The humidity must have been over ninety percent. I stepped inside and sighed. At least it was cooler than on the street. I headed for the elevator.

"Accessories, please."

I found what I needed and hurried back to the apartment. That was Thursday and I had one more chore before I headed for the beach. I pulled out my Murphy bed and rearranged the pillows under the sheets, hoping when my parents got home—they'd both come in late—they'd think I was asleep. If it worked, I could repeat the performance when I auditioned on Monday. Then I'd have to come up with a plan if I got the job.

FAITH A. COLBURN

September 13, 1937

Monday evening, I waited for my parents to leave—Mom to the
bank to scrub floors and Dad off to the races. I really thought
about telling them, but I just knew Dad would raise a fuss like he
did when I won the contest—and we just had to have an income
from somewhere.

I'd been learning how to knit, so I worked on a muffler to keep
myself from pacing. Mom had already left for the bank, but I was
beginning to think Dad intended to hang around all night. I kept
purling when I should knit, constantly ripping out.

"Darn!" I said to myself.

"What?" Dad asked.

"Nothing. I just made a mistake."

I jumped at a knock on the door. Finally, I thought as Dad grabbed
his crutches and hobbled out with one of his racing buddies.
Betting on the races, even though it drove Mom crazy, seemed to
give Dad an outlet for his nerves, and he did bring in a little
money. Maybe Mom should let him alone so he wouldn't go any
crazier. But I didn't have time to think about that.

The minute the door closed I tore around the apartment getting
ready. I had an hour before my audition. I folded the dress, the
green one, and packed my shoes in a paper sack that I tucked
inside my swim bag, along with the gun and some change. I made
my bed up, left the apartment building in the last rays of a bright
day, and walked to the club, swinging and singing a new tune—
Let's Call the Whole Thing Off. I wished I could.

I smiled at the doorman as I stepped into the club, then hesitated for a moment when the strong smell of stale beer and tobacco smoke struck me. Soon, though, my eyes adjusted to the dark and I located the bar.

"Hi," I said to the barman. "I'm here to audition."

He looked me over, thoroughly, without a word. I guessed I would have to get used to that.

"C'mon," he said. "The dressing room's over here."

He led me across the club to a dressing room behind the stage where the band was busy tuning up.

"Here it is. I'll tell the manager you're here."

I came out transformed into something. I wasn't sure what. Something unlike me. I'd followed Helen's instructions, but my face seemed that it might crack if I smiled. The green satin slipped and slid over my body and I wanted to grab it so it wouldn't slide off. While my parents were gone, I'd practiced walking in the ankle-strap heels, but as I stepped onto the stage, I hoped I wouldn't trip.

I introduced myself to the leader of the band. "I'm here to audition."

After giving me that appraising look, he nodded. "We're just tuning up, as you can see. I'll let you know when we're ready. Did you bring something to sing?"

"No, but I know most of the standards and a lot of the new stuff as well."

"Anything in particular you'd like to start with?"

"How about *Sing, Sing, Sing?*" *Might as well start with something that has already succeeded.*

"What key?"

"How about B flat?"

"You got it."

As I waited for the orchestra, the manager Fred Newman, came up and introduced himself. I towered over the short, squat nightclub manager with receding gray hair and sharp gray eyes. "And that's Bob Long," he said, gesturing toward the orchestra leader. "He never gets around to saying his name."

"He didn't."

Taking my hand, he said, "I think he's just in awe of all the beautiful Italian names."

"I am for sure." I grinned. At least he wasn't looking me up and down like I was a cream puff that he wanted to eat.

"Oh, that's right, you must be, let's see, maybe Welch?"

"Irish and Welch. How did you know?"

"Your name seemed like it could be—British anyway. Well, I've heard the Irish can sing too."

"We can," I said.

"Okay Bobbi, it looks like Bob's ready for you. Let's see what you can do." He released my hand and stepped off the stage.

At the mic and looked back at Long. By then I knew the drill.

"You ready?"

I nodded, and he started the orchestra on the first notes of the song. On the third bar, I came in strong, swingin' and singin' and snappin' my fingers. As I moved with the swing, the green satin shimmered like liquid—and it still felt like it could slide off. I tried to ignore the sensation.

After the song, Long barely paused before he led into my theme, *Blue Moon*. I entered at the end of the introduction, singing slow and smooth like Greta'd taught me.

When the orchestra paused, Newman clapped and stood, coming forward.

"You jumped right into that second number without a flinch. That's good. I'd like you to hang around and sing the first set with the orchestra, just to see how you adapt to each other and how the crowd responds to you. Can you do that?"

This looked hopeful. I couldn't believe I could get the first job I tried for, but I would take it if I got it. "sure," I said.

"Okay, relax for a while. See if you can get Bob to say more than a couple of words. We open in about fifteen minutes, and you'll go to work a few minutes after that."

I turned to Long when Newman went back to his office. "How did you know what key for *Blue Moon*?"

"You did *Sing, Sing, Sing* in B flat, so I was pretty sure the A would work for *Blue Moon*. Besides, I actually managed to get away from here during the summer to go dancing with my wife at the Pavilion. You do good work, Bobbi. I'm glad to be working with you."

Embarrassed, I reminded him I didn't have the job yet.

Long smiled, and that's when Tony Falgione stepped up.

"Hello Bobbi. I sure didn't expect to see you here."

"What on earth are *you* doing here?" I demanded when I caught my breath.

"I work here Bobbi. Looks like you will too. I'm the bouncer."

I didn't know what to say. I'd kind of brushed him off before, and now here he was again—and I'd have to see him almost every night if I got the job. When I didn't say anything, though, he let me off the hook.

"It's okay Bobbi. Seems like you have a lot going on. It's nice to see you, though."

"Nice to see you too," I mumbled. I couldn't imagine how this would go well.

The band cut our stumbling around short, starting the first set with its theme. Tony hustled off to troll the club, looking for trouble, and Long introduced me as a guest artist as I stepped up on stage after that first number.

After the set, I glanced around, but I didn't see Tony. Newman handed me off the stage, led me to a table. We sat.

"Okay Bobbi, how old did you say you are?"

"Nineteen, sir."

"You just stick to that and you've got a job if you want it."

"I want it, sir."

He smiled. "It's twenty dollars a week. You'll be working from eight to four every night but Sunday. Can you do that?"

"Sure. When can I start?"

"How about tomorrow night?"

Not eager to burn any bridges, I said, "I can't, I can stay tonight, but I'm singing at the Pavilion right now, and I owe them another week after this. I have Mondays and Thursdays off, so I can be here this Thursday, Monday and Thursday next week, and then full time after that. Is that alright?"

Newman nodded. "So I can expect you ready to sing at eight Thursday?"

"Yes, sir."

"We're closed Sundays and Mondays, but otherwise you'll be working. Right?"

"Yes, sir."

"Call me Fred."

"Okay, Fred."

"When you're not on stage, I want you talking up the customers. You can take a break to freshen up your makeup and all that stuff, but mostly I want you out on the floor."

"Yes, sir."

"Okay, go freshen up for the next set and I'll see you later." Fred got up and walked away while I sat still for a moment, then took off for the dressing room to make sure everything was still in place. That darned silk made me feel naked.

October 5, 1937

My only fight with the boss began after only a week of singing. I should have anticipated the groping, but the East Bandstand at the Pavilion had kept me off the floor, away from the crowd. So a few days into my first nightclub gig, I'd had a rude surprise.

"Bobbi, you can't go around smacking my customers," Fred growled, scraping his hands over his scalp and scrubbing them across his face.

"But, Mr. Newman, he had his hands all over me. I feel like I need a bath. He smelled like a distillery."

"I know, Bobbi, but you still can't hit my customers."

Everything had been going great. Mom had headed for bed early the nights she didn't work, exhausted from walking the streets looking for a job that just didn't exist, and from working half the night at the one she had. The made-up bed had worked so far, but I knew my luck couldn't last long. I wasn't counting on some drunk trying to maul me. Should have known, but I guess I'd tried not to think about it.

Anyway, this very drunk customer had grabbed me as I left the stage, weaving my way through the tables to my dressing room. Without a second's thought, just on instinct, I spun around and slapped him, leaving finger-welts across his cheek. Trapped in the knot of men standing around him, I was caught. He had my upper arms in his grip and his face pushed into mine. I almost gagged on his beer and cigarette breath.

Where was Tony?

He spotted me about the same time I spotted him. He had a hand on the jerk's shoulder before you could say Jack Robinson. The guy took a swing, but found himself propelled, barely standing, toward the back door—without ever connecting.

Panting and blinking back tears, I ran for the dressing room. I was straightening my dress and looking at the bruises coming up on my arms when Fred pounded on the door. He pushed past me when I opened it and started growling. He'd been so quiet and calm when he hired me, I didn't know he had it in him. We stood eyeing each other. At last I took a chance. I flung my head back, looking directly into Newman's eyes.

"I'm not some cheap floozy that guys can just paw at whenever they want. If they don't keep their hands off, I'll make sure they do."

"Look, you're here to entertain my customers."

"By singing to them."

"Not beat up on them. I want you talking to them and mixing with them."

"Not if it means they get to paw me."

Fred stared at me for a moment, eyes narrowed.

"Bobbi, you're good, I'll admit it. In just one week I've had a dozen guys tell me they heard you at the Pavilion and came to the club just to hear you sing. But you've got to talk to them. Let them see you."

I took a deep breath, wondering if I'd overstepped. "Fred, I really want this job, but not if I have to let your customers paw me."

"But that's . . . ." He stopped, looking at his shoes. Again we stood eyeing one another without speaking. At last Fred broke the silence, and I took a quiet breath.

"Okay. Tony is a pretty big boy."

I nodded.

"I'm going to have him escort you around between sets, just to make sure my customers keep their hands to themselves—and you do, too."

I knew that could be complicated, but so far Tony hadn't made any claims on me—it was only one date after all. Maybe he had a steady girl by now. Anyway, I'd be glad for the protection.

"Okay." I sagged a little. "Thank you, Fred. Thank you. You won't regret it."

"Okay." He stepped out and closed the door behind him.

I could hear him muttering to himself through the thin walls of the dressing room.

"Dames. Maybe hiring this little girl wasn't such a good idea."

The last words I heard were something about "adding a little class." I hoped he meant *I* had a little class.

When I walked out for my next set I felt tired like I'd never felt before. Tony stood waiting for me, and from then forward I became "Tony's girl," at least for Fred's customers' benefit. I really liked having the big guy around. Always well groomed—shoes shined, narrow hands well manicured—he wore a huge ring I wouldn't like to get socked with. He would hand me off the stage at the end of my sets and walk around the crowded lounge with me, sort of delivering me at a table and standing aside while I talked and flirted with the customers. He hardly ever spoke, but he occasionally took my elbow and guided me away from someone he didn't like. I trusted his judgment, glancing up into his eyes with a whispered, "Thank you." He was smooth, and I hoped I'd learn to spot the troublemakers myself. Fortunately, he never, ever asked me out or tried to do anything romantic. I was sure he had a girlfriend.

As it turned out, Tony was the least of my worries.

October 14, 1937

By the time I finished my last set every night, I could barely hold my head up. Not only was I up way past my bedtime every night, I was also getting up a couple of hours after I got home from the club's four a.m. close and going to school—to keep up the pretense for my parents. I'd never been one to sleep in on the weekends, so they couldn't believe that first Saturday when I just lay in bed, trying to sleep, long after they'd rolled out and gone about their day. Since my bed was in the living room, though, I didn't get a whole lot of rest. Sunday was better, but I knew I couldn't keep up this schedule for long.

Like I said, I wanted to have a couple of paychecks to turn over before I told my parents what I'd been doing. It had worked but became more and more difficult. Fortunately, while Mom either cleaned the bank building or slept, Dad was out messing around with his friends. I was not looking forward to telling my parents, but the money from the Pavilion would run out in a week and Mom's checks wouldn't cover the rent. I wanted just two more nights—until I got paid.

When I left the lounge my second Thursday night—eager to drop on my bed and sleep, at least three hours, maybe three-and-a-half—I would have run if I could. One more sleepless day and night, then I could sleep Saturday morning, work my shift, and collect my check. Then I'd tell them, quit school, and sleep. . . and sleep . . . and sleep.

My usual brisk stride became a plod as I trudged the half-block to Euclid Avenue and turned left. I did not notice how sparse traffic had become, or the stifling cloud cover, or the mist in the cemetery on my left. Rain had soaked the streets during my shift and damp pavement deadened the sound of my footsteps. The air felt especially cool and damp as I passed the cemetery gates. The atmosphere, the mist, the dampness, and passing a cemetery felt vaguely ominous, and I quickened my pace. I wanted to hurry anyway, so I could curl up in that inviting bed, already laid out— but faster wasn't very fast.

I took another left onto 123rd street, head drooping. The dark car parked just inside the LakeView Cemetery entrance, behind the stone pillars where Jack and I had stopped and kissed during the summer, didn't really reach the level of my consciousness, nor did the man pacing and smoking there. Trudging along the edge of the graveyard, I focused only on getting home, anticipating the warm bed and a few blissful hours of sleep. In my haste, I'd left everything in the dressing room and only stuffed my key into my pocket, so I could move more quickly. My purse with its tiny pistol tucked away remained on my dressing table.

When I reached the cemetery entrance, a man reached out from behind a pillar and grabbed my left arm. I gasped in shock. My forward momentum swung me past him and allowed me to jerk away, but I'd been thrown a little off balance and the man lunged after me, closing his arms around my neck and shoulders in a hard embrace. Too stunned to scream, I struggled silently. In an instant, he had a hand covering my mouth and nose, grinding my lips into my teeth—taking my breath away. You can't think when someone grabs you like that. As I tried to break free, a glimpse of my pistol flashed through my mind—but mostly I just fought. He lifted me off my feet and I kicked wildly, hoping to connect with his shins.

"Be still, you little bitch," he snarled—hot breath warming the back of my neck. My skin stood up in goose bumps.

As I squirmed and struggled, he dragged me backward toward the passenger side of the car. He held me around the shoulders with his right arm, and reached inside with his left, releasing his grip on my mouth, and fumbling for something in the glove box. Screaming, I kicked and struggled. I smelled something cloyingly sweet—something that made my eyes water. In the moment when he brought a damp cloth over my nose and mouth, I realized my hands were free and my body remembered what Jack had taught me.

"If you don't shut up and stop fighting me, I'm going to knock you out."

I went limp just like I would in the water, allowing myself to fall while I pried his fingers loose. He lost his grip and I landed on his instep with the square heel of my shoe. Dropping into a runner's crouch, I took off for the club with the beast howling and pounding along behind me, following the margin of the cemetery. He paced me. Afraid to look, I could hear him running—close behind me. We tore along for a block, two blocks. He seemed to be dropping back a little bit as we started the third block. I glanced over my shoulder. He was still there, still following. We ran another block and I couldn't hear him anymore. I looked again. No kidnapper—but I didn't slow down.

At the club, I pounded on the door and nearly fell into Tony's arms when he jerked it open. Without a word, he gathered me up and carried me, still panting and crying, to a table next to the bar. Setting me down, he dragged a chair over and pushed me into it, then stepped behind the bar and poured an inch of Drambuie into a glass, bringing it back and setting it down in front of me.

"Drink this, then tell me what happened."

I hesitated.

"Don't worry. It'll just give you a little buzz."

I took a deep breath and a little sip. "Thanks, Tony."

"So what gives? You look like you've seen a ghost."

"I have, sort of. Somebody tried to . . . tried to . . . ."

"Tried to what?"

"I don't know. This man jumped out from the cemetery and grabbed me. He dragged me to his car." I stopped, burying my face in my hands.

"Have another sip."

I looked up at him, taking a gulp of the smooth liqueur. I choked and tried to talk and cough at the same time.

"He had his hand over my mouth. Couldn't breathe . . . kicking at his shins . . . then I just dropped."

"You must have connected."

"Guess so. I'm not sure what I did."

I finished the Drambuie as he turned over another chair, turned it backwards, and sat.

"I'll be alright now," I told him. I didn't even convince myself.

"Right. Did it occur to you it might have been the Torso Murderer?"

"No. Nothing occurred to me except getting away." I began to tremble. "What if it *was* the Torso Murderer?" I crossed my arms on the table and laid my head on them with a groan.

"If it was, you may be the only victim to escape." He reached for my chin and raised my head to face him. "I need to take you to the police."

"What're they gonna do *now*."

"Maybe catch the guy."

"I didn't see him. He got me from behind."

"There might be something else that'll help. Something you haven't thought of."

"Oh, Tony! I'm going to have to quit. What if he comes back? What if it *was* the Torso Murderer? How am I going to get home?"

"One thing at a time. I'm going to take you home, but we need to go to the cops first."

"I need to let my folks know."

"Then we'll go there first."

"Aw Jeez! They don't even know I'm here."

"What do you mean?"

"I was gonna tell them I got the job when I could show them a paycheck."

Tony stared. "Your folks don't know?" He frowned. "How old are you anyway?"

I cringed, hesitating while I decided what to tell him.

"Fifteen."

"Fifteen!"

"Shshshsh. Fred'll fire me."

Tony shook his head. "Fifteen! No wonder you didn't tell your folks."

"Well, neither one of them can get a job. Dad broke his leg. I can't lose this job."

"Never mind that now. You alright?"

"Yeah, I'm okay, Tony. I'm just scared." I thought for a moment. "I need this job, but I can't walk these streets. I don't know what to do."

"Let's not worry about that now. You need to get to the police." Tony stood. "We'll figure the rest of it out later."

He disappeared into Fred's office, leaving me to picture what might have happened to me. Wishing I had another shot of that Drambuie, I visualized the way the remains of the Torso Murderer's victims had been described on the radio. My shoulders sagged and I dropped my face into my hands just as Tony came back jingling a set of keys.

"Okay, honey, here's what we're gonna do," he said, taking my arm and leading me to the door. "I'm gonna take you home and I'm gonna walk you right up to your door and see that you get there all safe and sound. Then I'm gonna wait and take you and your folks to the police station. Okay?"

"Doesn't Fred need you to help clean up?"

"Fred'll be fine. I told him what happened and he says you don't need to some in until Friday." He ushered me into the passenger side of his deep blue Chrysler DeSoto.

"Thanks for sticking up for me, Tony," I said as I ducked in.

"Hey, I've got a little sister, about your age. I'd want someone to take care of her."

By the time Tony got me home, the sky had lightened. I knew Mom would be up, she always takes the early morning hours to clear her growing despair and try to find some hope. I suspected that she would have given in to terror.

When I turned my key in the lock, my parents started shouting. I looked back at Tony. He just shrugged as I stepped inside.

"I'll wait here."

Mom wiped red-rimmed eyes and blew her nose while Dad began the inquisition. "Where the hell have you been until five o'clock in the god-damned morning and who was that guy dropping you off?"

Before I could answer, Mom had recovered enough for her own snarling observation.

"He must be at least twice your age. I ought to get the hairbrush."

I leaned against the door, waiting for an opening. This yelling and screaming was familiar, but it wasn't usually directed at me.

"I don't understand you," Dad yelled, slamming his hand on the back of the couch, raising a cloud of dust. "You've never been like this, staying out all night. We thought you were dead! What's gotten into you?"

He resumed stalking the apartment while Mom took over, dripping sarcasm.

"What have you been doing with that . . . that . . . that . . . man?"

"I got a job, just like you wanted," I said when Mom paused to take a breath.

"Jesus Christ! What kind of a damn job keeps you out all night with some guy? You're not a slut!" Dad snarled, grabbing and twisting my arm.

With his nose inches from mine, I cringed, but held my ground. "I've been singing in a nightclub for twenty dollars a week. I didn't want to tell you until I'd earned a couple of paychecks."

Dad released my arm, stepped back, and stared, but Mom didn't miss a beat. "You're doing *what?*"

"I sing. I sing every night but Sunday and Monday. I can make us a decent living."

Mom took her turn staring. "You're only fifteen, Bobbi," she began slowly. "You can't get a job in a nightclub."

"I *did* get a job in a nightclub. Where else did you *expect* me to get a singing job? I'm working at LakeView Jazz Club."

Dad exploded. "Not anymore, you're not. I don't know who would hire a fifteen-year-old anyway."

"I told them I was nineteen."

Mom wasn't done yet. "So you go out with the customers after work," she snapped.

"No . . . ."

"It sure looked like you were with *someone,*" she hissed.

"That was Tony, the bouncer."

"Oh, that's better. She's going out with the bouncer."

"No. He just brought me home tonight because it was late."

"This morning," Dad growled. "He brought you home this morning."

"Right. Look at you. Your hair's a mess, your lips are all swollen. That must have been some goodnight kiss."

"Mom, Dad." I looked from one to the other, dreading what I had to say next. "He was protecting me."

"From what? Your other boyfriends?"

"Aw, come on. He was protecting me from the guy who jumped me on the way home, over by the cemetery."

"Sure he did . . ."

"No, Mom, look at the back of my head. I got away and ran back to the club 'cause it was closer, but I must have banged my head into him. It hurts."

Mom grabbed my arm and spun me away from the door. Parting my hair, none too gently, she discovered the lump and clots of blood crusted in my hair. She nodded at Dad, who dropped into a chair with his elbows on the table.

"This stops right now," he said when he could speak. "I don't want to go looking for pieces of you when the Butcher gets done with you."

"Look, we can do this later. Tony's waiting outside to take us to the police station. He thinks we should report this."

"Tony's waiting?" Mom snarled, dripping sarcasm.

"Wait a minute. Wait a minute. We do need to go to the police," said Dad. "Maybe Bobbi can help get this monster off the streets."

After a thoughtful pause, Mom agreed. "And Tony'll take us?"

"Yeah, he's waiting outside—if all the yelling and screaming didn't drive him away." I inclined my head toward the door.

"Let him in, let him in," Dad said.

October 16, 1937

When I opened the door, I found Tony leaning across the hall, arms folded across his chest. He eyed me.

"Everything okay?"

"Okay for now, but I'm gonna get a lot more yellin' at. You heard."

He grinned. "Couldn't help it."

"C'mon in."

He pushed off against the wall and stepped inside the now quiet apartment where my parents gave him a critical looking over. Stretching himself up to his full height, Dad spoke for both of them.

"Thanks for looking after our daughter."

"Any time."

Dad frowned. "She says you're willing to take us to the police station?"

"She may be the only victim to escape the Butcher. Maybe she can help catch him."

"We want to be with her."

"Of course. If you don't mind, I'd like to stay with you too—just in case there's something I can do to help. Fred wanted me to do whatever I can."

"Fred?"

"The manager—actually, the owner."

Dad swung forward on his crutches. "Sure. Let's just go so we can all get some sleep."

"Tony grinned."I'm all for that."

We trooped downstairs to Tony's car and settled in for the ride downtown. When Tony parked in front of the station, he jumped out and hurried around to help Dad with his crutches.

"Thanks," Dad said as he began stumping his way into the building, jabbing the crutches into the steps as if he wanted to crush them to rubble.

By ten to seven, we were all inside staring at the desk sergeant across a scarred counter.

"Somebody tried to grab my daughter off the street," Dad announced.

"When was this?"

I stepped forward. "A little after four this morning."

The sergeant frowned. "And what were you doing on the street at four in the morning?"

So this is how it was going to be.

I narrowed my eyes, daring the officer to make something of it. "Going home from work."

"Where do you work until four in the morning?"

Tony stepped up to the desk. "She's a singer," he said, "and a damned good one."

"And who are you?"

"I work with her at the LakeView Jazz Club."

The man smirked. "Work with her, huh?"

"Look, you knucklehead," Dad snarled, leaning across the counter, "you've got a killer out there making prime cuts out of Cleveland citizens and you may be looking at the only one who's ever got away. Don't you think you ought to get somebody out here to find out what she knows?"

The man stared back at Dad. "Might have been some john just wanted a little free lovin'."

Dad looked like he was going to crawl over the counter, but Tony was quick.

"Look, Sergeant," he says, stepping up beside Dad, "this was over in the Torso Murderer's favorite part of town. Bobbi here is *not* a hooker, and I suggest you get someone to talk to her. Now."

The guy backed up a step, frowning and taking in Tony's tough stance. "It *is* kinda quiet right now. I guess I could get someone up here."

"Do it," Dad said.

"Okay, okay."

The officer opened a door behind the counter and yelled, "Got some dame up here thinks she escaped from the Torso Killer . . . Yeah . . . She's just a kid . . . Okay."

He gestured toward a beat-up wooden bench across from the counter. "Have a seat. Someone'll be out."

The bench felt like a granite shelf, but I'd never been in a police station before, so I took a good look around. Behind the sergeant's desk were three photos, President Roosevelt, Governor Davey, and Mayor Burton. Do you suppose it would have hurt any of them to smile when they have their picture taken? Since there wasn't much to look at, I studied the desk sergeant. His uniform seemed a little tight around the neck and he adjusted his tie from time to time as if to relieve the pressure. When he glanced up and noticed me watching him, his already-ruddy complexion brightened and I looked away. He didn't seem very busy, but I remembered that he had said it's quiet right now. Seemed like all he had to do was make mysterious marks on sheets of paper and move them to another pile.

After about half-an-hour, Dad ran out of patience. "I'm gonna go up there and jump down that desk sergeant's throat and dance on his liver," he grumbled.

Just as he started scrambling to his feet, though, a plain-clothes officer stepped through a door at the end of the hallway. "You the people think you saw the Torso Murderer?"

I nodded.

"About time," says Dad.

"Will you come back?"

We all started for the back of the station.

"Not all of you."

"We're her parents, and this guy was there," Mom said.

"We're all comin'," Dad growled.

The officer grimaced, but turned and led the way. When he got back to his desk, he robbed other desks of their extra chairs. I looked around at the harsh open office lit by buzzing fluorescent tubes. Most of the scattered gray, metal file cabinets and desks had a covering of heaped papers as well as bits and pieces of other stuff that might have included dried-out sandwiches and cold cups of coffee. I wondered what awful things had to happen to bring other people into this room. It almost smelled like fear. When we were all seated, I focused on the detective.

"I'm Detective Lieutenant Able," he said. "Maybe we can start with your name and address, Miss."

I introduced myself and my parents and gave our address.

"And who's this?" he asked, inclining his head toward Tony.

"This is Tony Falgione. I work with him at LakeView Jazz Club. I ran back there when I got away."

"So he wasn't actually there."

I glanced at Mom. "No. He wasn't there when I was attacked, but he convinced me to come here."

"You didn't want to report this?"

"Didn't think about it."

"Okay. Just tell me what happened."

"I'm not sure I can be of any help. I was just walking home after work."

"And what do you do?"

"I'm the club's canary."

"Okay. So what happened?"

"I turned onto 123rd Street. It had rained while I was at the club, and it was foggy. I couldn't see much, but somehow I felt . . . I don't know . . . kind of spooky." I paused a moment, closing my eyes, trying to remember. "I didn't see anything."

I stopped again, eyes fluttering open. "No. That's not right." I shuddered. "I *did* see something. I just didn't really notice it. There was a shadow just inside the gate. I saw a cigarette glow, like someone was taking a drag, and then a spray of sparks, like he threw it on the ground and ground it out."

"About how tall was this figure?"

"Well," I hesitated, closing my eyes again. I reached a few inches above my head. "About this much taller than me."

The detective frowned. "That's very precise."

"There's a mark on that pillar. We noticed it last summer. It was like somebody had marked Jack's height there."

Able sighed. "Who's Jack?"

"My boyfriend."

His face seemed to light up. "And what were you doing in the cemetery with Jack?"

"Looking at statues and stuff. His grandfather made some of them."

"We'll get back to that later. What happened next?"

"Well, like I said, I was feeling kinda spooky, even though I didn't really notice anything—just a shadow. I was really tired."

"Yeah?"

"So I started walking faster. Something just didn't feel right. Then when I got to that pillar—I hadn't really noticed anything, you see—he reached out and grabbed my arm."

"That's when you ran?"

"I was moving fast enough, I jerked away, but he jumped out and grabbed me . . . kind of around here." I gestured around my chest. "And he had his hand over my mouth and nose. My lips are all split."

"What did he look like?"

"I don't know. He grabbed me from behind."

"So how'd you get away?"

"Well, he lifted me off my feet and I was kicking," I leaned against the back of the chair and looked at the ceiling. "But he dragged me backward into the cemetery." I looked back at Officer Able. "He had a car hidden in there."

"Did you see what kind of car?"

"I don't know. Dark color. Black, maybe brown or dark blue." I dropped my face into my hands and rubbed my forehead with the tips of my fingers. "I think it had only two doors. I don't know if that helps," I frowned. "and no spare tire on the fender."

"Maybe we'll have you look at some pictures later. What happened next?"

"He opened the passenger door." By then, I was gulping for air. Tony touched my elbow for just a second and that steadied me. "He reached into the glove box and got some kind of rag or something . . . I started screaming . . . He put that thing over my nose. It smelled really sweet."

"Ether. It's a wonder you didn't pass out."

"That's when I got away."

"How? What did you do?"

"I don't know." My hands trembled and I blinked back tears.

Tony reached over and took my hand. "Just take your time, Bobbi. You're safe now."

I nodded and continued. "I . . . I'd been fightin' an' kickin'. . . an' that didn't do any good. He just hung on tighter." I looked down at my hands, clutched in my lap. "I know," I said finally, raising my head, and smiling. "I went limp. Just let myself fall. See, when you're swimmin' and somebody grabs on to you, you just sink . . . ."

The cop frowned.

"Anyway, it musta surprised him, 'cause he lost his grip. And *that's* when I ran. I was still pretty close to the club, so I ran back there. I could hear him pounding along behind me, but I lost him after about three blocks."

"And she came beating on the back door of the club and kinda fell inside when I opened it," Tony added.

"Yeah, I was really scared." Without even thinking, I ran a rough hand through my hair and winced. "Oh, and I got this."

"What's that?"

"I musta banged my head into him somehow, because I've got a bump and I have some blood in my hair. I don't think it's mine."

"We'll want a sample of that blood. We can get his blood type at least, so before you leave, I'll take you down to the lab." He'd been taking notes and he shuffled some papers." Can you remember anything else? Anything at all?" After a long pause, Detective Able cleared his throat. "Okay. Let's go back. You say you saw a shadow before you got to the gate."

"Well, I remember it now, but somehow I was just so tired I didn't pay any attention—like I didn't even notice."

"Alright. Can you describe him? You're sure it was a man?"

"Oh yes! Definitely a man, but I never saw his face. He was just a shadow—then when he grabbed me, he had me from behind. Even when I got away, I never turned around." I stopped to think. "Well, I did turn around to look, but he was not very close. I was running and I could hear he'd dropped back—he was kinda howling."

"Howling?! Like a wolf?"

"Yes. No. I don't know. It was a horrible noise—like he was in pain—like somebody was sawing off his leg with a rusty saw."

Dad rubbed his thigh where it had been broken.

"What did you see?"

I closed my eyes, thumbs under my cheekbones, fingertips massaging my forehead. For several moments, I just sat thinking. Tony reached over and rubbed a soothing hand over my shoulders.

"You alright, Bobbi?"

"Yeah. Just thinking," I mumbled. I raised my head, speaking very slowly. "He . . . his clothes must have been really big for him, 'cause they were flapping around him. It was dark, but it looked like maybe a work shirt and work pants—maybe boots."

"Can you describe his face?"

"Uh," I took a shuddering breath, "it looked almost like a skeleton."

"What do you mean?"

"Like holes where his eyes should be and . . . and like just a jaw 'n no cheeks."

"No what? What about a nose? Did he have nose."

"Yes. A big nose."

"Anything else?"

"Um. Yes. Remember that mark on the pillar? Last summer, Jack noticed a whole bunch of cigarette butts right inside the gate. We talked about how somebody must have stood there waiting for something—and there were tire tracks."

"I was going to get back to that. I think it was this Jack guy who tried to grab you."

I looked at him in stunned silence. Tony touched my elbow for just a steadying second.

"We don't know him," Mom said.

"Ella," Dad warned.

"No," I said, glaring at my parents. "That's just dumb. He's my boyfriend. Why would he try to grab me."

"It wouldn't be the first time," said Able.

"No. It's not him."

"What makes you so sure?"

"This man's hands were hairy."

"I thought it was dark."

"I tried to pry his fingers off my mouth—while I was fighting him. And his voice. Sounded . . . I don't know . . . like blowing in a gallon jug, you know, across the mouth. An' he had long hair, cause it kind of flopped over his forehead."

"I think we're gonna have to check this Jack out. See if he has an alibi."

"I'm tellin' you it's not him. None of what I just said fits him."

"Maybe, but we need to check."

"He's in Chicago. Goin' to college."

"What's his name?"

"Jack."

"Last name?"

"Mosso."

Able raised his eyebrows. I couldn't quite fathom the cat-eating-the-canary expression that crossed his face. "Jack Mosso?"

I glared at him. "Yeah. But he's out of town."

"Maybe he came back."

"You're barkin' up the wrong man."

"I'll be the judge of that."

"Oh for cryin' out loud. I told you. Don't you have any suspects after all these murders?"

"We've got a couple, but can't tie 'em in. Now you've given us a lead."

"You oughta see where your suspects were last night."

"We'll be checkin' on Mosso and his family, too."

"His *family?* What's his family got to do with it?"

"Maybe nothing."

"Just let 'em do their job, Bobbi," said Tony.

"But this is nuts. Jack'll be furious if they interrupt his studies."

"How furious?" Able wanted to know.

"What's the matter with you people? Not like that."

"You don't know Bobbi," said my mother.

"I do know. I saw that monster's face. I know it was blocks away, but it looks nothing like Jack. Jack has long, slender fingers. This guy's hands were like hairy sausages—and that voice. That awful, scary voice. It's not Jack. Period."

"I think it's too late Bobbi. They're gonna check on him whether you want 'em to or not," said Dad.

"We are," said Able. "Now let me see you down to the lab—and then we'll look at some cars."

Two hours later, I'd had the blood picked out of my hair, packaged and labeled, and I'd looked at dozens of pictures of cars. I hadn't realized there were so many kinds of cars. I could barely hold my head up when the detective finally offered to show us out the door.

"Just leave Jack alone," I pleaded on the way down the hall.

"We'll check every lead—including your boyfriend." He paused, writing something down. "Did you have a fight with him?"

"No, of course not."

"Let's go, Bobbi," Dad said. "If Jack's innocent, there's no harm done."

"But messin' with his whole family? What for?"

"It'll work itself out, Bobbi," said Tony, taking my elbow and steering me along behind Detective Able—just like he did every night at the club. "I'm sure they'll check on the other suspects too."

"You did what you could, Bobbi," Mom said. "When they see that nobody in the Mosso family looks like your description, they'll find somebody else. At least you gave them some idea of what that monster looks like."

By the time we were tucked into the car, we were all yawning. Nobody said a word during the drive back to our apartment.

Tony dropped us early in the afternoon and I hoped to flop into bed immediately, but Dad hadn't forgotten about my new job. As soon as I closed the apartment door behind me, he started in on me

"What were you thinking anyway?"

"I was thinking that I don't want to live on the street. I was thinking that I could pull my own weight. I was thinking that this might be my big chance to make my own living. "

"To let every drunk in Cleveland paw at you night after night?"

I smiled. "It's not like that. I can stare most of them down, but last Saturday some guy tried to feel me up and I whipped around and slapped him. Fred wasn't too happy about that, but I said I was there to sing and I wouldn't put up with any of that stuff."

"Good for you, but that's not good enough. It won't stop them."

"No and Fred didn't like my methods anyway. So he ordered Tony to come get me at the ends of my sets and follow me around while I chat up the customers. Everybody thinks he's my boyfriend, so they leave me alone."

"I can imagine," Dad said. I could see him remembering the burly bear of a man with whom he'd just spent half a day. That only took him a minute, though, and then he was right back at it. "But I don't like this. You're only fifteen. I don't like you hanging around the bars until all hours. You need to be in school. You can't learn when you're out till all hours."

"I know, Dad, but this is a chance for me to get a start. I'm not crazy about all the drunks, either, but Tony does a good job of protecting me. He says he has a little sister who's about my age."

"I don't want you on the streets," Dad said. "It's not safe. Look what happened tonight. We'll get by. I'll find something. Soon."

"But what if you don't? There aren't any jobs out there. We all know that. You've been looking all summer. I can make a living for us until things get better."

"We've had this talk," Dad said. "You're staying in school."

"Yes, we've had this talk but things have changed. It will be months before you can work again, if at all. That's not your fault. It just is. I don't see any restaurants reopening. When they do, you'll be able to take over. But now, I'm quitting school because I can't sing until four a.m. and get to school by nine."

"I don't want you hanging around with this Tony guy," Mom butted in. "Next thing we know you'll be in trouble."

"Aw Mom, he's just like the big brother I never had."

"Big brother hell."

"He won't hurt me, Mom. Besides, I'm making twenty dollars a week. We can get by on that and I can save something . . . ."

"How much?" Mom asked.

"I get twenty dollars a week."

Mom looked at Dad. "Maybe . . . ."

"Nothin' doin.' she needs to finish school."

"Dad, I know you want to take care of us, but everything's gone phooey. I'd like to finish school, but I really don't have to. I can be a singer without finishing school. Many of the big names don't have high school diplomas."

The argument dragged on with Dad tearing at his hair, frustrated with his inability to sway my logic. By four-thirty, Mom had given in, knowing that our situation had become desperate the moment Dad stepped in front of that pick.

"Look, Dad," I said, "I know you want me safe. I will be safer living here with you than if we're all out on the street. So let me take care of that. But I still need to walk to and from the club. I know the hours are just grim, but if you could walk me over there and come get me when it's time to come home, I could keep working."

"You can do that, Paul," Mom said. "Like she says, it'll keep us all off the streets—and I'll need you to take me to and from work too, you know. I'm not walking around in the dark all by myself anymore."

Dad shook his head and I noticed a tear running down the side of his nose. "I don't like this. I don't like it one bit."

"C'mon, Dad. We're all doing the best we can."

"I can't stand it." He tore away and walked into the bedroom.

Next morning, I slept . . . and slept . . . and slept. Even my parents' bickering couldn't disturb me. When Mom rustled around getting ready to go job hunting and Dad headed out right behind her to look for what's not there, I barely opened an eyelid. That evening, though, I noticed he was missing in action even though he'd agreed to walk me to work. Mom had already left for the bank as I got ready. I'd got my stuff when I ran back to the club, so I had my purse, but I was still scared.

My hands were trembling when I headed for the door. I'd waited as long as I could, so I trudged down the stairs with my hand on the handle of the pistol and my finger in the trigger. I nearly dropped everything when Dad stepped out of the shadows by the door, dropping his cigarette and grinding it out on the pavement.

"You got everything you need?" he asked.

I guess I was a little wild-eyed when I turned in his direction. "I thought you weren't gonna be here."

"I told you I'd walk you, didn't I? I just got back from taking your mother." He checked his watch, and I noticed how he cradled it in his hand. *His own personal dragon's egg.*

"But I was waiting upstairs."

He shrugged. "Sorry. Goin' all the way up those stairs and then back down—I'm gettin' blisters under my arms."

We walked about a block. "Dad?"

"Yeah?"

"Thanks."

"Least I can do."

We walked on another couple of blocks. I kept my hand hidden in the folds of my skirt, wrapped around the gun, finger on the trigger.

"Dad?" I stopped walking. "Maybe you should take care of this. It didn't do me any good last night—I forgot it in the club until after I ran back for help."

I held the pistol out to him.

"Where the hell did you get this?" He set his crutch under his arm, grabbed the gun and shoved it into his jacket pocket.

I started walking and he followed. I wasn't sure I wanted to talk to him about it. "Pawn shop."

"Can't believe he sold this to a little girl."

I glanced at the roofs of buildings outlined in twilight after-glow. "I'm not a little girl anymore."

Dad had caught up and he looked over at me. "No, I guess you're not."

We walked some more in silence. I noticed the air cooling. It wouldn't be long before winter.

"Where'd you get the money?"

"From the fifty dollars you made me save from that contest check."

"Figures."

"Well, I thought it would protect me."

"It would have. But you've got to have it in your hand."

"I know that but I was just too tired to think. I feel better with you here."

We walked the rest of the way in silence.

When we reached the club, Tony opened the door, "You alright? Didn't think you'd be here tonight."

"Sure. I slept really great—right around the clock. I feel wonderful . . . Dad's gonna walk me from now on."

"That's good," he said, stepping back, still eyeing Dad.

I stopped. "You the doorman, tonight, too?"

"Just like to get outside when I can."

As the men exchanged greetings, I noticed Tony sizing Dad up—
like he does the customers every night. When Dad turned to leave,
he spoke up.

"Mr. Bowen, would you like to watch your daughter sing?"

"Well, yes, I would, but I really can't afford the cover, and after
this, my wife will tear me a new one if she gets off and I'm not
there to walk her home."

"Tell you what. Why don't you and the wife come some night when
she's off and you can both watch her. I'm just the bouncer here, but
Mr. Newman was pretty shaken up by what happened to Bobbi. I
don't think he'll have a problem with hosting you."

"That would be nice," Dad said, "but I really like to pay my way."

"Seems like it's been pretty rough—with your broken leg and all.
But you're spending the day lookin' for work and then walkin' her
over here and then walkin' her home at our ungodly hours."

"What? Walking my daughter over here so she can be ogled and
touched by every man in town?"

"Aw, don't think that way. Bobbi's beautiful and talented—and
there's a . . . she's kind of fresh—new."

"Naïve?"

I blushed and studied a crack in the sidewalk.

"Dad, I've got to get changed."

Neither of them acknowledged me, instead they kept talking about
me as if I wasn't there.

"Yes, that, but . . ." Dad hesitated. "But how long can she stay that
way around here?"

"I intend to stop it."

"Stop what?"

"I keep the men's hands off of her."

"So she told me and I'm grateful. But this is no place for young—women."

I laid a hand on Dad's chest. "Dad!"

He went on talking, ignoring me. "I know. I used to run a place like this—maybe a little worse. It was during Prohibition and there was an illegal back room off my restaurant—the restaurant I managed."

"Well, Mr. Bowen, I, that is we, do our best to protect her. Go ahead one of these nights and see how we do."

"Maybe I will."

"Dad! I've gotta get changed. I'll see you at four?"

"Yeah, yeah," said Dad as he turned to leave. "See ya at four."

I touched Tony's arm. "Guess he gave you kind of a hard time." Before he could answer, though, I went in and practically ran to my dressing room. All that talking about me was embarrassing.

The following Tuesday, I noticed my parents sitting at a back table, but I didn't have much chance to talk to them. Every time I glanced their way, though, I saw Dad watching me. When we passed a table full of men who had obviously been drinking all afternoon, I snuck a look at Dad and saw him begin to rise from his seat. As one of the men reached for me, I turned and looked at him. I have a special look for reachers. The guy carefully withdrew his hand and sat. When I glanced back at Dad, he was saying something to Mom, but they were too far away to hear.

They slipped out between my second and third sets. They even danced a little before they left. I knew I'd hear about their visit later.

The next afternoon, sure enough, when I woke up, I found them both sitting at the kitchen table—an unheard of event. I sighed, "Okay you guys. Let's hear it. What did you think?"

"I like that Tony guy," Mom said. "I didn't get a good look at him the other morning. I was thinking about other stuff—he's a handsome man."

"He's okay," I admitted.

Dad leaned forward, elbows on the table. "You've got that look like your mother— that scares a man half to death."

Mom frowned at him. "I don't scare anybody."

"The hell you don't." He looked back at me, still assessing. "I notice Tony has a really light touch."

"What do you mean?"

Dad closed his eyes for a moment as if gathering his thoughts. "He didn't seem to say much. I noticed that—every time I saw somebody I didn't like—he'd . . . without looking at you or saying anything, he'd touch your elbow and guide you away from that table."

I cocked my head at my dad. "He *is* pretty smooth. Notices a lot of stuff I don't."

"I hope you're paying attention." Dad grinned. "I saw him once just casually step between you and a bunch of loud-mouths. He *is* really smooth."

"Just like a big brother."

"Big brother, my ass," Dad muttered.

"Bobbi," Mom blurted. "He's in love with you."

Dad grinned. "I think so too."

"Aw, he's just doin' his job. And he's good at it. Besides, I'm pretty sure he's got a girlfriend."

Mom gave me a long, critical look. "Might be the best protection you've got. I don't suppose you're in love with him."

"Mom. I'm goin' out with Jack."

"He's gone, Bobbi. He'll be gone all winter. Maybe Tony'll grow on you."

"What kind of loyalty is that?"

"How do you know Jack'll be loyal to you—big college man like that?"

I frowned at Mom and glanced at Dad to see him make a little, almost imperceptible, shrug.

"This is about me."

"Yes it is, Bobbi. It's about who can take care of you."

I just stared. I opened my mouth and closed it. I didn't know what to say. I opened it again. "I guess I'm doing a pretty good job of that right now, don't you think?"

Dad grinned, but didn't say a word.

 Mom kept looking at me, eyes narrowed. "Look Bobbi, he's a good looking man—a little bulky in the shoulders. You could do a whole lot worse."

"You bet I could. But I don't love him so just drop it, will ya?" I looked around the kitchen. "I just got out of bed. What's to eat around here?"

October 28, 1937

I only managed to see my old friends when they drug me out of bed on an occasional Sunday afternoon, and we headed out for window shopping or just hanging around listening to music on the radio. It bothered me more than I'd thought it would. I'd always been a bit of a loner. I'd had very little interest in boys when the other girls were consumed with them—until Jack. But that fall, all they wanted to talk about was my job—the glamour and the gowns (I still wore Mom's.) and the men (They couldn't keep their hands to themselves.). It was good to see them, but mostly they made me sad.

On stage, I allowed the music to move me, dancing stage right to the instrumental numbers and immersing myself in the techniques I'd learned from Greta, when I sang. Looking into the lights without squinting required conscious effort, but it had become second nature. My bare shoulders and arms made the spotlights easier to bear, once I got used to the feeling. I'd sweat off my makeup every set, but I'd gotten used to that, too, and nobody bothered me on stage. In some ways, I had come to feel like I'd always imagined the street artist must have felt. I knew I was surrounded by people moving and talking and breathing, but I felt alone on the planet with the band behind me melting into nothing but a sound that moved me. But when the music ended, I had to step back into the crowd.

One night in late October, I had just finished a set when I noticed a kind of nervous hush. As Tony handed me off the stage, I saw four men moving toward the tables next to the stage. The people already sitting there got up and moved. Puzzled, I looked at Tony.

"That's Big Al Puccinelli," he said.

"Yikes! What's he doin' here? I thought the Mob hung out at Anthony's."

"He said he's here to hear you sing."

I looked up at him. "What if he doesn't like me?"

Tony smiled, his lips a thin, tight line. "I'd worry more about what if he *does* like you."

"Oh," I said, barely breathing. "Oh."

We'd just reached my dressing room, so I stepped in and sat in front of the mirror. I gazed into my own eyes. They looked as frightened as I felt.

"Oh man," I whispered to the mirror. "Could it get any scarier?"

As I sat staring at myself, I remembered the night, before my audition, when I'd heard about the Torso Murderer's latest victim and how scared I'd been. I remembered my decision not to let fear rule my life—and how I'd been attacked, less than two weeks later. The beast had remained quiet ever since, but I didn't expect him to stay that way. Dad had probably kept me from turning up in pieces, but he couldn't protect me from a mob boss. What was I supposed to do now? I guessed it was too late to run.

I checked my makeup and stepped out, ready for my usual schmoozing between sets. Tony and I worked the back of the club, trying not to be too obvious about avoiding Puccinelli. As I stepped up on stage for my second set, I glanced toward the mob boss's table and saw him staring back at me. I looked down at the hem of my dress, making sure I wouldn't step on it in my panic as I climbed the steps.

Working my way through the set, moving back and forth at the front of the stage and making brief eye contact with people in the crowd, my attention stayed riveted on Puccinelli whose eyes never seemed to leave me. I'd always taken for granted that my job involved being seen as well as heard and, even though it sometimes made me cringe, I figured it went with the job. That night I felt very looked at and absolutely vulnerable. By the time Tony collected me again, I needed a dressing room stop to powder the sweaty shine on my face that hadn't come from hot spotlights.

As I faced my mirror, I hoped Puccinelli was satisfied and that he'd go home without wanting anything from me.

Before I'd refreshed my lipstick, though, Tony tapped on my door. "You ready? Puccinelli wants you to join him at his table."

I groaned. I just wanted to make a living. That's all I wanted. Just to make a living. "I don't suppose I can refuse," I called through the door.

"I wouldn't."

"No, I suppose not." I looked around my little dressing room then refreshed my lipstick and stepped out, reaching for Tony's hand. "I'm ready."

He gave mine a little squeeze. "You'll be alright," he said.

"I hope so."

"Bobbi, you realize I can't stay with you like I always do—without being obvious. It'll just be you and Puccinelli."

I stared at him, my mind buzzing in alarm. Well, what're you gonna do? I let it buzz for a minute or so, then took a huge gulp of air and forced myself to breathe evenly. I squared my shoulders, straightened my back, and let go of his hand.

"Let's do it," I said, noticing a strange look in Tony's eyes.

I walked out like usual, on Tony's arm, smiling and nodding at the customers as we made our way to Puccinelli's table.

I'm sure as hell not gonna let Puccinelli know he scares me to death.

I sat carefully on the chair Tony pulled out for me and gave him my most ravishing smile as he stepped away. Then I turned my attention to the mob boss. Alfred, "The Owl," Puccinelli. Big Al. I looked him over. Clean shaven, hair carefully parted and slicked back, red rose in his lapel.

THE RELUCTANT CANARY SINGS

He doesn't look so scary. He's kind of handsome. How mean can the guy be? Well, handsome is as handsome does. Seems like he's done some pretty nasty things. I can't think about that now. Need to stay alert.

"Good evening, Mr. Puccinelli," I began. "I hope you're enjoying the LakeView.

He gave me a long, unnerving look from of the corner of his eye, head cocked to the right. The part of my mind that still functioned thought the owl nickname must have come from the way he cocked his head.

"It's kind of a dump, don't you think?"

Torn between loyalty to Fred and Tony and my desire to avoid upsetting the dangerous man across the table, I took a moment to answer. "Well, it's not the Ritz, but I've enjoyed singing here and I hope Fred will keep me on."

Puccinelli continued appraising me. It wasn't quite a stare-down, but I sweat bullets in those few moments.

"I'm here because the wife sent me. She's heard about you and she wanted me to see if the rumors are true."

"Gee, what rumors, Mr. Puccinelli? I haven't done anything particularly scandalous—except singing in a bar, of course."

"Oh, nothing scandalous," he said. "She heard you could sing and that you're presentable."

"Presentable?"

"You don't look like a floozie."

"Oh."

"Listen, I've got a proposition for you. We're having a little Halloween party at my place Saturday. We'll have an orchestra and some singers. That singing soda shop guy and . . . ."

"You mean Sammy Sansone?" I interrupted. *Yikes! I gotta keep my head.* "I'm sorry," I said. "I didn't mean . . . ."

"As I was saying, Sammy Sansone and the Carlo Palatino orchestra. And the wife wants a female vocalist. Somebody new—you."

"That would be *great!*" I said, thinking for a moment only of working with a big-name orchestra and a well-known singer. Then, remembering who I was talking to and my permanent job at LakeView, I stopped. "But, I work here every Saturday, and I don't want to lose my job. Saturday's our big night."

"Don't worry about that. I'll make Fred an offer he can't turn down."

"Oh, but he's been real good to me. I don't want to let him down."

"I'm sure he'll do alright for one Saturday. You're not going to work here all your life anyway, are you? He'll have to get along without you some day—so we're all set?"

Sammy Sansone. It's just a party. I'll be alright.

"Okay, as long as it's okay with Fred," I said. "But I don't know where to go."

"I'll send my driver for you a six. That way you can meet everybody and practice with Palatino and Sansone before the party starts at eight. You'll have a place to change."

"Okay," I said, "I'll be ready." I thought for a second about whether I wanted Puccinelli to know where I lived. I guessed it would be easy enough for him to figure out if he wanted to, but why make it easy.

"All my gowns and makeup and shoes and stuff are here," I said. "I'll meet your driver here, if that's alright. Is it a costume party? Do you want me in costume?"

"No."

"Great. I'll see you next Saturday."

"Yeah," Puccinelli said. He gestured to his bodyguards. The four got up and left the nightclub, leaving me in a kind of breathless vacuum. I remained seated for a few moments, nerves tingling. I'd be completely alone at the party—no Tony to look out for me. I thought I could hear a waterfall roaring over the edge of the world; then Tony was right beside me, holding out his hand.

"You alright? You look a little pale."

"Huh?" I looked around to get my bearings and noticed all eyes in the club seem focused on me. "Oh. Yeah." I took Tony's hand and stood.

"What happened?"

"He wants me to sing at a party—at his place."

"Good God, Bobbi, you can't do it. I can't be there to protect you."

"I'd already realized that, Tony. But I don't know how to turn him down." I turned toward the stage. "I'd better get to work."

When I looked back into his eyes as I started up the steps, he looked almost as frightened as I felt. I stopped.

"I'll be okay, Tony."

"Yeah," he said turning toward his watching-post at the back of the club.

By the time I got home the next morning, I'd decided not to tell my parents. I was ready with a lie. It seemed like I did more of that every day. I told them I had to go to the club early on Saturday to rehearse some new pieces. Tony would take me home, I told them. I didn't need the uproar and what could they do anyway? I hoped all Puccinelli wanted was a singer for his Halloween party.

At Puccinelli's on Saturday, I was nearly blinded by the crystal chandelier in the entrance hall. I tripped on the threshold and nearly sprawled on a cat that yowled and tore off across the checkerboard floor. If Puccinelli's driver hadn't grabbed my elbow, my grand entrance would have ended in a splat. Once righted, I thanked the driver and gazed around the foyer. Before I could appraise my surroundings a thickset man with an obvious bulge under his left arm strode into the hall, heading directly for me. I caught my breath.

"Bobbi. Right?" he asked.

"That's right," I said, gripping my hatbox a little tighter.

"I'm Michael," he said. "I'll take you into the hall."

I glanced out the tall, mullioned windows as Michael led me away. *My gosh there are a bunch of scary-looking guys standing around like a flock of ravens. I wonder what they'd do if I tried to leave.* As I turned away, one of them glanced at me, grinned and winked, as if he'd heard what I was thinking. My heart took a little flop, like dropping over the top of a ferris wheel. Turning from him, I noticed another man standing by some bushes and staring in the window.

"Oh my God," I murmured. "It's Jack." I kept walking.

"I'm sorry," said Michael, "I didn't hear."

"Um," I said. "I was just looking out at the grounds. What a gorgeous place."

"Yeah," said Michael. "They hired a landscape architect. Some famous guy."

My heels echoed across the empty ballroom as Michael led me to the stage, but my glimpse of Jack had me completely distracted. Was it really him? I had no time to think about him, though, because Sansone was already introducing himself as Michael disappeared. Though I couldn't help feeling excited about meeting Sansone, I really wanted a minute to think about what Jack was doing at Puccinelli's mansion must mean. No time for that, I told myself. I grasped Sansone's hand and smiled.

Palatino's band had made a name for itself already, too, and I wanted to sing with them more than just this one night. I knew the pay would be better, so I turned on the charm, trying to ignore where I was and who else might be there. During a break while the band set up, I sat on the edge of the stage swinging my feet, waiting and thinking. Sansone sat beside me.

"So. How'd *you* get in this crowd?"

"Darned if I know," I said. "Puccinelli just turned up at the club where I'm singing and told me he wanted me at his party. He's not a man you wanna turn down."

"Ain't that the truth."

"How about you?"

"Well, I'm just a soda jerk over in Akron and his cousin comes in a lot for chocolate milkshakes. He saw me one night singing in a club and told Big Al. Funny how these things happen."

"I'm not sure how tickled I am. I've heard some really scary things about Puccinelli and his crowd. Well, I'm tickled to meet Carlo— and you, of course."

"That's just my point. Here's this guy you're really scared of—and for good reason—but he can give you opportunities you'd work a lifetime to get."

"Yeah, if nothing awful happens to me in the meantime."

Sansone grinned. "Nobody's ever given me any trouble around here. It'll be nice to have somebody else to do some of the numbers, though. By the end of the night, I'm pretty much pooped. How about a couple of duets? Are you up for it?"

I sparkled. "Yeah. I'd like that. Any suggestions?"

"How about *"I'm Gonna Sit Right Down and Write Myself a Letter?"*

"Yeah, I know that one. What key?"

"How about B?"

"That works for me. What else?"

"Maybe *I Can't Give You Anything But Love?* —We ought to do something slow. Or how about *Stardust Melody* or *The Very Thought of You?*"

"I know 'em both. What key?"

"I do 'em both in A flat."

"*The Very Thought of You* would work for me. I've been singing it longer."

"Okay," Sansone said, jumping up. "I'll get a score and we can figure out who's taking what lines."

As Sansone conferred with Palatino, I sat where I was and thought about Jack.

So if he's a member of Puccinelli's crowd, no wonder he always disappears when my friends come around.

I had a hard time thinking of the man who taught me to save lives as someone who might take them.

Before I could begin to make sense of it, though, Sansone came back and we got to work. By the time we'd looked over the scores and decided how we'd divide them, the band had set up and tuned up. After they played through *In the Mood* to warm up, Sammy (he'd told me to call him Sammy) and I stepped up on the stage.

I glanced at the baby grand piano. Of course someone with Puccinelli's money would have a grand. When I looked over the raised lid at the pianist, though, I gasped. I *had* seen Jack outside—and there he was, right in front of me, grinning. I stopped and stared.

"What's wrong?" Sammy asked.

I flushed, still looking at Jack. He winked. I glanced at Sammy.

"Uh." I swallowed into a dry throat.

"You look like you've seen a ghost."

"I did, sort of . . ."

"I've never seen their pianist before. You know him?"

"I think I do. Hold on a minute."

I stepped over to the piano. "What're you doin' here?" I whispered. "I thought you were in Chicago."

Jack grinned at me. "Same as you." He glanced toward the back of the room. "You better get to work. Big Al's watching."

I peered into the dark back of the room and quickly stepped back to Sansone's side.

"You alright? You need a glass of water or something?"

I looked back into Jack's eyes, frowning. Sammy laid a hand on my forearm and I turned to him. "What? No, I'm fine," I said. "Let's just get to work. Puccinelli's watching."

I looked over my shoulder once more as we stepped to center stage and started through *I'm Gonna Sit Right Down*. When I forgot where Sansone was supposed to come in, he shouted, "Hey, ya gotta let me sing too."

"Oh yeah. Sorry. Let's do it again"

I tried to ignore Jack, but his presence filled my mind as we sang it again from the top. This time Sammy sang over my lyrics and I stopped to wait for him, with Jack a presence I could almost feel on the back of my neck. I wondered if he were watching me.

"Alright," Sammy said, "let's take it from the two bars before 'and close with love.' We got it that time. "Now let's do *The Very Thought of You* and come back to this afterwards. Is that okay?"

So we switched styles, moving into the opening bars of *The Very Thought of You.* I looked deep into Sammy's eyes, but I saw only Jack's eyes smiling at me and winking. His presence made me do the very thing I sang—forget to do the ordinary thing I normally did with barely a thought.

"Hey," Sammy teased, "you better look away or you'll make me flub." I smiled and kept singing. Let Jack put that in his pipe and smoke it.

Sammy's eyes melted into mine as his voice took the next lines about daydreams and kings. Any other time singing with such a well-known star would be *my* daydream—another step into better gigs and more money, but with Jack just a few feet behind me, my other daydreams left me confused.

As Sammy and I sang the next verse together, free hands joined, mics separating our intense gaze, I got caught up on the longing and fear in the line. I'd feared for myself when I walked into the Puccinelli palace, but what about Jack? This must be his home turf—or maybe Puccinelli hauled him in like he did me.

As we finished the song, I noticed Puccinelli standing at the back of the hall again, holding the cat that nearly tripped me when I arrived. He walked up to the stage.

"You do that later tonight and you'll have all my tough guys cryin'," he said to Sansone, "and that ain't so good. They need to be on their toes."

Sansone grinned, "Okay, boss. She's good isn't she?"

"Yeah, just fine. Be in the dining room at eight sharp. The wife don't like to be kept waiting."

Once he'd closed the door behind himself, I took a long, shuddering breath. "Where'd he come from? Should we change songs?"

"He does kind of slip up on you," Sammy said. "But you get used to it."

"I'm not so sure I want to be around to get used to it. Did you see those guys he had hanging around outside?"

"You'll be alright. They're just there to protect Puccinelli."

"Right," I said and stepped back center stage to continue the rehearsal, giving Jack a long look before I turned to Sansone.

When I entered the dining room an hour later, changed into Mom's midnight blue gown, I realized I was in for a feast like Mowrey's used to serve before the Depression. Tiffany stemware and Wedgewood china made for classic place settings bordered by solid silver flatware. Seated conveniently next to Sammy I kept asking questions about how we'd handle the evening, glancing often to the head table where Jack sat close to Puccinelli. Sometimes, I caught him glancing in my direction.

"There will be requests," Sammy said, "and sometimes they'll ask for one or the other of us specifically. So if we know it, we sing it. If we don't, we'll ask if the other can sing it. Otherwise, we'll just alternate, at least if that's okay with you."

"Works just fine for me. Will we have any breaks?"

"Yes. We work for an hour and break for half an hour. We'll do four sets."

"That's good. I never get that kind of breaks at the lounge."

"Well, these people are dancing and they really go after it, so they're okay with a break now and then."

Once the guests had finished eating, we all moved on to the ballroom where I sang and swung for the rest of the night with nice long breaks for chatting up the crowd. I looked for Jack in between, but he always seemed to be hanging close to Puccinelli and another man I assumed, by the resemblance, to be his father— or maybe one of his brothers.

During the second set, as the orchestra played *In the Mood*, Sammy grabbed me and we danced the number on stage with the crowd stomping and clapping along.

As the band launched into *Sing, Sing, Sing*, I stepped back up to the mic, grabbing it as I hit the first phrase. Yup, I'd be alright and I wouldn't get eaten—and I'd think about Jack when I got home.

At the end of the evening, as the band packed up, Palatino grabbed my elbow. "Hey Bobbi, I'm thinkin' about hiring a canary to sing with my band. You interested?"

"Might be. What're you gonna pay?"

"Don't know yet."

"Give me a call at the LakeView when you decide. I'm definitely interested."

I was thinking about the offer when Michael, the scary guy who met me at the door, appeared almost magically, to take me back out to the car and tuck me in. Palatino played at Danceland. Radio WNAX did a weekly broadcast of the Saturday show. It would be a good move for me—except, of course, I wouldn't have Tony. As Michael led me out, I looked back for Jack, but he'd disappeared.

Once in the car, I leaned against the door post and closed my eyes, exhausted. I felt the car pull out and slumped a little lower.

"How ya doin' Bobbi," the driver asked.

My eyes popped open and I stared at the back of his head for a moment. I leaned over the front seat.

"Jack?" I shouted. "I sure didn't expect to see you here. I mean— What are you doin' *here?*"

"Now you see why I didn't want to meet your friends."

"But how . . . ?"

"Al's my uncle."

"But your name. You're not a Puccinelli."

"Uncle on my mom's side."

I leaned back and thought about that. Now I understood why the cops were so eager to pin the Torso Murders on Jack.

"Do you like it?" I asked, finally.

"Like what?"

"The Family."

"Probably as much as you like your family."

"Yeah."

"So you're okay with my family?"

I thought about that for a long moment. "Not really. Your uncle scares me to death."

"So you don't want to see me anymore?"

I thought some more, remembering our lifeguard lessons and the trip to the gallery—our talks on the beach. He was different.

"You're not your family," I said finally. And I realized it was true. I felt safe with Jack like with no one else—except Tony.

He hadn't mentioned having the cops hassle him. I wondered if they mentioned me. I hoped not. I leaned over the back of the seat, then climbed over.

"What're you doing?"

I slipped down next to him. "I haven't seen you for two months. I don't want to sit in the back seat like you're a cab driver," I snuggled against his side.

He put his arm around my shoulders and pulled me in close.

He grinned down at me. "I like this better, too."

"I looked over my shoulder at him. "You gotta stop startling me like that."

"I thought you liked surprises."

"Mmmm. Sometimes. It's wonderful to see you."

"I had no idea Uncle Al had you singing tonight. When you got out of the car," he kissed the top of my head, "I almost dropped my teeth."

"Dropped your teeth?"

"Aw, Grandpa used to say that."

I snuggled closer. "It's great to see you. How's school going?"

"Just fine. Strangest thing. The cops dragged me out of class one day. Wanted to know what I was doing—when was it? Wanted to know what I was doing a couple days in September. Was I back here in Cleveland."

Here it comes. I slid down in the seat a little bit, but he didn't say anything more, just frowned as if he were puzzled.

"So what were they looking for?"

"Damnest thing. Somebody got away from a kidnapper, I guess. They thought it was the Torso Murderer and somehow they got the idea it was me—or somebody in my family. I guess they checked alibis all over the place."

"Wow. That's weird. Hope everybody had alibis."

"Hauled one of my brothers in, but couldn't make it stick."

"Hmmm," I said.

We drove in silence for a while. When we got to my apartment building he opened my door and I stepped out.

"Well," I looked at my toes, "see ya at the lake?"

"Prob'ly not, Bobbi. I'll be in Chicago."

He took my hatbox from me, walked to the door, and turned to me. "Been nice knowin' ya."

"What? Just like that?"

"How do you want it to be?"

I dropped my chin. "I dunno, but you were worried just a minute ago if I would want to see you anymore."

"I don't know either, Bobbi. I don't. But I'll be gone."

I stood back and looked at him. "That hasn't changed. So?"

"You'll be workin'."

"That hasn't changed either. If you're worried we'll lose contact, we could write letters."

He hesitated, frowning. "I'm not much of a letter writer."

He stood with his head down. "What about that bouncer—Tony, I think?"

I stepped closer, looking into his eyes. "What about Tony?"

"I hear you're getting' pretty close since I been gone."

"That's just nuts. He's Fred's Compromise."

"Fred's Compromise?"

"Well, yeah. When I started singing there, some guy," I hung my head in embarrassment, "he couldn't keep his hands to himself." I could feel a flush working its way up my cheeks, remembering the smell of the man's breath and the slimy feel of his hands on me. "I didn't even think. I just smacked him. Left welts on his cheek."

Jack smiled. "That's my girl—but what's that got to do with Tony?"

I explained about Fred coming to my dressing room and chewing me out, and the deal he made to have Tony look out for me.

"So you're not sweet on him?"

"Of course not. He's old."

I stood with my hands on my hips. "Were you gonna say anything or just go back to Chicago an' be mad?"

He hesitated. "Go back to Chicago, I guess. I still don't guess I'll see you anymore."

"Why?" I restrained myself from stamping my foot.

"You're gonna be singin.' You're not a little kid anymore, Bobbi. The guys are gonna be after you."

"So?"

"So maybe I'll see you in the spring—if you still want to see me."

"I will."

"We'll see."

I took my hatbox and walked inside, holding the door open to watch him pull away.

Monday evening, Tony met me at the door. "Are you alright? I waited for you until—God, I don't know what time. I would have gone to your apartment, but I knew you hadn't told your folks."

With a start, I remembered that Tony was going to take me home when Puccinelli's driver dropped me off. "Oh, Tony. I'm so sorry. I forgot. I was exhausted, I just had 'em take me home."

He stared. "Do you think that's wise?"

I sighed. "Aw, I don't know, Tony. They can always find out where I live."

"Just take care of yourself, Bobbi. I've been worried about you all weekend."

"I'm really sorry, Tony."

"Aw, it's alright. You better go get ready."

I lingered a moment, my hand on his sleeve, then turned and walked through the tables to get dressed and made up. Back in my dressing room though, I thought about Tony waiting for me, probably sitting alone in his car, even after the club closed.

I'd been taking him for granted and that wasn't fair. I wasn't sure what to do about it though. I didn't want to wander around that club without him to protect me. I should tell him I'm seeing someone. But I don't think he wants to *date* me. I don't care what Mom says. I shrugged. Too late to do anything about it now.

June 15, 1938

By summer, I still hadn't heard from Palatino and my patience was running out. Worse yet, I hadn't heard from Jack. After our little conversation on Halloween, his absence felt ominous. If that weren't enough, my friends had nearly become strangers. My weird hours had left me exhausted and my friends' homework and school activities had kept them busy so I hadn't had anyone to talk to about it. We'd spent time together, on and off, on Sundays and the occasional evening—early—but we hadn't really talked in months. It was partly my fault, maybe *all* my fault. I'd been pretty closed-mouthed and our lives were so different—I just didn't feel much like confiding in them. With the arrival of summer, though, we found time to go back to the beach and I was glad at least for their physical presence.

One bright, sunlit Sunday we were lying around on the sand— Kate under an umbrella I'd bought to keep her from sunburning like she usually did.

"Okay, Bobbi," she said, "we've been waiting for almost a year. We expect you to tell us everything about your life. It's so much more exciting than ours."

"There's not much to tell. I go home exhausted and I get up exhausted. My feet hurt all the time and that darned corselette pokes me under my arms. Sometimes I feel like a mole. I sleep during the day when everybody's out doing stuff and I prowl around at night, dodging other women's husbands."

"You sure have a dark outlook," said Helen.

"Everybody just loves you," said Mary Teresa.

"I don't know if I'd call that love. I walk around that club and smile and grin and when I walk away, I hear 'em talkin' about my 'honkers' and sayin' how they'd like to get in my pants."

Mary's eyes widened. "They don't all do that, do they?"

"Of course not, but it doesn't take many to ruin a night."

"Gee Bobbi, that must get real lonely," Kate said.

"You're around people all the time. New people. Not the same old faces," argued Mary Teresa, "that must be fun."

I stared out at the waves, listening to the shrieks of people on the rides in the amusement park and the calls, back and forth, of people on the beach.

"Well," I told them, "you can be very lonely in a room full of people. You have the noise and the lights and people chattering at you, but none if it means anything because they don't know you and you don't know anything about them."

"What about that bouncer guy? That Tony we met last summer. He seems nice. Didn't you say he escorts you around to keep you from beating up on the customers?" Mary teased.

"Tony's sweet," I said. "He's like a big brother, you know? He really kind of saved me, especially at first—not just from the rude customers, but from just drifting off into nowhere like a piece of bark you throw into the lake—he took us to the police station that night."

"I think he's sweet on you to take such good care of you," Mary said.

"Aw, he's just a sweet guy. I'm learning a lot from him, though— what to look out for, who to avoid, and how to stay out of their way. But he's old. Must be at least twenty-five."

"That's not so old, Bobbi. He's pretty good lookin.'"

I thought about that. "Guess I never gave it much thought. I guess so. Mom says he is—great big shoulders and arms."

"I s'pose he's kinda clumsy."

"Not at all. You remember when we all went dancing. He's smooth, and quick—like J . . ." I caught myself still thinking about Jack.

"Maybe you oughta get closer to him," Mary hinted, not very subtly.

"Wait a minute," said Kate, raising a hand. "Like who, Bobbi?"

"What?"

"You said like—something. You started to say somebody's name."

"No. I was just saying Tony's smooth and quick."

"You're holdin' out on us again, Bobbi. C'mon. Spill it."

"No, there's nothing to spill."

"Is it a customer? Maybe a member of the band? Come on, Bobbi. You know all our secrets. Who's the lucky guy."

"There's no lucky guy," I said. "Just forget it."

Mary noticed me getting upset. "You were going to say Jack, weren't you? What have you heard from him?"

"Nothing, Mary. He just went off to college and that was the end of it. A nice summer romance, I guess."

" Aw, we're sorry, Bobbi," Kate said. "We just thought—I don't know what we thought."

"You never mentioned him," Helen said, "Not that we saw you very much."

"I still think about him sometimes," I admitted, "but . . . ."

"Well, you get to wear those gorgeous gowns," Mary reminded me, interrupting with a change of subject.

"Yeah, I loved that at first and the wolf whistles. I couldn't understand why women don't take that as a compliment. But now

I just feel like a piece of steak laid out in front of a dog. Listen, I need to go out and swim. All I've done for the last nine months is sleep and sing, sing and sleep."

"Do you hate singing now?"

"No," I said, standing on my knees. "I still love to sing and I still have music in my head all the time. I just," I stood. "I'd just like to do it for myself or like at the Pavilion last summer. Singing all the time—it's just a job—work." I ran into the waves, swimming hard, as if I hoped to reach the edge of the world.

I spent the next half hour like an otter, rolling and diving, floating on my back and undulating with the waves. I couldn't get it out of my mind—swimming with Jack, held tight against his lean body, his arm over my left shoulder and under my right arm, showing me how to tow a drowning victim. I wondered what he could be doing in Chicago and whether he'd come back and just decided not to look me up. When I'd finally exhausted myself, I rejoined my friends, trudging up the beach, panting.

"See? I'm completely out of shape."

"Your mom said you sang at a couple of Al Puccinelli's parties. What was that like?" Helen asked as I dried myself.

"Terrifying," I said, tousling my hair with my damp towel.

"Wasn't one of them on Halloween?"

"The day before. That was the only time. He had a whole flock of bodyguards, all dressed in black. Outside of the mansion like a flock of crows. One of them winked at me—scared the bejesus out of me." I smiled, remembering how Jack took me home. "But I got to sing with Sammy Sansone there. And the Carlo Palatino orchestra. He asked me if I'd like to sing with his band at Danceland—but I haven't heard anything yet. Singing with them was a lot of fun, but you know, Puccinelli has a frightening reputation and he sneaks up on you."

"What? Like a ghost or a goblin?"

"Sort of, he's just quiet. He doesn't walk heavy like a lot of guys—like most guys. And he doesn't talk at you while he's coming. He's just somewhere else and then, suddenly, he's there. It always made me jump."

"That would scare the stuffin's out of me," Mary said.

"Just *being* there would scare me to death," Helen added.

"Sammy says no one's ever given him any trouble."

"Did anybody notice she calls him Sammy now?" Kate asked, grinning.

"Well, he asked me to."

They all giggled. I stretched out on my towel, eyes closed, absorbing sunlight.

"I can't remember when my skin's been so white," I said as I visualized Jack's deep tan.

"So when will you get out of the LakeView Jazz Club and move on to someplace where people dance?" asked Helen.

"They dance at the LakeView," I said to the sky, "just not a whole lot and they don't seem to have much fun."

I kind of dozed off, then started speaking again, kind of in a trance.

"You wouldn't believe the diamonds and pearls at that party. Oh my gosh! The rich guys with shoes shined like mirrors! Starched shirts their wives didn't do on their ironing boards."

"You should have snagged one of them," Kate says.

"I've thought about it. *I* could throw the parties and invite happy people and dance and sing when I want to—and paint when I want to." I rolled up on my elbow and looked at them. "I just didn't know who I'd be getting mixed up with—and they kept me onstage most of the time anyway."

And Jack was there and I was thinking about him.

"Didn't anybody ask you to dance when Sammy sang?"

"Aw, I'm like a piece of furniture to all those rich folks, or a finely-tuned car. I don't think they'd pay much attention to Puccinelli if they weren't afraid of him."

"Afraid like you?"

"I've kind of gotten over being scared." I lay back down with my arm over my eyes, thinking. "He carries this cat around all the time."

"Puccinelli?!"

"Big fat long-haired cat—and he's got this *big* ruby ring and he's always strokin' that cat."

"You *oughta* be afraid," Helen said.

I waved them away. "You know me. I ain't scared of nothin'."

"We know," Helen said. "That'll get you in trouble one of these days."

"Aw, maybe I'll find me a dumb pig farmer and get married and not have to worry about the killers and the gangsters and the men who can't keep their hands to themselves," I said. "I could sit out in the country with an easel and paint pictures of flowers and lakes."

"And pigs," said Mary.

Helen rolled up on her elbow and looked at me. "I don't think any pig farmers are goin' to show up at the club and sweep you off your feet," she said.

"Guess not."

Ralph and Ed and a couple of their friends came jogging up the beach, providing a welcome interruption in the conversation.

June 22, 1938

A few days later, I was at the lake alone, hoping Jack would find me. Midweek, the amusement park sat quiet, mostly. I heard a group of kids playing volleyball on the beach, but mostly just waves washing up on shore. As I sat on my towel, hugging my knees to my chest, I noticed the lake's musty fishy smell, I daydreamed and wondered why I hadn't seen Jack yet. I thought he must be out of school. Maybe he had another girl—a college girl.

I wished I could call him. I'd had a big argument with Mom and Dad about getting a telephone. We'd needed a phone when Dad broke his leg and we didn't have one, I'd said. I told them they could give the number when they applied for jobs. I could give the number to band leaders who might want to pay me more. Since I was paying for it, I got it, but I wondered what good it did if Jack didn't know the number, anyway? I thought I'd have seen him by then.

I wondered if he still thought I was sweet on Tony. Did he believe me when I told him about Fred and his fresh customers? How could he have known Tony'd been escorting me around the club in the first place? I couldn't get the last time I saw him out of my head, jivin' with the band there at Puccinelli's place. I still couldn't quite believe I'd found my gentle pianist at that mobster's house. But, I reminded myself, he belongs there. I closed my eyes and imagined him ticklin' the ivories in a tux, watching me in a shimmering evening gown, singing an old torch song to his accompaniment. I'd sit beside him on the piano bench and at the end of the song, I'd . . . .

"Hey Angel, what's a sweet thing like you doin' out here all by yourself?"

"Jack!" I squealed, leaping up and flinging my arms around his neck. "Where'd you come from? How long you been back? What've you been doin'?"

"Lookin' for you." He chose to answer only the last question.

I leaned my head back and looked into his laughing eyes. "I was afraid I'd never see you again."

Jack frowned. "Me too. I've been by your apartment and I never see you."

"You could always knock."

"Your parents probably wouldn't let you see me."

"Because of your family?"

He nodded.

"How would they know? I told them your name and they didn't say anything. Mom'd probably invite you to stay for dinner."

He spread out a towel and we sat while I gave him my fought-for telephone number and told him all about my summer so far. Not much to tell.

Before he told me anything, though, we had to talk about Tony again.

"I almost didn't come looking for you."

"Why?"

"I'm still hearing that you're sweet on that bouncer."

"Well, I'm not, but if you're so convinced I am, why *did* you come looking for me?"

"I remembered what you said last fall."

"Like?"

"You asked if I was gonna ask you or just go off and be mad. So I'm askin'."

I held his eyes, almost starting a stare-down. "There's nothing between Tony and me."

He eyed me. "But what about after hours—you go to other clubs with him."

It hadn't occurred to me that he'd know I visited other clubs. We all did.

"I don't go with Tony. Tony goes with *us*. He's an alligator."

"What the hell are you talking about?"

"An alligator's a cat who digs swing and . . . ."

"I know what an alligator is. What do you mean he goes with *us?*"

"Oh. Sometimes, when we finish up for the night—or even between sets—we go to other clubs and listen to other bands." I hesitated. He was a musician, but not the same kind. I wondered if he 'd understand. "We try to learn from them."

"We?"

"The band, the Bob Long Band from LakeView. Not everybody goes, some go one night, some go another. Every once in a while, I go too. It's fluid. Sometimes Tony comes along. That's all."

"How do I know that?"

"Because I'm telling you, damn it!" I calmed myself down and looked into his eyes. Listen, it's a way to get to know people in the business, make connections, learn stuff to make me better. I'm working. That's what I have to do."

He gave me a skeptical look, but I guess he decided to leave it. Instead, he filled me in on his year at school and his fights with his father. He'd resigned himself to majoring in business he told me, and taking as many music courses as he could fit in—until the head of the music department called his father.

Alarmed, I asked what he'd said.

"He told my old man that if he'd just let me study music, I could be playing with Arturo Toscanini before long."

I stared. "Toscanini? Really?"

"Yeah. Mom and Dad love listening to the NBC Symphony Orchestra on the radio."

"So your dad was impressed?"

Jack gave my hand a quick squeeze, grinning. "Yeah, I'm majoring in music now—or I will be next year."

"So why did it take so long to get back," I asked after a few minutes of snuggling into his arm around my shoulders, my own jealousy sparking.

"I got to perform with the Northwestern Symphony Orchestra. The spring concert was late this year."

We chatted for a while about his music career—and mine. Then Jack suggested we get a bite. He admitted to skipping lunch so he could look for me.

"Lucky you chose the very day I came down here," I said, as we walked, arm in arm, between the sycamores.

"No luck about it," Jack replied. "I've been here every day this week—since I got back."

I stopped walking and stepped into his arms. "Really? I'd have called you if I knew the number."

He kissed the top of my head. "I know, Bobbi. I'm just glad I found you."

Back in the yellow Packard, Jack drove us to the Mayfield Street Soda Fountain where we'd met for our first date, almost a year before.

"What's college like?" I asked him when we'd given our order.

Over hamburgers and fries, he told me about going to classes all over campus and about his professors. He told me about an economics professor who seemed to have his lectures memorized. When a student interrupted with a question, he floundered for the rest of the class. He told me about his dorm and his roommate from Nebraska.

"Nebraska! Where's Nebraska?"

"It's right smack in the center of the country. You've seen stuff about the dust storms in the news reels?"

"I hardly ever go to the movies, Jack."

"Well, you've heard about 'em and that's where they are. Morey's from some little town out there. His dad's a farmer and he talks about growing corn and taking little pigs in the house when it's cold an' . . ."

"Pigs!" I interrupted, giggling.

"What about 'em?"

"Oh, my friends and I were just kidding around that I'd marry a rich pig farmer and not have to worry about money anymore."

Jack grinned. "I'll have to introduce you to Morey."

"I never dreamed a pig farmer could be smart enough and rich enough to go to college."

"But he is, Bobbi. He's really smart. He's in pre-med because he says it's hard to get well-trained doctors out in the country."

"A doctor!"

"Yeah. He works full-time and takes classes and I really have to work to keep up with him. His grades are excellent."

"I thought farmers were dumb."

"Not this one, Bobbi. But I don't want to talk about Morey. Tell me more about Tony."

"What? There is really nothing to tell about Tony. I don't know who you're talking to, but I go to the club and sing and he walks around with me between sets to keep me from beating up on the customers. That's it."

"You sure?"

"Look. I don't know who told you that Tony escorts me around, but whoever it was ought to know that I never—*never*—see him alone outside of the club. Never. Like I told you last fall."

Jack stared at me for a long moment. "I guess I'm just jealous. Tony gets to walk around almost every evening with my girl on his arm and *I* haven't seen you in what—eight months. And the last time I saw you, you spent the evening with Sammy Sansone."

"*Your* girl? I like the sound of that."

"Listen," he said taking my hands, "I want to be alone with you, but there's just no place." He stopped, thinking. "When do you have to be at the club?"

"Seven o'clock, but I probably better—I'll call Mom. They still haven't caught the Butcher."

"The Torso Murderer?"

"Right. Mom's still terrified he's gonna get one of us."

Jack frowned. "How're you gettin' to the club?"

"Dad walks me over and comes to get me when I'm done."

"I'm not sure I like that."

"It's alright, Jack. I don't want to talk about it."

"I'm gonna take you tonight. You go call your mother."

While Jack paid the bill, I used the pay phone in the corner. Mom wanted to talk about it, but said Jack was waiting and hung up before she could fuss.

"We could just drive," I suggested as we climbed in the Packard.

Jack had a better idea. "A movie. You said you seldom see a movie. Think of all the music."

At the Euclid Beach Park Theater, we found ourselves alone at last in balcony seats watching a musical, *Romance in the Dark*. As we unfolded our seats, I grinned. Romance in the dark must have been what Jack had in mind and it was just what I wanted after all the months without him. As soon as we found seats, his arm snaked around my shoulders. I leaned into him as the house lights went down and the news reels started.

When the movie's theme song began, Jack pulled me close, turning to gather a handful of hair. With his face inches from mine, he hesitated—a beat, two beats, looking into my eyes. He brushed my lower lip with his—just a touch, like a drifting feather. He kissed the corners of my mouth, his touch light and cool as snowflakes falling on cedars. I melted against him as he settled in for a long, deep kiss. Then he pulled away, looking into my eyes and frowning as though he was deep in thought. I held my breath. I didn't know how to kiss. I probably disgusted him.

"What's wrong?"

"Nothing," he whispered. "I was just wondering if you like to French kiss."

"French kiss?"

"With your tongue."

"Ick." It was involuntary. The idea seemed gross. Somebody's tongue in my mouth? Even his.

"I guess not."

"Never tried it."

"You've never . . . Bobbi have you ever done *anything*?"

"Umm." I didn't know what to say. I was afraid if I told the truth, my inexperience would put him off. But if I lied—maybe he'd think me a slut.

Oh well, I thought as Jack solved my problem by kissing me again, tongue barely penetrating, brushing the inside of my lower lip. That wasn't so bad. I felt goose bumps raising the hair on my arms and a chill that traveled up my neck, making my scalp tingle. Experimentally, I touched the tip of my tongue to his.

"You really haven't, have you?" Jack asked, raising his head and looking into my eyes.

"Was it that bad?" I whispered.

"No, Bobbi, it was just fine. I'm gonna love teachin' you."

"You don't mind?"

"Mind? No. I don't mind."

He transferred his hand from my hair to my waist, pulling me closer with a powerful left arm. In only a few moments, the iron arm of the theater seat began cutting into my side. I began to squirm.

"What's the matter?"

"The darned arm of this chair. It's digging into my ribs."

"Damn!" Jack said. He let me go and leaned back to study the piece of solid iron that separated our seats. We watched the movie for a few minutes but must have he kept thinking about our problem. He leaned over to whisper his solution in my ear. I smiled to myself, nodded, and slipped over onto his lap. He'd found the answer, we fit together perfectly with my right arm around his neck and my knees over the offending arm.

"This is better." He wrapped his left arm tightly around my back, cushioning me from the other side of his seat. I couldn't believe how careful he was of *my* comfort. I leaned my head on his shoulder and hummed along with the movie score—between interludes of passionate kissing. When his free hand roamed to my chest, palm gently massaging my breast, though, I gasped. We couldn't do this, but those goosebumps were rising again and I could feel myself flush. As he started unbuttoning my blouse, I realized I was panting. I took a huge gulp of air and reached for his hand.

"Not here, Jack. The usher . . . ." I couldn't believe I hadn't said, "*No. No. A thousand times no.*"

"It's dark, Bobbi."

"He has that little flashlight."

"Aw come on, Bobbi, I just want to touch you."

"Shshshsh," I whispered, moving his hand back to my waist and kissing his neck. "Everybody already thinks I'm a slut because of where I work. I don't need to give them any more ammunition."

"They don't either."

No point in arguing about it. He didn't hear the remarks about my anatomy I heard when I walked around the club.

I held his hand for a few moments. When I released him, he began to roam again, and I knew I would spend the summer, until he went back to college, fighting both of us, probably myself most of all. At least he didn't try to unbutton any more buttons that night. By the time the house lights came up, though, we were both panting. I jumped back to my own seat and straightened my rumpled dress.

"Just a minute," said Jack when I stood to leave.

"What?" I asked, sitting.

"Give me a minute to—um—compose myself."

"Oh." I remembered the lump I'd felt when I was sitting on his lap. "Are you alright?"

"Yeah," he growled, "more or less."

Back in the car with the cool spring air ruffling my hair and Jack's arm around my shoulders, I sang one of the new songs from the movie.

"You really got that fast," he said. "Had you heard it before?"

"Nope. Just liked the sound of it."

We drove around East Cleveland for a while, but I had to work, so we grabbed a quick bite and Jack dropped me off, stopping long enough for a goodbye kiss. When I turned to get out of the car, I noticed Tony standing by the club, watching. I smiled, glad to be seen, finally, with my boyfriend and glad to let Tony know where things stood—in case he'd forgotten our visit to the police.

"That's Tony," I told Jack. "You should kiss me so you know he knows."

He did—with passion.

August 16, 1938

After our movie date, Jack would show up or call in the afternoons
when his family didn't have him running errands. We'd swim and
lie around on the beach or go to the movies. We tried to spend
Sundays together—unless Jack's family had other plans for him.
Those precious Sundays, we often ended in the Packard parked
along the lake somewhere, watching the waves. During those
interludes, I learned how exquisite Jack's touch on my naked flesh
could feel—but I always managed to keep myself clothed below the
waist.

I knew the stakes. No one would take care of me if I got into
trouble. Jack might try but I was far from sure of his parents. *My*
parents might try, but they couldn't even take care of themselves. I
hated thinking that way, always wondering what everything
would cost me, but my existence had been too precarious for too
long. I couldn't forget. The shriveled up old woman down the
stairs, a woman who looked like she'd never had a generous
impulse in her life, haunted my mind. I remembered her when I
thought about how I had to rein myself in all the time. I really
wanted to trust.

One day, the thought of trust stopped me cold. Trust what, I
wondered. Jack maybe, but I knew it was more than that. My
future? My friends had a wonderful future imagined for me—
singing with the big time orchestras, lots of money, my choice of
good-looking men. I could see it too, with all the glamour. But I'd
never cared much about glamour and I didn't see the love
anywhere in that future. All those people listened and danced, but
they didn't know me—didn't care to know me. They had their own
agenda for me, and they stuffed me into that pattern.

So I kept gritting my teeth and keeping my knees together—even
though it was against every impulse in my body.

Toward the end of the summer, Jack showed up and I heard something out of kilter in his voice.

"What's wrong?"

"Bobbi . . . I have to leave."

"Leave? I know. In a couple of weeks."

"No. Now. Dad and Uncle Al have something cooked up."

"When? Right this minute?"

"Tomorrow."

"No Jack. That's too soon."

"I know Angel, but I've gotta do it. I know you have to work tonight, but I wanted to say goodbye."

I stood mute, thinking.

"Bobbi?"

"I'm sick."

"Sick? Are you alright? You never get sick."

"I'll tell Fred I'm sick. I've never missed a night. Not since I started. "

I hated lying to Fred, but I really wanted a last night with Jack before he left for another nine months. Parked along the lakeshore later that evening, I wanted to know if I'd see Jack at all during the winter—maybe during Christmas break.

"I wish I could go with you—take art classes."

"You talk about art all the time," Jack said, "music's art too, you know and you've got a terrific voice."

"Aw, I'm just tired of being ogled and having some man reaching for me all the time. Besides, when you make it a job, it isn't fun anymore. It would be nice to just stand somewhere in front of an easel, looking at beautiful stuff and playing with colors and shapes."

"Mmm," murmured Jack, nuzzling my neck. "I'm not crazy about all the ogling either—unless I'm right there to protect you."

Jack tried to take full advantage of our last few hours. He'd turned the radio to soft music, and I allowed him more freedom than usual. After a few passionate kisses, teasing with his tongue, his hand cupped behind my head, he roamed down to tickle my neck. When he squeezed my breast, I shuddered with a chill that ran up my neck and into my scalp. His hand slid down to rub my belly. By then, he'd found every spot that made me shiver. At least I thought he had. He moved up again to give the other breast a light squeeze. With my fingers threading through his hair, I pulled him close for a deep kiss, my breath coming in gulps.

Jack fumbled with my buttons and I just couldn't stop him. When they were finally undone, he sighed and reached inside my blouse, sliding it down my shoulder, along with my bra strap, and running light fingers down my shoulder and over the swell of my chest. He stroked my naked breast with light fingertips and teased my nipple, making me gasp and arch my back.

He looked surprised when I straddled his lap and unbuttoned his shirt, nuzzling his neck and rubbing trembling fingers over his chest, following the swells of his muscles.

"Oh," I said, surprised, "yours stand up too."

"That's not all that stands up, Bobbi," he said, taking a sharp breath when I turned my attention to the buttons on his trousers. I'd been intimidated the first time I'd seen him. He sure didn't look like my father had when I'd nursed him. But I'd learned to love the velvet texture of his skin.

As I stroked him, he fumbled with layers of skirts and slips and petticoats.

"Jack," I cautioned.

"Shshshsh, Angel. I just want to touch you. I gotta show you how good that feels."

Frustrated, he lifted me off his lap, breathing hard. "Here," he said, "lean back against the door."

"But I can't reach you."

"That's alright—for now," he said, kneeling on the floor and sliding his hand up my inner thigh. I gasped, arching my back when he insinuated his fingers inside my panties. When he leaned forward to kiss me and I noticed that the music had stopped. The announcer had come on almost shouting with excitement. For once, I ignored it.

"Oh Jack, we can't," I said as he threw my skirts up over my chest and started to separate my legs.

"We can't stop now," he murmured. He searched for my mouth again.

Oh my god, I thought. I can't stop. I want this but . . . oh, I can't. Tortured with indecision, I knew I should stop him, but oh no, I had no desire to stop him—ever.

 And then I heard it. The words Torso Murderer smashed through my confusion.

I jerked my legs together and tried to sit up.

"I won't hurt you. Just relax."

I kept struggling, flailing to sit. It was almost like I was fighting for my life in the cemetery again. It only lasted a few terrifying moments, but I'm sure Jack thought I'd gone crazy.

"Listen!" I screamed when I finally got my brain back. "Listen to the radio—the Torso Murderer."

"Bobbi, you're alright." Jack was still trying to resume the interrupted kiss and nudge me back down on the seat.

"No I'm not! Listen."

Sighing, he pushed himself up to sit, reaching for my hand to help me up, just as headlights flashed over the back of the car.

"Jesus, Mary and Joseph," he growled in exasperation, as he spotted a cop climbing out of a marked car and walking over to us.

"Cover up, Bobbi," he said. "We've got company."

I straightened out my clothes, as best I could, although I couldn't button my blouse before the officer flashed his light in the car.

"You need to get straightened up and get out of here," he said, blinding us with the flashlight.

"What's up, officer," Jack said, cool as a cucumber. "We're not breaking any laws."

"No, but the Torso Murderer has killed a couple more people just down the beach a little ways. Coulda been you."

"That's what I was trying to tell you," I said.

"Just get out of here," the officer said walking back to his car and pulling out.

Once the other car had moved on, Jack tried to pick up where we'd left off, but I was staring over his shoulder, watching for movement.

"It's okay, Bobbi," he said, "calm down. We'll be alright."

"No we won't! He came after me once. He's right here."

Jack straightened up, looking carefully 'round the car. "What do you mean, he came after you?"

"He did—or someone did, Jack. Please, Jack, let's get out of here."

Once we were moving, Jack demanded an explanation. As I began to relax, I told him about my near abduction during my first month at LakeView.

"Why in hell didn't you tell me?"

"Didn't come up." I shut up, wondering if I dared tell him I'd brought the cops down on his family—until Jack glanced in my direction.

"Everything alright?"

"Yeah. I just lied, kinda." I sighed and told him. "Remember when the cops came to check your alibi?"

"Yeah. Pop said they were interviewing everybody in the family— all our employees." He looked across at me for a moment and back at the street. "Weirdest thing. They wanted some big guy with fat, hairy fingers." He looked at me again. "Wait a minute. That was you?"

I cringed. "I'm so sorry, Jack. I didn't tell them it was you."

"What *did* you tell them?"

"I mentioned that we'd been in the cemetery and saw all those cigarette butts and tire tracks and they just decided it was you."

Jack gave me a grim smile. "Yeah, the cops know my Uncle Al. My brothers were really ticked off about it."

"I didn't know then. It never occurred to me they'd suspect you. I told 'em . . . ."

"I know," he interrupted. "No harm done. But why in hell didn't you tell me?"

'I didn't know how to reach you in Chicago and then I was afraid to tell you. Jack, I'm so sorry. I told them it wasn't you, but they just ignored me."

"It's alright. Keep 'em on their toes. So he tried to grab you at the cemetery?"

"The 123rd street gate."

"I shoulda made sure you were safe."

"Nothin' you could do about it."

"Hell you say. I'll think of something."

"I'm alright."

"I'll take care of it," Jack said, leaving no room for doubt.

The mood completely destroyed, Jack sighed and turned for my apartment.

When he pulled up in front of the building, I cupped his face in my hands and kissed him. "Jack I really wanted . . . ."

"I wanted it too, Bobbi. I been wantin' it for a while." He tickled my earlobe with the tip of his finger. "I guess we'll just have to wait."

"But it's so long."

"Guess you're safe for the winter. C'mon. I'll walk you to the door."

We stood, holding each other. Jack reached down and kissed me, meeting my tongue in a slow sweep.

"You're really good at that," he said. "Damn," he said, turning and walking back to the car. "I guess I'll see you in the spring."

Standing in the doorway of my apartment building watching the yellow Packard disappear around the corner, I knew I'd like to spend more time with the boy who'd almost become my lover— before the Butcher intervened. I wished they'd catch the beast so I could feel safe.

The next day when I arrived at the club, Fred called me into his office to tell me that he'd made arrangements with a taxi company to pick me up at my apartment, bring me to the club, and take me home.

I frowned. "Why's that, Fred?"

"Aw, that Torso Murderer got some more people."

"Well yeah, but that's expensive."

"I got a great offer on a package deal."

"What kind of package?"

"Do you want the taxi service or not?"

"I do, Fred. Thank you. I'll feel much better. Dad'll be happier, too."

"Good," he said, turning back to his paperwork.

As I walked to my dressing room, I remembered how Jack had said he'd "take care of it." I wondered what he had to do with Fred's sudden decision, because I knew he had something to do with it.

PART III: CLEVELAND, OHIO

September 28, 1938

Not only did the band rehearse after the four a.m. closing, they often went to other clubs, sometimes between sets, sometimes after-hours, to hear other musicians, often jamming with them. I'd been pretty conservative my first year at LakeView. I'd gone out with the band between sets and, very occasionally, I went with them to an after-hours spot. That's apparently what Jack had heard about. But after he went back to Chicago, I got involved in a lot more after-hours jam sessions. Recognizing the fierce competition for good gigs, I took advantage of those opportunities to learn—new styling, new arrangements, new music and new ways to use my voice. I picked up bits and pieces of styles, imitating like a magpie.

I found I didn't need Dad, or a taxi, to take me home at night. One of the band members usually made sure I got there safely—and I could almost always count on Tony when the others didn't. When I told Dad I didn't need him anymore, we had a knock-down, drag-out about it at home, with Mom and Dad reminding me I was sixteen and I needed my sleep. After a few heated arguments, I just went my own way—like Dad always did—and my parents, unwillingly, got used to my already-weird hours. Often I worked until well into the morning—sometimes having breakfast with the orchestra at noon and catching a bus home to sleep.

Fred grumbled about his "canary" wandering off when he wanted me schmoozing the customers between sets, but I reminded him that the rest of the musicians had always done it and that I learned a lot of new stuff that kept my performance fresh—and I was *usually* there to schmooze. Besides, I reminded Fred that he saved some money on taxi fare.

It only occurred to me later that Jack might be saving the money and he'd wonder who took me home when I didn't use the cab. I hoped we wouldn't have another fuss about it—especially since Tony often went along.

One night in March, at the DownBeat Club, we listened to a new canary in town from New Orleans, Denise Delacotte. As the girl went into an exciting series of jazz riffs, scat-singing improvised sounds around the melody of *One O'clock Jump,* I couldn't help yawning.

"I can't hardly listen anymore, Tony."

"You want me to take you home?"

"I think I could learn something from her—but I'm just too tired."

"C'mon, I'll take you home."

As we started to get up and put on our coats, the girl ended her set, stepped down from the stage, and grabbed my arm.

"Don't leave now."

I smiled at her. "Girl, I'm pooped."

"Aw, Come on. I don't hardly get to see another girl. C'mon. Sit down." She pulled up a chair and we three sat. "Here, have a cigarette. That'll wake you right up." She offered a flask. "Have a snort."

"I don't . . . ."

"Sure ya do. It'll perk ya right up."

I took the flask, taking a sip and grimacing. Denise shook out a cigarette and held out the pack. I hesitated for a moment and took one. Tony gave me a quizzical smile and lit them both.

I took a shallow drag and coughed. "That tastes *awful.*"

"But it's so soothing."

Taking another drag, I wondered what was so soothing. I was working my throat to keep from gagging.

"I don't think I've ever heard anyone sing to *One O'clock Jump.*" I wanted to change the subject.

"Oh, I was just scattin' around."

"There aren't any words, are there?"

"No. Just whatever sounds I make. Don't you have any scat singers around here?"

"Sure we do. I've just never heard anybody do a song that doesn't have any words at all."

"Listen, I'll tell you a secret. I don't have the breath to hold out the notes—but I'm really good at improv. I scooted over to the LakeView once between sets, so I know you're a canary, too."

We talked for a while—until Tony suggested we go for breakfast. Denise and I kept chattering on the way to the all-night diner. When we learned they were no longer serving breakfast, I ordered chicken.

"You know, just a few months ago, chicken was a luxury we had when we got some kind of windfall—when Dad got a day job of some kind or he won some money at the track." I shook my head. "I really like having my own money—saving some of it and not worrying about it so much."

Denise admitted to beginning her career when there weren't any other jobs—like me.

"Things had gotten ugly at home. You know. No money, no jobs and just fighting and fighting. So I ran away; I was almost out of school anyway. I had this copy of *Billboard* and there was a page devoted to Walkathons where they were advertising for contestants. I got my friend Adrian to sign up with me and persuaded my friends Christian and Claire, who also danced in the Walkathons, to recommend me to the promoter, so Adrian and I were off to Baton Rouge."

"That must have been scary."

"Just the getting there. We hitched—but at least I had Adrian to protect me. You know. They feed you seven times a day and you get free doctors. I figured we'd make enough dancing, even if we didn't win, and selling pictures of ourselves. We did okay."

"How long did you do that?"

"Oh, I don't know. Six months. Then one of the singers got sick and I volunteered to take her place. It all worked out and here I am."

I barely noticed Tony's silence. He didn't say much anyway, so we talked about our jobs until we finished our meals. Tony dropped Denise at her hotel and me at home, so we could all get some sleep.

After that, we spent as much time together as we could, for the two weeks Denise and her band remained in Cleveland. I learned more about my friend's singing career and how she got on with the Freddy Morris band and I talked about the contest, Dad's broken leg, and singing at LakeView.

We were at the Mayfield Street Soda Fountain one afternoon, chattering as usual, when I caught Denise's eye. "I don't want to be a canary," I blurted. "I want to be an artist."

"What?"

"I want to be an artist—like Pablo Picasso or Paul Gauguin."

"Who's that?"

"You don't know Paul Gauguin?"

"Or that other Pablo guy."

"Well, let's go to the art gallery. I'll show you."

We finished our sodas and climbed on the bus for an afternoon of looking at art.

Denise stood looking at Picasso's paintings. "That's whacky."

"Yeah. I guess the 'modern' artists threw out all the old ideas and did a lot of experimenting. Just look at the way Gauguin uses color," I said, leading her on to those works.

"You could do stuff like this."

"Aw, I don't have time."

"Sure you do. You could experiment, too."

"What do you mean?"

"Take a sketch pad with you to the clubs. Draw the bands and the lights and the crowds."

"And the dark."

"The dark?"

My eyes were shining with enthusiasm. "Yeah. The spotlights make the dark blacker. And you get lots of blue."

"That's the cigarette smoke."

"Yeah, but you get color—sort of like pink clouds."

Denise stared at me as I rambled on, thinking out loud about drawing or painting the clubs and the bands—and the dancers.

"I wish I knew how to do oils," I concluded.

"So? Make it up. You said that's what the modern artists do."

"Aw, I don't have the money for oils and canvas anyway."

We spent another hour at the gallery—until it closed—while I concentrated even more than usual on techniques.

"I gotta go home and get my sketch pad," I said as we walked out of the building.

Denise went with me and when we arrived at the apartment, we found both my parents at home. Mom looked up from cooking dinner.

"Hey, I wondered where you were. Where you been anyway?"

"I've been hanging around with Denise here."

"Hi, Denise. I don't think I've met you before."

"She's singing with the Freddy Morris Band over at the DownBeat. I don't get to hang around with a girl singer very often, so I've been with her."

Mom gave us a little nod of approval.

"Dinner's about ready. We're having spaghetti and meat sauce. There's plenty. Why don't you stay for dinner, Denise?"

"Sure," said Denise. "I haven't eaten a home-cooked meal in months."

Once we'd eaten and chatted with Mom and Dad for a couple of hours, I grabbed my sketchpad and we headed for LakeView.

"You realize I haven't had a wink of sleep since I went to work last night?"

Denise grinned, handing me her flask. "Me neither, as you know—but you don't go on until eight."

"Well, it's six o'clock now."

Denise opened the door for me, taking a swig from her flask as I stepped through with my sketchpad.

"We'll just crawl under the tables and nap for a while."

So that's what we did, not crawling out until we heard the band tuning up. While I scurried to my dressing room, Denise caught a late bus to the DownBeat Club.

We spent the next afternoon sleeping at Denise's hotel, but after my last set, I found my way to the DownBeat with my sketchpad. I dragged a chair to the edge of the dance floor where I could see the band and the dancers. I began sketching Denise, the band, and the stage behind them.

It's funny. When I started out to draw things, I began noticing all kinds of stuff that had been background for months. I'd seen the blue color in the clubs—the mist of cigarette smoke drifting into the spotlights. Now I paid attention to the band and the glint of those lights on brass, on the keys of the saxophone or the bell of a trumpet. I saw shapes—the voluptuous figure of the string bass with parallel lines of strings slashing its length, and the pale curve of fingers caressing those strings.

Even my hearing seemed more complex. I'd always listened to the music, to the singers and the soloists, the rhythms and harmonies. But this night I began to hear voices speaking. Very few words— just tones and cadences. I found myself matching the strokes of my pencil to those cadences, the depth of fill to the tones.

Sketching in this atmosphere gave me an entirely different feeling than anything I'd done in school. Dazzled, I drew and smudged, scribbled and filled as fast as my fingers and my new awareness could work. I'd never felt such delicious solitude.

When Denise finished her set, she stepped down to watch over my shoulder.

I wasn't a street artist, like I wanted to be, though. I couldn't work with someone watching, so I asked Denise to move.

She brought over another chair.

"Okay. Sorry. Must be hard to stand up and sing if you can't stand someone watching you."

I smudged the shading around the edges of the stage.

"That's different," I said as I smudged away. "If I flub, you can't see it." I looked up at the band and back at my sketch. "The sour note is just gone—Damn it! I can't do faces."

"Do 'em like that Pablo cat."

"Wouldn't fit—aw, I'm never gonna be any good at this!"

"Look, the faces are just a smear in this light anyway. Give it some time, Bobbi. Keep drawing and learning. You'll get it."

"But this is awful."

I looked up at Denise, cringing a little at the look in her narrowed eyes.

"Bobbi, do you like my singing?"

"Yeah. I've learned a lot from you."

"Do you think I woke up one morning and said, 'I want to be a scat singer?'

"I don't know."

"Well, I didn't. Remember, I started by filling in for someone who got sick. When I found out I didn't have the breath to hold out a note . . . ."

"Maybe I can help you with that," I interrupted. "I had a voice coach once."

"Maybe later. What I'm talking about is how hard I worked to do what I do."

I gestured toward my drawing. "But this is hopeless."

"Dammit, Bobbi. Just because you were born with perfect pitch and a voice and breath to go with it doesn't mean everything's gonna be easy for you."

"Maybe it won't *ever* be there for me."

"If it's worth doing, it's worth working for—that's the best wisdom I ever got from my French-Indian grandma. She said it all the time."

I looked down at my drawing and up at the bandstand and I remembered how I'd felt just a few moments before. I couldn't imagine what had happened in that few moments, but there it was. The instant someone else saw what I was doing, it became trash. How did that happen? How could I retrieve that great feeling? I looked over at Denise.

"When I was little, my dad and I used to go to the art galleries. One afternoon we saw this guy with an easel set up on the street, just sketching what he saw—people hurrying all around him."

"Yeah?"

"I told you about the sketch of Dad and me."

Denise sat waiting. She didn't say another word until I looked at her.

"That must have been a great time with your dad," she said.

"It was. And it was just so peaceful and calm—that guy just in his own world."

"So you'd like to live in that quiet space, too?"

I frowned. "Yeah, I guess so." I looked down at my sketch pad. "I was so focused on drawing—I heard you singing," I looked back at Denise, "but I felt—separate somehow."

"Just keep trying, Bobbi. Maybe that Pablo cat couldn't draw faces either. Maybe that's why he made fractured people."

"He could . . . ."

"Never mind, Bobbi, you will too. Just give yourself a break."

I sighed. "I guess." I sat up and straightened my shoulders. "Let's get some food. I'm starving!"

I closed my sketch pad, slung my purse over my shoulder and we left the club as it closed, striding up the street to a diner, just a few blocks away, arm-in-arm, just two girl singers.

By the time the Freddy Morris band moved on, I had my own flask, compliments of Denise. I'd filled it with Drambuie, remembering the taste from the night when Tony poured it for me. By the time she left, I had a sketchpad full of drawings I didn't quite like, but I didn't quite hate, and an empty space my new friend had filled with understanding. We'd never talked about the difficulties of singing with all-male bands—the long hours and lack of sleep, the boozing, the drugs, and air thick with cigarette smoke, the passes and the groping. We only talked about techniques and tones, new ways of entertaining, but underneath the banter and the cigarettes and booze, I knew, for once, that somebody understood me—even the fact that I wanted something different.

When I wasn't working or sleeping, I sat in the clubs with my sketch pad, my flask, and my cigarettes. At least my drawing time gave me some quiet. Interestingly enough, no one bothered me when I had a sketch pad in my lap, but once I'd spent a couple of weeks with Denise, I knew what it was like to have someone know you, and I felt more alone than ever.

November 20, 1938

Two months after Denise left town, I walked rain-drenched streets on my way to Mileti's Grocery. Mom wanted some onions and a can of tomatoes and I wanted to get outside during the daytime. I hardly saw the sun except when it rose. Heavy clouds scudded across the tops of buildings, promising a deluge—maybe before I got home. Stepping along to another new song I'd heard somewhere, I thought about my last night with Jack and how the Butcher had interrupted—and not a peep out of him since. Maybe they'd catch him before he struck again.

Reaching for Mileti's door, I glanced at the news stand outside. I saw Jack's face under a banner headline on the *Cleveland Plain Dealer*. Stopping mid-stride, I took a hesitant step closer to read: "Student Murdered in Gangland Slaying."

"No."

Suddenly, empty space, filled with roaring silence, enveloped me. A car passed on the street; people talked about the weather; a delivery truck door clanked; a paper sack, blowing by on the sidewalk, rustled. On top of all those normal sounds, I heard the roar of water falling over the edge of the earth, falling down and down without end, without sense, without emotion. I'd always known it was there, a rampaging torrent that rushed me to the very brink.

I took another step forward and picked up the paper. "Body found in Chicago's meat packing district has been identified as Jack Mosso, nephew of crime boss Big Al Puccinelli from Cleveland."

I flopped the paper over so I could no longer see the face and looked up, eyes burning with tears I tried not to shed.

"How much?"

"That'll be a nickel."

I fished in my pocket and pulled out the required change, handed it to the newsboy, folded the paper again, tucked it under my arm, and stepped inside the store, my song gone. I don't know why I didn't run screaming for home. My mind had become a complete blank, filled with the sound of rushing water. I shuffled to the produce aisle as if half asleep and stood staring at the bins of fresh onions, potatoes and squash—until an old woman I'd seen there before laid a cool hand on my arm.

"Can I help you find something, dear."

I glanced around the store, trying to remember where I was and why I was there.

"Are you alright?"

"No," I told her. "Yes."

I couldn't move. My feet felt like they'd grown roots into the grocery aisle. The old woman must have gone to get Mr. Mileti while I stood there, unaware. I turned automatically at the sound of my name.

"What?"

"Are you okay?"

"What?" I managed to focus on his face. "Oh. Yes. I guess. I need an onion."

I took a random onion from the bin and moved on to the canned goods, biting my lips. I took a can of tomatoes and went to the checkout counter where I stood in line, paid, and left the store without a word. Everyone seemed to be following me with their eyes. I heard someone murmur, "I wonder what's eating her."

Outside, I walked to our apartment on sodden streets. Alone there, I put the grocery sack on the counter and sat, hands folded on the table. Dry-eyed, I didn't move. I heard nothing of the noisy city outside the window. It felt like I'd opened a box of silence, wandered in, and closed the door. Even the roar of water had gone.

Eventually, I opened the paper, spreading it on my lap. I traced the line of Jack's cheek with my fingertip. I looked and looked. I tried to compare every detail of the grainy newsphoto with all the details I knew so well—details I'd learned with my fingers and my lips. I felt his breath on my cheek.

This is the only picture I have of Jack. It's the only one I'll ever have.

 Not sure I could stand to read the article, I began anyway. I needed to do something, to find the mistake, to make this go away.

"Body found . . . ." I'd already read that. I closed my eyes for a moment, then opened them and lifted the paper.

 "Jack Mosso, a music student at Northwestern University . . . ." Looking at my own fingers on the newspaper, I felt Jack's long, slender fingers stroking my face, cradling the back of my neck drawing me in for a kiss. I remembered the sound of those light fingers on the piano, accompanying my voice during the party at Puccinelli's.

Raking my fingers through my hair, I read on.

". . . was found Tuesday by a Wilson and Company worker on his way home."

I couldn't stop my mind from going places I didn't want to go.

What if they beat him up?

I groaned.

What if they broke his fingers?

I took a long, shaky breath and read on. I had to know.

"Mosso was shot twice in the head in a murder resembling a gangland assassination."

THE RELUCTANT CANARY SINGS

It would have been instant. At least he didn't lay there suffering.

Unhinged, my mind careened around among the things we'd done together, the feeling of his hands on me, his smell, the sound of his voice; and all the things we'd promised to do together, the gigs in Hawaii and Cuba and, maybe, Europe. In one instant, he was holding my hands across the table at the Mayfield Street Soda Fountain and in the next we were boogieing at Danceland, or swimming together like a pair of otters. I closed my eyes and we waltzed at the Trianon Ballroom and swung at the Savoy. I imagined all the concerts he would never play; all the times we would never perform together. The image of Jack in a tux, his fingers skimming over the melody of *Stardust* and then handing it off to me, filled my mind. We finished the song and I joined him on the piano bench.

I threw the newspaper across the room and covered my face with my hands.

All he wanted was music.

My mind wandered around in a kaleidoscope of images, accompanied by sounds and smells and tastes. I saw us at the soda fountain, sharing a strawberry soda, and at the beach, soaking up sunlight. I smelled the lakeside air with its bouquet of fish and popcorn balls and grease from the Euclid Beach rides. I felt his body against mine in the water and heard his laugh. And finally, I felt those long, slender fingers gripping my hair and pulling my head back to kiss my neck.

I groaned, remembering the times we'd parked the Packard along the beach late at night. *If only I'd let him love me the way he wanted.*

I wished I could cry, but tears wouldn't come. I felt something hard and sharp in my chest and I couldn't sit still any longer. My throat hurt and I couldn't stop swallowing. I picked up the newspaper and stepped across the living room, into my parents' bedroom. I rummaged around in Mom's sewing basket.

She came in right then, but I wanted her gone.

"Whacha lookin' for?" she asked, hanging up her coat.

"Got it," I said.

I smoothed the page and cut out the photo, ransacked my little corner of the apartment until I found my scrapbook, and placed it between the pages. I sat on the chair by the window, folded my hands on the scrapbook, and sat staring at the brick wall across the alley. I kept trying to swallow away the painful constriction in my throat. I couldn't stay still.

I stood and rearranged all my things. Almost everything whispered to me. The blue dress I'd worn on our first date. I shifted the hangar inside the wardrobe. A funny-looking shell Jack had picked up and handed to me. A movie ticket. The pamphlet from the art gallery. I stared at it, focusing on the desolation of that one little flower. Now I understood those blacks and browns and grays.

Some part of me noticed when the afternoon sun slid behind a cloud, dimming the light in the room, but I paid no attention. I'd had my little excursion into the daylight.

By then, Mom was staring at me.

"What're you doin' there, Bobbi?"

"Just cleanin' up a little."

"Looks like a regular spring cleanin'."

I kept working until Mom picked up the newspaper.

"Your father will want to read this," she said. She smoothed out the front page and noticed the hole where I'd cut out Jack's picture. I kept working while she read.

"Bobbi." She closed the distance between us and tried to get her arms around me.

"Not now, Mom. I've gotta get this stuff cleaned up."

"Bobbi, stop. This is *your* Jack, isn't it?"

I kept on rearranging.

"Yes it is."

I stepped past Mom to grab my scrapbook. It was mine. I didn't want anyone to touch it.

"You must be devastated."

I stopped for a moment, looking at Mom. Then I shook my head and went back to picking up scraps of newsprint from the floor.

"I'll call Fred," Mom said, reaching for the phone.

"What for?"

"To tell him you're not coming."

"Why not?"

"Bobbi, you need time to get over this."

"Nothin' I can do about it." I stood and stared at Mom without really focusing.

"I think you should stay home. You were really close." Mom stopped to think for a moment. "Did you ever . . . ."

I stopped and hung my head, remembering that last night before Jack left for Chicago. "No. We never. I wish we had."

"Bobbi."

"Never mind. I'm going to work."

"Not now."

"No. When it's time. Mom. I want to finish this."

I must have looked crazed. Mom stood and watched me for a while. "As you wish," she said, turning to peel and chop the onion.

How could I stay home and do nothing all night? I'd drive myself crazy. Maybe I was already crazy, but I knew I couldn't stay there with nothing to do but think about Jack's face with those two red spots growing on his forehead.

At the club, I went directly to my dressing room, without greeting Fred or Tony. Applying makeup, I stared into the mirror, dabbing some astringent to the puffiness under my eyes. Noticing the lines in my cheeks seemed gaunt, I applied a little extra rouge under my cheekbones. That would have to do.

As usual, Tony met me at the door when I stepped out. How could that be? How could he do what he'd always done? Nothing should be the way it was.

"What's wrong?"

"Nothin.' Why?"

"You look—I don't know—tired."

I tried to smile. "I'm okay."

"You . . . ."

"I'm okay, Tony."

I stumbled when he handed me up on stage, but caught myself, straightened up, and strode to my place behind the mic, staring out at the crowd as the band played the opening bars of *Blue Moon*. I felt my face crumpling and my throat tightening as I sang about the one who appeared before me—the only one I'd ever hold. I hoped nobody noticed. Too late to back out now, I clasped my hands, white-knuckled, to keep myself standing until the end of the song, then stepped aside at its end.

With a lot of hand clasping, I got through the set and returned to my dressing room with Tony holding onto my hand over his arm. I couldn't talk, but his steady presence helped, just like it had at the police station. Slumped in front of the mirror, still trying to swallow the painful lump in my throat, I looked at burning eyes that stared back it me. My head felt like it would explode.

"I wonder if I'm getting a cold," I murmured to myself, hanging my head.

Trying not to think, I sat without moving.

Fred stuck his head in the door. "Bobbi, are you alright?"

I jerked upright. "Why wouldn't I be?"

"You don't have the . . . ." Fred paused staring at me. "Energy—you look beat."

"I'll try to do better." I *felt* beaten.

"You need a night off? Don't you feel good?"

"I think I'm coming down with a cold, but I'll be alright."

Fred continued to stand, watching me, as if he thought I might shatter. Finally, he caught my eye in the mirror and then looked away when I glanced up at him.

"Just a little off tonight, Fred."

"Huh," he said, leaving and closing the door.

Through the flimsy door, I heard him telling Tony to watch out for me.

"Yeah, I know," says Tony, "something's up, but she's not talking."

I wished someone had watched out for Jack. I couldn't help wondering what Puccinelli sent him to Chicago to do.

It doesn't matter. It got him killed and there's no way to change that now—maybe there never was.

The next day, I woke up at about two, unable to remember why I felt so exhausted and empty. A single ray of sunshine crept from between the heavy drapes I'd made to block it, but I flopped onto my stomach and pulled the covers over my head. I just couldn't wake up yet—didn't want to wake up.

The image from the newspaper flooded back, catching me unaware, and I stiffened in pain, groaning under a weight that squeezed the breath out of me. I tried to go back to sleep, but sleep wouldn't come. I lay very still and tried not to think, but that didn't work either. I rolled over on my back and stared at the ceiling, seeing only Jack—across the table at the soda fountain, holding my hands; lying on the sand, panting; dancing at the Pavilion, smiling and excited, eyes shining. I remembered the hesitation in his voice—how he almost whispered when he told me that he wanted a career in music and how he'd reddened, my sophisticated college man, blushing like a kid asking for his first date.

I lay there, thinking of my future without Jack. Singing, of course, there would be no escape from that. I'd have to keep working. I had to do something to make a living. But singing in nightclubs would feel pretty bleak if I couldn't look forward to summers with Jack— and more after graduation. We'd never made promises between us, but we'd had dreams. We'd dreamed a lot of dreams that would never come true, at the beach and in the yellow Packard.

I climbed out of bed and got dressed.

"You want me to scramble you an egg?" I hadn't even noticed Mom rustling around in the kitchen as I awakened.

"What're you doin' here?"

"Your dad and I decided I should stay with you today."

"What about looking for work?"

"I don't suppose I'll miss any jobs I didn't miss yesterday." She paused. "How about an egg?"

"I'm not hungry."

"You gotta eat something."

"Later."

"Where you goin'?"

"Euclid Beach."

"But," Mom studied me for a moment, "wind off the lake's chilly today."

"I'll wear my coat."

"Don't think the streetcar's running anymore. It's November, Bobbi."

 "It goes out on Lake Shore Boulevard. I'll walk from there."

"You'll freeze. The wind's blowing a gale off the lake today."

I hadn't noticed. I shrugged into my coat and left the apartment in silence. At Lake Shore and 159th, I stepped off the streetcar and leaned into a blustering wind as I trudged to the beach, holding my coat tight around me. The wind started my eyes watering and soon tears poured onto my collar. I found myself a spot and sat with my arms around my knees and watched whitecaps pound onto sand. I buried my face on my knees, sobbing and listening to the heavy rhythm of waves stalking the shore.

I didn't hear the old gentleman approaching, long coat flapping in the wind, until he spoke.

"Whatever it is, give it time," he said. "It'll get better."

I gasped, scrabbling backward to get away. I hadn't thought about the Butcher in days.

"It's alright," he said. "I won't hurt you."

I looked up at him. Maybe it wouldn't matter if it *were* the Butcher. I was already scattered all over the city and I doubted all the pieces would ever come back together.

"Where'd you come from?"

"Probably the same place as you—walking the beach and thinking."

I remained all curled into myself. He looked at me for a few moments.

"I'll leave you to your grief," he said.

I gave him a bleak smile. It's about all I had to give.

"Just don't let it defeat you," he said and continued walking.

The surge of waves kept whooshing up on the beach and whispering away, taking all sense of time and place with them. I didn't know how long I'd been sitting there when I realized I had no more tears to cry. The sun had hidden behind clouds all day, so I couldn't tell if it had set, but the air seemed darker. I got up, scrubbed my face with my hands and walked back to the streetcar stop, hoping I hadn't missed the last one. Soon I'd have to get ready for work, so I'd better get home.

Back at the apartment, Mom was busy making dinner. "It'll be ready in half an hour."

"I'm not hungry."

"Bobbi, if you plan on working tonight, you'll have to stay on your feet for another twelve hours."

I looked at her without speaking. Her own personal cash cow. *God! I'm weary!*

"I know you're taking a cab now so you don't have to walk, but . . . ."

I glanced over my shoulder as I heard Jack's voice. "I'll take care of it," he said, as clearly as if he were right in the room. But of course, he was not there and my heart did a hard thump. Now I knew what it meant when someone said her heart fell.

I looked at Mom. I guess I wasn't being fair.

"Alright, alright. I'll come to the table. Call me when it's ready."

I flopped on the couch, hoping I could nap. But there was Jack again. I closed my eyes, but he didn't go away. If anything, he looked more real—a handsome face with two bright red spots on the forehead. When Mom called me, I was staring at the ceiling, at Jack's face.

"C'mon Bobbi, you've gotta eat somethin'."

Remembering my parents still depended on me, and thinking I couldn't stand to look at Jack's ghost anymore, I dragged myself to the table and ate a few bites of Mom's pot roast.

"Bobbi, you haven't eaten enough to keep a bird alive," Dad said when I asked to be excused. "Your mother got that roast especially for you 'cause she knows you love it."

"I gotta get ready for work."

I gathered up fresh clothes and a towel from the chest of drawers in the corner and waited in the hall, leaning against the wall by the bathroom door. When it opened, I slipped in, locked the door, and took a quick bath—and tried to appreciate how hard my parents were trying to take care of me.

Later, at the club, I repeated my previous night's wooden performance. I felt wooden, concrete maybe, but it was the best I could muster. Fred asked again if I needed some time off. I could afford to take a day or two; my parents wanted me to; I had a little money in savings; but what would I do? Lay around and remember Jack, maybe. Sit on the beach and weep. I conjured a smile for Fred.

"I'll be alright."

For the next seven hours, I forced a smile and hoped it didn't look forced. Consciously putting more intensity into my voice and more energy into swinging with the music, I got through another night. By quitting time I'd succumbed to exhaustion like I'd never felt—even when I was just starting, going to school in the daytime and singing at night. At the end of my last set, I made an early call for a cab and climbed in without changing to my street clothes. I stumbled up the stairs and across the apartment where I stripped and crawled into bed, lying on my back and staring at the ceiling until I dropped off some time after sunrise.

For the rest of the week, I managed to choke down a few bites of food each evening before leaving for the club and a few hours of sleep after I returned. On Sunday when I refused to get out of bed, Mom called Mary Teresa, explaining what had happened and asking her to drag me off to do something—anything—to help me remember I was still alive.

When Mary arrived, she came directly to my side and sat on the edge of my bed.

"Your mom told me what happened, Bobbi. I'm so sorry." She paused for a long moment, stroking my back. "But you can't just wallow in it."

"Christ! It's only been a week! Is that all you think he's worth!" I exploded. "Just leave me alone. Let me wallow in peace."

Mary looked up at my mom. "Maybe she does need a little time," she suggested.

"I'm just worried."

"Well, I know—but maybe a week?"

Having people talk about me when I'm right there annoys the heck out of me, but that time I didn't have the energy to care. The worst images had stopped swirling around in my head and I just wanted to sleep. Was that too much to ask?

Mom nodded and Mary left. Thank God!

I made it through the next week and there was Mom again, with the telephone. I wished I'd never fought for it. Soon, Mary sat on the side of my bed.

"What's the matter?" I snarled. "Am I cluttering up the living room?"

Mary stared at me for a long moment. "*Now,* you're wallowing," she said.

"Why not? All he wanted was music. Is that too much to ask?"

"I know, Bobbi, but you making yourself sick won't change that."

"I just can't get over—he was here, and then I go to get a tomato and he's gone."

"What?"

"We were just so good together."

"You'll get over it and you'll be good with someone else."

"Not like that."

"Nobody'll be just like him, but," she took my hand, "just give it time." She paused for a moment to let that soak in. "Let's go see what Kate and Helen are doing."

"I don't feel like it."

"Of course you don't, but you will." She stood and tugged on my hand. "Come on. Get yourself out of that bed and get dressed."

"I don't want to."

"But you're going to. I'm not leaving until you come with me."

"But . . . ."

"Just get up." She'd almost pulled me out of bed by then.

"Let go. I'm falling."

"You gonna get up?"

"Yeah, alright. I'm getting up. Just let go so I can get my feet on the floor."

Once out of bed, I stood passive while Mary grabbed clothes out of my dresser and off the hangars in my wardrobe—underwear, slacks, shirt—holding them out to me, one garment at a time until I put them on. I followed Mary down the stairs and into the sunlight, squinting and shielding my eyes with my forearm as I stepped out onto the street.

"God it's bright."

"Well yeah. You've been holed up in that dark apartment for two weeks with the covers over your head. Come on, Bobbi. It's time to get out in the sunlight."

"What am I gonna do without him?"

"Go on, Bobbi. You're gonna go on."

I nudged a cigarette butt with my toe.

"God this city is filthy."

Mary kept walking.

"Look at all the newspaper blowing around and the grime on the sidewalk."

"C'mon Bobbi," said Mary.

Of all the places to go, we ended up at the soda fountain, once we'd found Kate and Helen. In the neighborhood, I guess it was the only place.

"We sat at that table," I said, pointing.

"We're sitting over here," Mary said, taking my elbow and steering me to the other side of the shop. "And you're not to think about that other table."

I just stared at my friends and slid into the back of the booth where they'd maneuvered me. They must be crazy. Did they really think I wouldn't be thinking about that other table?

After an afternoon in the soda shop, remembering, talking with the girls about the times I spent with Jack, I actually began to think about him without feeling like I would collapse. In a few weeks, I could get through whole hours at a time without crying. I focused on my singing, adding new songs to my repertoire and again taking lessons. For a long time, I sang every song for Jack.

Eventually, I began to feel comfortable with the idea of moving on and singing with some of the big name orchestras—making more money—maybe finding some guy to take care of me like Mom said. Didn't matter who. Not anymore.

January 9, 1939

By the time I could even think about more than just surviving, Dad had healed enough to get a few odd jobs here and there. He would buy some groceries and bet on some races. He added fairly consistently to the family finances by throwing in his wages and his winnings. Mom kept up with her scrubbing, so we got by okay. I made a little more than Roosevelt's new minimum wage—just a bit more than I'd made at the Pavilion. My parents made minimum, but among the three of us, we did pretty well. My life seemed stable for once—with a big hole in the middle.

I kept singing at LakeView through the holidays, wondering if Palatino would ever call. I hoped he'd meant it when he said he wanted a girl singer. I needed a change, someplace where I hadn't always imagined I was singing to Jack, or with Jack. I'd wanted the job when Palatino brought it up, but by January, I *needed* it. I hadn't heard that he'd hired anybody else, so I still had hope, but I wondered if I could give him a subtle—or not so subtle—reminder.

Between sets one night after the New Year, I suggested a trip to Danceland, since nobody had checked out the scene over there in ages. Long and a couple of the other guys jumped in Tony's car—it seemed like Tony was always there. I wondered for a moment how Fred felt about his bouncer taking off with the band, but forgot about it in my eagerness to talk to Palatino. We buzzed over to the other club.

A big barn of a place, like the Pavilion, Danceland fairly jumped with activity. I took a good look at the stage where I would work if I got a job there. I found it nice and roomy, especially when Palatino got me up there to sing a number or two. I noticed an air of professionalism with the band's logo stamped on the fronts of all the band's boxy music stands. A quick scan revealed the dressing room, stage left, where I could step off to repair my makeup without winding through the crowd—if Palatino offered the job. For the first time in months, I smiled when we headed back to LakeView.

A couple of weeks later, Palatino showed up at the club by himself—at the beginning of our last set. He took a table by the stage and sort of nudged Tony aside to hand me down at the end of it.

"Aren't you leading the band anymore?"

"Sure I am, but it's Monday; Jimmy's doin' it for the last set. You ready to come to work for me?"

"Give me the low down."

THE RELUCTANT CANARY SINGS

"Monday through Saturday, eight to four, station WNAX broadcasts live on Saturday. I can pay you twenty-five a week."

"When do you want me?"

"As soon as I can get you. At least by the Saturday before Valentine's Day. We're planning a special program—do you know *My Funny Valentine?*"

"Sure. Maybe I can come over sometimes between sets to rehearse with your band?"

"Smooth. See ya when ya can get over."

I smiled to myself as Carlo left the club. I'd get great exposure from the radio show. I'd make twenty-five percent more than Fred paid. Yes I did calculate stuff like that. I'm my father's daughter. I might be heading for the big time—money and security.

I glanced around the club on my way to Fred's office to tell him the news. *I'd sure miss Fred and Tony looking out for me, though.*

When I told Mom she'd have to save a little less for a couple of weeks so I could take a cab to Danceland for rehearsals between sets, she exploded.

"We have to keep saving, Bobbi. You can't just spend money like that."

"Mom. When I go over to Danceland as their featured singer, I'll be making twenty-five percent more than I'm making now—almost seventy-five percent more than Roosevelt's minimum wage. But I've gotta sound good that first night or I might not have any others."

"Well, I don't like it, Bobbi. What if you don't get the job?"

"I already have the job, Mom. I just need to be ready—and Danceland is too far to get there between sets. I'll take out the five a week I've been taking and another five spot for the taxi."

"I'm against it."

"Fine. But that's what I'm gonna do. I'll give dad the rest of my check, like usual."

"That's another thing. You shouldn't let your father manage your money."

"Mom, I don't have the time or energy to worry about paying the bills. I just want to work and sleep and spend a little time with my friends—before they forget me."

"Give it to me."

I stared at Mom, narrowing my eyes and wondering why I was afraid to turn my money over to her.

"We can be saving at least half of what we all make together."

"We are."

"And if you're working at Danceland, we can save three-fourths."

Ah, that's why.

"That's just it, Mom. I want to save money, sure, but I don't want to live like we have been anymore."

"Remember what happened when your father broke his leg."

I glared at Mom. "I remember every night when I step on that stage. That's why I'm taking this new gig."

Mom glared back. "Your father will think he's got a sure thing and bet it on a horse race."

"No he won't Mom. He knows how hard I work."

"You think that'll make any difference?"

"I have to think it will." I stood and walked into the kitchen, ran and chugged a glass of water, then looked back at Mom, still sitting across the room.

"I think school's out. I'm goin' down to Mary's.

"You're gonna regret this."

"I may. Surely I may."

A couple of days later, over dinner, I suggested that we could afford a bigger apartment when I started at Danceland. Mom glared at me.

"I'd like to have my own bedroom. I'm too old to have Dad running through my bedroom all the time—and maybe we can afford something with a bathroom." I didn't care about the telephone any more, but it was handy for all kinds of reasons.

"I'll start looking when you get your first check," Dad said. "I agree that we can afford it."

"Don't encourage her," Mom snapped, "we need to save more."

"Mom, we're crowded in here like sardines. We've saved some money and can keep saving. No reason we can't save fifteen dollars a week. That's not chump change. In six, maybe seven years, we could buy a house with that if we wanted to—bought and paid for. But I'm done with this apartment."

"You. Both of you," said Mom. "You're gonna ruin us. What if you lose that job, Bobbi? Then what'll we do?"

"We'll look for another one. That's what we'll do. And remember, with this gig at Danceland, I'll be on the radio every Saturday night. That'll make it much easier to get the next job with a better band. Things are getting' better. I'll bet Dad gets a job by the end of summer."

"You *are* betting."

"We've got enough coming in, Ella," said Dad, glancing at his pocket watch.

"If you'd sell that damned watch . . . ."

 Dad ignored her, cutting her off mid-sentence. "I think Bobbi's right. I'm seeing more restaurants opening. It's just a matter of time and I'll be working again."

"But what if you're not?"

"Ella, I'm tired of you running me down."

"I'm not. I'm just facing reality."

"Damn it! Reality is that Bobbi's making most of the money—almost a fortune with this new job—and if she wants a bigger apartment, she's gonna have it!"

Mom slammed her fork down on the table, threw up her hands, and stomped toward the bedroom.

"If you won't listen to me, I'll just go to bed."

With Mom out of the room, Dad and I discussed what kind of apartment we needed.

"Let's stay in this neighborhood if we can, Dad. All my friends are still here. I'll have to figure out how to get to and from work, but it's not a big deal. There must be some better apartments close by."

Dad agreed and promised to start looking right away—and by March we had a larger place where I had my own room and we shared a bath—just the three of us. We moved our few remaining belongings into a furnished apartment that looked pretty spiffy compared to our old one.

As soon as we'd moved, Dad and I got together, while Mom was out stocking up on groceries, and added up the bills. Even the increased monthly rent only cost one of my weekly checks. With the cost of a telephone—and I had to invest in some new gowns since I changed jobs—we could still save half the income from all three of us.

Once I felt secure in our decision, I got so excited I had to show off.

"Dad, I'm gonna run over and get my friends, so I can show 'em our new place."

"Sure thing, Bobbi. I saw somebody tearing the boards off Mowrey's and I wanna go over there and see if they're opening it up again."

"Dad! That'd be great."

"Yeah—if I could get my old job back—hire your mom to wait tables again. She's really good, you know."

Mary was off making wedding plans with Ralph that Tuesday afternoon when I went looking for her. After catching up on Mrs. Calibri's burns and how well they'd healed, I went to look for Kate, who was also off with her boyfriend, Ed. When I finally located Helen, I heard the announcer on Helen's radio chattering about war in Europe.

"What's he talking about?"

Helen grimaced. "Apparently Germany has invaded Czechoslovakia."

"I thought they got all that stuff settled twenty years ago."

"I dunno. Seems like the Germans aren't satisfied."

"Didn't they start the last war? Hope they don't get another one started."

"Me too," Helen said as she grabbed her purse. "Let's go do some shopping."

We spent the afternoon wandering in and out of Cleveland's department stores as Helen helped me select new costumes for my new gig. As we looked at gowns and accessories, Helen bubbled over with enthusiasm for my new opportunity. I raised my left arm while she zipped me into a gown.

"It is a good chance to make more money—quite a bit more money—and the Saturday radio show gives me a *lot* of exposure. Unless we have another crash, I should be in good shape."

"Is that all you think about?"

"What *should* I think about?"

"Well, Bobbi, you're going to be a star—you *are* a star!"

"Hmmm. I'm not sure I know what that means."

"It means. It means—everybody loves you."

"*Loves* me? I can't tell you how many of those people, who love me, have fondled my rear as I walk past them. A lot of them go for the front, too, but I can usually stare them down." I unzipped the dress. "I really miss Tony—and Fred."

"I don't suppose you can avoid the crumbs."

"I learned a lot from watching Tony and who he avoided, but I can't avoid 'em all." I stepped out of the dress. "I think I'll take this one."

"How about these other two?"

"Nah. I'll have to wait for another paycheck or two. "Mom'd have a conniption fit if I bought more than one dress at a time. Remember they're her dresses and I've pretty much ruined them. She's already having a cat about the apartment."

"But the ones you've been wearing are all old."

"And they're getting sweat stained and worn. I know, but I'll get by with them for a while. I need a new corselette."

"I thought you hated those things."

"I do. Believe me I do. But it's harder for them to pinch when I'm packed in tight."

"Pinch!"

"Yeah. My old one's wearing out and sometimes I've got big bruises on my butt at the end of the night."

"God! They can't all be like that."

"No, of course not, but it's simply amazing how the ones who are manage to work their way up to where I step off the stage. Then there are the ones that slip into my dressing room and insist they're gonna take me out after my last set and show me a good time."

Helen grimaced. "Yuck! How do you handle them?"

"I haven't had to fight one of them off yet, if that's what you mean. I guess I'd do lot of kickin' and screamin' if they ever got physical."

"You need Tony."

"I know, but he still works at LakeView."

It seemed to me that talking about Tony made him materialize, just like magic. A couple of nights after our shopping expedition, I had stepped out of my dressing room and found him waiting for me. He offered his elbow.

"I don't suppose the management around here would mind too much if you flirt with this customer for a while, would they?"

"I think it would be alright."

He led me to a table where he'd left his drink and ordered one for me.

"So what're you doin' here? You quit LakeView?"

"I would if I could get on here."

"Really? Why? Do they pay better over here?"

"I don't know. I could look after you like I did at LakeView."

I stared at him for a few moments, frowning.

"I really do miss having you to look out for me."

"Doesn't hurt to have a big guy walkin' around with you, does it?"

"Sure doesn't." I sipped my drink. "But I might not stay here for long."

"Somebody givin' you a hard time?"

"No more than the usual, but things are opening up now. People are makin' more money and goin' out more."

"You wanna get on with one of the big-name bands?"

"That would be nice."

"D'ya ever think about settlin' down and gettin' married? Quittin' the business?"

He'd hit a nerve. Not that Jack and I ever talked about marriage, but the idea hung in the background. I probably wouldn't have quit singing, but I could have done it with him.

"Did once."

"That guy dropped you off at the club that night? Jack Mosso, wasn't it?"

"Yeah." He'd remembered the police visit.

"What happened to him? He run off?"

"Got killed. Murdered."

Tony took my hands and held them, looking into my eyes. I could see him putting things together. "Not the Torso . . . ."

I interrupted. "He was Al Puccinelli's nephew."

"Al Puccinelli's—How'd you end up with him? That party?"

"Not like that. Met him at Euclid Beach. He wanted to be a concert pianist."

"Sure he did."

"He did, Tony. You don't know him."

"That family, Bobbi."

"Not everybody's their family. They got him killed."

Tony remained silent, watching me square up my shoulders and compose myself. I stared back at him, wondering what he was thinking.

"I don't know how many times I've seen you do that. I'm still amazed."

"Do what?"

"You'll be scared or hurt and you'll just stand yourself up and look like you've got the world by the tail. You almost make me believe it."

"No point in whining."

"But who holds you and takes care of you when it gets to be too much?"

His gaze caught me and held me. I could almost hear water falling off the edge of the world. I looked down at our hands, joined together on the table. I felt the warmth of those hands enveloping mine and I relaxed just a little.

"No one," I whispered, "not since Jack."

This time it took me a little longer to straighten up. Tony held onto my hand for a moment longer, catching my eye, as I got up to go back to work.

"Bobbi, you don't have to be tough all the time."

"Tony, I have to go circulate."

I heard the roar of water recede just a little as he released my hand.

"I know, Sweetie, but just remember. I'm here if you need somebody."

"Thanks, Tony. I'll remember that. You're a good friend."

From then on, Tony turned up once a week—to make sure I was doing alright, I guess. He never stayed long, only long enough to meet me at my dressing room door and escort me to a table for a few moments' chat. Without realizing it, I began to look forward to his visits. I even talked to him about things that mattered to me.

One night he caught me when I'd been thinking about getting out my sketch pad again. I hadn't picked up a pencil since Jack died. That thought reminded me how much I'd wanted to finish high school, so when Tony asked about my parents, I flared.

"Damn it, Tony. Why couldn't my parents take care of *me?* I'm so tired of supporting all of us!"

He took my hand. "I know, Sweetie, you've really been behind the eight ball."

I wailed like a self-indulgent little fluff. "I didn't even get to finish high school."

I ducked my head when I realized the people at the next table were looking at me.

"I'm sorry for that, Bobbi. I know you really wanted to graduate." He squeezed my hand. "But you're doin' alright for yourself without it."

"I'm not, though. I *hate* being up all night and never seeing the sun. It's gonna be summer soon and I'll be sleeping instead of swimming—even on the weekends."

"I thought you liked being a night owl. After hours, you went to those other clubs all the time."

"It's what you gotta do to make a living, Tony. To keep up with what's goin' on, keep the act fresh, look for better gigs."

He ran his thumb over the back of my hand. "I guess I should have realized that. Guess I don't know much."

I touched his cheek. "How would you know, Tony? I have to look like I'm havin' fun—all the time."

I laid my hand back on the table and Tony took it. "Maybe you should have been an actress."

"I wanna be an artist!" I stood to go back to work. "But I don't know how."

As I stepped up on stage, I looked back over my shoulder. Tony still sat, looking at his hands where I'd just pulled away from him.

Poor guy. He's trying to be my friend and all I do is complain. I stepped onto the stage and grabbed the mic.

By the time I'd been at Danceland for a couple of months, I heard that Italy had invaded Albania, but I didn't pay much attention. Dad had actually landed the job managing Mowrey's and he'd taken over the rent, utilities, and groceries. It had been a long time since I'd seen him so happy, and for the first time in almost two years, my money was mine. I hadn't realized just how heavy the weight of the whole family had been until it was gone. My chance to finish high school had gone, too, and with it any chance to attend college or art school. Singing was still my meal ticket and I kept doing it, trying to make myself more marketable.

During the next few months, I tried to ignore the rumbles of war from Europe. Even though the U.S. remained neutral, Dad talked about the war in Great Britain and France. Tony sometimes mentioned it, too, wondering if Roosevelt would get into it. Maybe everyone would get drafted Sometimes I wondered what would happen to the crowds at Danceland if the U.S. got into it. Would everything dry up like it had after the stock market crash?

I'd been at Danceland for another eight months when I went to the DownBeat one night after hours, watching and listening to the Jimmy Jones orchestra. When Jones asked me up to sing a couple of numbers with the band, I performed *Deep Purple* and *Begin the Beguine.*

"Good," said Jones when I finished the second number, "you can do those Latin rhythms."

"Yeah. So?"

"C'mon. Let's grab a chair." He turned to his first saxophonist, Glen Porter. "Hey, bring your gobblepipe up here and do *Moonlight Serenade.*"

When we were seated, Jones took my hand. "Dollface, my canary's about to quit me—gettin' married. I need a female vocalist to take her place. You interested?"

I retrieved my hand. "Might be. What's your story?"

"We've been touring all around the Great Lakes, up and down the Eastern Seaboard—Atlanta, Miami, Atlantic City, New York, Philadelphia—you name it."

"I think I saw your bus outside."

"Yeah. I give my canary two seats—so she can sleep."

"Cabbage?"

"I'll pay you thirty dollars a week."

"I'll have extra expenses on the road—food, wear and tear on wardrobe."

Jones hesitated. "No, Bobbi, I pay hotels and meals—if those expenses aren't paid by the hiring agency. So you won't have any living expenses to mention."

"But I have to buy gowns and makeup. The guys don't have that expense—at least not nearly as much."

"You drive a hard bargain."

"People know my name from the radio show."

"Locally."

"WNAX broadcasts around the lakes, into Pennsylvania and New York."

"Okay, okay, thirty-five a week. And don't you tell the guys, either."

I glanced at the band, just finishing up the number, wondering what it would be like to live on a bus with fifteen men.

"When do you need me?"

"Kitty's leaving us before our Halloween gig in Atlantic City, so if you could meet us there that'd be great."

"That'll give me about a month to wrap up here, pack up my gowns—you've got somewhere in the bus to hang them?"

"Yup."

"Okay, I'll do it."

We made arrangements for Jones to call with final instructions. I stepped out of the club, humming, and hailed a cab. Thirty dollars a week and that extra five would keep me looking snazzy.

PART IV: ON THE ROAD

April 7, 1940

By the time I joined Jones in Atlantic City, Dad had had his old job back at Mowrey's, full time, for about six months. He did hire Mom to wait tables, just like he said he would. As soon as they could afford it, they separated again. Their lives became immeasurably more peaceful, and so did mine during the times I got back to Cleveland. Those times, I stayed with Mom in our old apartment, the one Dad had found for us when I started at Danceland. It turned out she liked it after all. On Sundays in Cleveland, I usually helped Dad with the books and the stock. On the road, I sent a check to Dad every week to deposit in savings—I was well on my way to saving enough to buy that house.

On the bus early the following year, I watched wind-driven rain against the window turn the view outside into rivulets of spring green.

Well, I've made it a few months. It's been worth it. With Dad and Mom paying their own bills, and Jimmy paying mine, I'm saving a little bit. Dad says I've got more than two thousand in the bank.

I lit a cigarette and took another sip from my flask. I knew I shouldn't drink so much, but I didn't have to be on stage until the next day. The taste of Drambuie reminded me of what good care Tony used to take of me. I could almost feel his strong arms around me when I'd burst into the club after that guy tried to grab me—or his light touch on my elbow, steering me away from trouble. I sure wished I still had him to manage the crowds. As to Jack, it had been almost three years, but he still invaded my thoughts—especially after a gig in a really dressy ballroom.

My sketchpad had its own little spot under my seat, but I hardly remembered when I'd set out to draw my life in the nightclubs. By then, I could probably have afforded the oils; we'd recorded a few singles. My $7.50 a side wasn't much, but I could get a good set of oils and a canvas or two. Where would I store them on the bus, though? And I still didn't know how to use them. With Denise on the other end of the country, where she couldn't tell me to "just experiment like that Pablo cat," I felt silly for not just trying something until it worked—just like she'd told me.

Retching in the aisle woke me from a light doze. The trombonist's dog had thrown up and I grabbed my sketchpad. What a miserable way to wake up.

 I gagged, eyes watering, and yelled, "Damn it, Al, you been giving that dog booze again? Clean this mess up, you dig me?"

I turned to the window, mouth-breathing to keep my stomach down.

Jones, across the aisle, glared at Al and the dog. "Get that damned dog away from me and wipe up that mess." He faced front and yelled back over his shoulder. "I don't want any more bullshit on this bus. If that dog gets sick again, he's off the bus—for good. Got that?"

Al mumbled something and cleaned up the mess with an old undershirt.

"I hope that's yours," I said as he headed for the back of the bus with a paper sack full of soiled undershirt.

Once the disruption settled down, Jones slid over into my extra seat, nudging me with a shoulder. "How would you like to have breakfast with me?"

"Jimmy, we *always* have breakfast together—and lunch and dinner—along with fifteen other people. That's about the fourth time you've asked me that. The answer's the same—I *still* never mix business with pleasure."

"Damn," he says, "you sure?"

"I'm certain."

"You really like your job with the band?"

"You're not gonna fire me for not sleeping with you."

"Nah. I won't." He sat quietly a moment, as if looking for another pitch. "Hell, I guess I'll get some sleep."

"Good idea."

"I'd really treat you good."

"Jimmy."

"Alright. Alright." He slid back to his own double seat and stretched out as much as a tall man can stretch out in a pair of bus seats.

I'll bet he'd laugh his head off if he knew I'm still a virgin.

Before long, my gowns became a big problem. We played a few ballrooms in the South where the temperature sweltered and the humidity melted. I'd sweat big stains under my arms and they wouldn't dry-clean out. My dresses got rough treatment loading and unloading, dressing and undressing, all in a hurry, and Jimmy paid nothing for new wardrobe—I'd asked for more money to cover it, but he wouldn't budge. He reminded me I'd negotiated premium wages to take care of that. One night someone stepped on the end of my skirt and it ripped up the side, leaving another unusable garment to replace.

THE RELUCTANT CANARY SINGS

During a weekend gig in Cleveland, I called Helen and we haunted the sales, looking for gowns. I'd been hearing snippets on a radio, now and then, about Hitler's aggression in Europe and seen the Army and Navy recruitment posters. Cleveland was full of them. It was getting harder to ignore the possibility of war when it was posted in nearly every store window. We passed the posters with barely a glance, focused on finding work clothes for me.

In Halle Brothers we found a dress that fit, and I bought it, but the department stores just didn't have many evening gowns on sale. Helen knew of another gown, on sale, at Sterling-Linder, so we spent a couple of hours shopping there. I left with a second gown and some needed undergarments.

Afterwards, we went to the Mayfield Street Soda Fountain.

"Boy, this has been great. I appreciate the help."

"You've always had good taste, you just weren't interested."

"No, but I have to look good—and I'm learning what to put together."

We didn't say anything for a few moments, sipping our sodas. "I really miss you girls," I said finally. "I lost track when I started at LakeView and I've been pretty much on my own since." I glanced around the soda fountain, "This place hasn't changed a bit."

"Do you ever think of Jack?"

"Sometimes. Hell, all the time. Sometimes I even dream about him. But you know who I really think about—especially when I'm working the clubs?"

Helen shrugged.

"Tony."

"Oo-la-la."

"No. Not like romance. I miss having him look out for me."

"He did take pretty good care of you."

"Mom wanted me to marry him."

"You could do worse."

"That's what Mom said. But I don't love him—not like that. He really was just like a big brother."

"Have you met anybody?"

"Aw, most of the guys in the band are married, and living in a bus with a bunch of people doesn't show you their good side, anyway."

"Nobody in the clubs you play?"

"I completely lost my privacy when we started making records. When we did the Saturday broadcasts on WNAX, people knew my voice and, occasionally, someone would hear me talking and ask if I'm Bobbi Bowen and would I autograph something. But they didn't know what I look like mostly. Now, with the record jackets and the marquees everywhere, they know my face. So, no. Nobody in the clubs. Just people coming up to me *everywhere* wanting an autograph—having breakfast in a diner, checking into a hotel, having a drink. *Everywhere.*"

"But that's swell! Isn't that what you want?"

"I don't know, Helen. Of course, it makes me "salable." But I feel like somebody's watching me *all the time*, like one of those ant colonies with the glass on the side. I just want to put on a disguise and wander around being a regular housewife or something."

"Regular housewife? You?"

"You know what I mean."

We chatted for another hour, catching up on what had been happening with Mary and Kate. Both married, Helen said. Mary expecting her first baby. The guys both had good jobs. Helen had become department manager at Sterling-Linder.

THE RELUCTANT CANARY SINGS

We decided to see a movie before I went back to Mom's to catch a little shut-eye before I went to work. First we saw a news reel of Allied troops evacuating Dunkirk.

"Jeez. We're gonna be in it, aren't we?"

"I heard on the radio that Belgium has surrendered—Netherlands too, a couple of weeks ago," Helen whispered

After the show, we said goodbye. "Guess we're going on to Chicago after tonight."

"Where to after that?"

"I dunno. I just get on the bus and the driver takes us somewhere."

"You need to get another job like LakeView or Danceland, where you can stay in one place."

"Can't make as much money that way—at least not yet. It would be great to have a radio contract."

"Maybe soon."

"Maybe." I walked away, back to my unconnected life.

December 7, 1941 - Buffalo, New York

The Jones orchestra was on its way to Atlantic City when the bus driver yelled. "Hey, you guys, listen to this." After a minute of silence, he yelled again. "Hey, I think we're at war."

We all crowded up close behind him where we could hear Roosevelt's announcement about the attack on Pearl Harbor. A couple of the guys sat on the steps and Jimmy stood in the aisle, hanging on to the back of the driver's seat. Everybody else crowded in, leaning over the seats in front to get as close as possible. When the announcement was over they all went back to their places, mumbling to themselves.

"I wonder if people will stop going to the clubs," Al mused.

"I wonder how long before we're all drafted," Jones said.

For the rest of the afternoon, nobody slept. We all talked quietly about what would happen to the country—and to us personally. Starting the next week, we began to find out, as clubs and dance halls began cancelling our engagements. Instead, they would hire one or two of our headliners to perform with a house band or a local orchestra—for a night or a weekend, occasionally a week. That's how I ended up at the Firefly in Buffalo, New York, on a solo gig. I'd jumped at a whole week while I waited for things to pick up for the band. Money had become tight again and any job was welcome.

In February, I stepped into a night club in Buffalo, New York. I took the cold bluster of wind off Lake Erie with me and right away, I knew I was in trouble. Instead of a bustling place with someone behind the bar taking inventory and replacing depleted stock, a band tuning and setting up on stage, and a manager counting cash and preparing the till, I found the near-dusk of an empty hall— chairs still tipped on tables, sawdust still spread on the dance floor, lights off. Stepping back outside, grabbing the door as the wind caught it, I read the sign. Yes, I'd entered the right club. As my eyes adjusted to the dark, I spotted a middle-aged man wandering around, glassy-eyed and aimless.

"Hi." I walked over and held out my hand, "I'm Bobbi Bowen. Could you tell me where to find the manager?"

"Um," he said, staring at my hand like he knew he was supposed to do *something* with it.

"Where can I find the manager's office?"

"It's over there." He pointed vaguely toward a dark corner. "But he isn't there."

"Do you know where I can find him? Gene Olds, that's his name."

His eyes focused. "I guess that's me."

I squinted at him in the dark, "You're Gene Olds?"

"Unfortunately."

"Then you hired me to sing with your house orchestra tonight through Saturday."

"Let's go back to my office." He turned on his heel and walked away.

When we reached his tiny office, I examined him in the light of a small window. He looked rough. His hair stood up on end, like he'd been raking his hands through it. His jacket hung on the back of his chair and his shirt looked like he'd been clearing a basement in it. "What's going on? You don't look like you'll be open tonight."

"I won't and I won't need you this week at all. It's impossible."

 "What do you mean impossible? We have a contract. It wasn't impossible when you called me in Cleveland."

"I know, I know. But it's impossible now."

"No. I came all the way to Buffalo to sing with your orchestra. You can't back out now." I stood and leaned over his desk and caught his eye. "You called me, I didn't call you,"

He flushed and hesitated. "My lawyer says any agreements I've made are voided by the foreclosure."

"What foreclosure? What do you mean foreclosure? You didn't mention any foreclosure."

"The bank foreclosed on me at ten o'clock this morning. I didn't see it coming."

"Where's the sign and why aren't you locked and boarded up?"

"I ripped it all down after they left. I kept an extra key."

"So are you open for business or not? Do I have a job?"

"No. I'm just wandering around here trying to figure out how to get out of this."

"Look, I spent every cent I had on train fare and my hotel. You gotta pay me what you promised."

"I can't pay you anything."

"I don't know anyone here. I came because you said you had a job for me. I can't even get back to Cleveland. At least give me train fare."

"I can't. They cleaned out the till this morning. They took all the money I had in the safe. I keep all my funds here, so I don't even have enough for a cup of coffee."

He reached into his pockets and pulled out a handful of change. "Well, actually, I have enough to buy two cups of coffee and a couple of rolls."

I glared at him.

"There's a coffee shop and bakery about a block down. How about coffee and a roll?"

What a bizarre idea. I eyed him for a long moment. "You have got to be kidding."

He gave me a weary smile. "I can at least send you to some of my competitors. Maybe they'll have something for you."

"Okay." I sat. "Maybe a few minutes in a warm place where I can think will give me an idea."

"That's the ticket. Let me get my coat."

I got up, squared my shoulders, and turned my collar against the bitter spit of snow. After a short walk in the blistering wind, Olds held the door for me as we stepped into the heavenly aroma of fresh coffee and warm pastries. We found seats in a booth by the window where we could watch people scurrying before the gusts like lost newspaper pages. We ordered coffee and cream puffs. Once he'd paid the bill, Gene had two pennies left.

"Seed," he said. "So, Bobbi, you don't look very old. How long have you been singing in nightclubs?"

"About four years. I've been travelling a lot lately. With a regional orchestra—the Jimmy Jones band. We brought in good crowds.

"We were on our way to Atlanta two months ago when we heard about Pearl Harbor. After that, a lot of clubs cancelled the gigs we had lined up. We finished in Atlanta and went back to Cleveland— I've been singing with Jones for about two years—but we haven't worked much as a band since Pearl. I was eager for the job you had here."

We both sipped our coffee as I thought about how things had improved—until the war started. Since then, people had wanted to stay close to home and see what might happen next. The nightclub business dried up for a third time.

Gene apologized again and scrawled a list of other nightclubs in a notebook he'd grabbed as we left his club—the bank's club, I guessed. He gave me the manager's names and encouraged me to ask them for work. When he was done, I folded the page he'd ripped out and put it in my purse.

I asked Olds about himself and he talked about hanging on through the crash and the rough years. We fell silent, sipping the dregs of our coffee, reluctant to leave the warm shop.

"Well, I guess I'd better go see if one of these guys will hire me," I said at last. "I've got to get something today. Thanks for the coffee."

"Thanks for coming out with me," Olds said. "I feel a little less like just putting my head in one of the gas ovens."

"You'll figure it out," I said, reaching for my coat. Gene held it for me and put on his own while I buttoned up tight. "Well, see ya," I said as we separated outside the shop.

"See ya," he said, heading off in the opposite direction.

February 9, 1942

Hoping to stop in at least four of the clubs Olds listed for me—unless I got a job first, of course—I started walking. I buried my hands in my pockets and shrugged my coat tighter. Head down, I thought about how I got where I was.

What a drag to look for work in this weather. Sure would be nice to have a regular job like I did at LakeView. Nothin' wrong with knowin' where the next paycheck's comin' from. I really lucked out with that job. What would I have done without Tony and Fred? Can't count on finding a job with people like that.

I kicked at a newspaper page that had blown against my feet.

Wish I didn't have to walk into the wind.

I looked into a couple of the grim faces coming toward me.

Olds was nice, though.

By the time I arrived at the Orchid Lounge, the manager was busy in a meeting. Sitting alone at the bar, I aroused the usual curiosity. One guy, who had apparently been there for hours, slid down and perched next to me. He eyed me silently for a while. Hoping to discourage him, I turned a shoulder toward him.

"Hi honey. What're you drinking?"

I glanced at the bottles lined up on shelves behind the bar and rolled my eyes.

"Nothing, thank you."

"Come on, Honey. This is a bar. What can I get for you?"

Unwilling to get off on the wrong foot by being unpleasant to a customer, I sighed. "I'm not drinking anything."

"You here to pick up a john?"

"No! I am *not* a hooker."

He turned away, slopping his drink on the bar and carefully arranging his features into feigned indifference. But in a few minutes he turned back. "So-o-o-o-o whadaya doin' here?"

I couldn't help snapping my eyes when I faced him. "I'm waiting for Tom Reimer."

Again, he eyed me for several minutes. "Um-m-m-m-m, you his new squeeze?"

"No."

I looked at the manager's door and willed it to open. No such luck.

"Whadaya want Tom for?"

Patience waning, I responded a little more sharply than I intended.

"A job! I am looking for a job."

Apparently, he had to digest my words and think of a response, his head wobbling as if he'd nodded off.

"Well honey, you're pretty enough to bring my drinks," he said finally, laying a hand on my thigh.

Disgusted, I picked it up and put it on his knee. I got up and stood at the end of the bar. He slid down next to me.

"How 'bout bringing me a drink?"

"That's not what I do."

"Hmmm," he trailed off and remained silent, nursing his drink in slow motion. I hoped he'd lost interest, but after a few sloppy swallows, he was right back.

"So what kind of job you lookin' for?" He snickered as though he'd just heard something funny.

Catching the side of my tongue between my teeth, fully aware of the bartender's smirk, I closed my eyes. The man wobbled a bit on the bar stool and caught himself.

"So wha'd you say you do?"

"I'm a singer."

"Well," he said, leaning over the bar and winking at the bartender. "Whyn't you say so?"

Just then, Reimer came out of his office. "Who wanted to see me?"

"I did, Mr. Reimer. My name is Bobbi Bowen." Boy was I glad to see him, whether he had a job for me or not.

He smiled. "Come on in, then," he reached around behind me, lightly touching my waist to escort me into his office.

"Gene Olds sent me over here, Mr. Reimer. He said you might need a singer for a few evenings."

Reimer looked me over. "So why didn't he hire you?"

"He did. I came from Cleveland to sing with his house band, but he got foreclosed this morning."

Reimer stared. "Are you sure?"

"That's what he said. He was wandering around in there all by himself. They boarded it up and everything, but he said he'd ripped the signs and boards down. Don't know what he hoped to gain."

"He ran a good club." Reimer reached for a pack of Camels lying on his desk. He offered one to me, but I shook my head, and he lit one for himself. He leaned back and took a drag, letting it out in a rush. "

"Well, I guess that's one less competitor in the neighborhood." He stared at the ceiling. "Tough break." He looked at me through the smoke. "Tough break for you, too."

"Maybe a fresh new voice would get some of his regulars over here," I suggested.

"You're right, maybe I can make some hay out of this." He tapped his fingers on the desktop. "Old Olds," he said with a crooked grin. "I thought he was doin' really good."

"Would you like me to audition?"

"Hmm? Oh yeah, you were looking for work." He hesitated for a moment, opening the bottom drawer of his desk and putting his feet on it. "Nah," he said. "I think I'll play it pretty close to the vest. It's been kinda slow since we got in the war. Guys gettin' ready to ship out, stayin' close to home. Why don't you try me again in a month or so when people get over the shock."

"Maybe I could help you bring some of them in now."

"No honey, not this time. I've got me a band to pay, I'll stick with them for the time being."

"Well, I'm staying over at the Evergreen, if you change your mind."

"I'll remember that," he said, pushing up from his chair with a creak and walking me to the door. "You stay out of that wind now." We wove our way through the tables. "Oh," he said as he held the door for me, "you should try old Short over at the Buckeye. He's a ways over there, but he always seems to have a new female vocalist. Don't know why."

"I'll do that. Can I mention your name?"

"You'd probably better not. Short doesn't like me very much. Tell him Olds sent you."

I trudged into the wind feeling hopeful. But before I went to the Buckeye, I had another couple of clubs to visit. Olds had listed the next two as very good prospects. If they didn't pan out, I would visit the Buckeye first thing the next day. Even if the guy fired his vocalists every week, I only needed a couple of days to get myself home.

Three hours later, though, I was still hungry, still without a job, and out of time to visit clubs with any hope of catching managers. But I had an idea and I hurried to my hotel. Maybe I could get my money back and leave Buffalo right away.

Entering the hotel lobby, heels clicking on the tile floor, I thought that, if I could just get the hotel manager to refund my money, I could get a bus ticket back to Cleveland. I didn't know why I hadn't thought of a refund sooner. Excited at the prospect of home and relative comfort, I pounded on the bell at the front desk.

"Hi," I babbled when the manager came out. "I'm paid through Saturday but my job here didn't pan out and I wonder if you could refund my money for the rest of the week so I can get a bus back home. The club got foreclosed this morning so there's no job and I need to get back to Cleveland."

"You've already used the room," he said, interrupting my cascade of words.

"That's alright. I'll stay tonight and go back tomorrow. Just refund my money for Tuesday through Saturday."

"I can't do that. I've already taken today's proceeds to the bank."

"Well, you can pay me back tomorrow when the bank opens, and I can go home."

"No. Listen to me. I reserved the room for the week. I don't give refunds. I would have rented that room if I'd had a vacancy."

"Look. I came here for a job, but there is no job. I don't have the money to go home. Please just give me back the money for the nights I haven't used."

"I'm sorry. I don't give refunds."

"Please mister. I don't even have money to eat tonight. I need to get home."

"That's not my problem, miss. Times are tough all over. You reserved the room. You paid for it. Now you can stay here and look for another job. I've got to make a living too."

I went back to my room, feeling closed in, like I'd entered a house with many doors. Every time I tried one, I found it locked. I had a little change in my pocketbook. I took it out and counted it—four quarters, three dimes, a nickel, and two pennies. I dug around in the bottom, finally dumping everything on the bed. Shoving aside my lipstick, a compact, two clean hankies, a comb, and a handful of miscellaneous scraps I didn't even want to look at, I found another quarter and three nickels. One dollar and seventy-seven cents. That would buy me a bowl of soup. Actually, it would buy me several bowls of soup, but I didn't know how long it would take to find a job.

Taking the elevator down to the first floor and straggling into the coffee shop, I found a seat. For fifteen cents, I bought a bowl of soup—nothing substantial, just beef consommé, but I ordered extra crackers and took my time nibbling them. The meal didn't really fill my empty belly, but I wanted to hang onto every penny.

Back in my room, I tried to ignore my nerves as I planned a strategy. *Tony would be good at this.*

At that time of day, the clubs headed into their busiest hours. No one would talk to me anymore that night, so I sat down with a map of the city, compliments of a previous occupant of my room. I spread it out on the narrow bed and plotted all the clubs Olds had told me about. Using the phone book, I located a few more and pinpointed them on the map as well. Since I didn't know the city, I could only guess at which clubs might be the best prospects. I'd already visited some of the ones Olds had recommended. Dividing Buffalo into sections, I determined to visit all the clubs in the nearest quadrant during the next day.

Having a plan gave me some sense of control, but I couldn't entirely quiet my nerves. I decided to get some sleep and look the next afternoon. I didn't usually get to bed until after four in the morning, though, so I wasn't a bit sleepy. I tossed and turned for hours with my empty stomach growling at me. I finally got up and paced the room, trying to calm my racing thoughts—four steps to the window, six steps past the bed to the door, and six steps back.

What if I can't find a job? What am I going to do?

I knew my parents had no money to send me and, since the band wasn't working, neither did any of them. I finally collapsed, exhausted, and fell into a fitful sleep, dreaming of mounds of cream puffs that kept moving out of reach every time I tried to grab one of them.

The next morning, after a night of sleep interrupted by a burning stomach, I remembered the money I'd been saving for the past four years. Yes! Why hadn't I thought of that? Since I stayed with Mom in Cleveland, and Jimmy paid my hotel and meals on the road, I didn't have much for expenses. I'd taken care of my parents for a couple of years, so they'd taken care of me when they got jobs—whenever I had a gig in Cleveland—so I could save something. I would have Dad wire enough for me to get home.

I got excited at the prospect of eating breakfast and being home within hours. I jumped out of bed, got dressed, and rushed down to the front desk. Once I had the location of the nearest Western Union office, I scurried to the phone booth at the curb and dropped in a dime. Icy wind off Lake Erie rattled the folding door and I shivered as the operator connected my call. I watched a man with a briefcase in one hand, holding his coat tight around his neck with the other, pacing the sidewalk. He kind of jiggled and stamped to keep warm. He reminded me of a little steam engine as his breath rose in puffs and blew away. I heard the click when the operator made the connection.

"Hi, Dad. It's Bobbi."

"Hi, Sweetheart. What're you up to?"

"Dad, I've only got three minutes to give you the Western Union information. I'm out of money. I need you to wire me $20 for a bus ticket and a couple of meals until I get there. My job here fell through and I need to get back to Cleveland."

The silence that followed terrified me.

"You got a pencil and paper, Dad?"

"Honey, I don't have any money to send you."

"Just take it out of my savings." I heard a very long pause.

"There *is* no savings."

My stomach clenched. I felt like I was going to throw up.

"But Dad you told me just last week I had more than $2,000."

"It's not there anymore."

I leaned my forehead against the cold, metal face of the phone. I drove an image of my father, silhouetted in a betting window at Thistledown Racetrack out of my mind.

"How can it not be there? The banks haven't closed. I would have heard about it."

"No."

"Then where'd my money go?"

After another long silence filled with my father's breathing, I heard him clear his throat.

"You know where it's gone," he said at last.

"Tell me."

"Bobbi, I bet it on a sure thing."

"I only need twenty."

"It's gone."

"But it . . . ."

"It's gone, honey."

"It can't *all* be gone . . . . You usually win. You couldn't have bet *all of it!*"

"I had a tip."

"You don't bet on tips. You bet the odds."

"I had a tip and the odds were great!! I thought I could pay you back for the years you supported us."

"You *couldn't* have cleaned out the whole account."

He sighed.

"All of it? You bet all of it!?"

Nothing. I decided to address the crisis at hand and deal with my father later. I still couldn't believe he'd lost all my savings.

"Dad. I have no money." I reached in my coat pocket. "I have thirty-seven cents. I have no job here. How'm I gonna get home?"

Complete silence. I was about to scream when he finally cleared his throat again and said, "You're a star now, Bobbi. You'll find something. You always do."

I hung my head and gave the side of the phone booth a tentative kick. I'd spent $1.30 to call my dad. That would have bought me a meal—but there I was with nothing, my savings all gone.

"Dad," I said, "that's four years working all night, never seeing the sun, never swimming with my friends, dodging hands grabbing at me." I choked. I leaned against the wall of the booth. "What have you got on you?"

"I'm sorry, honey. I just paid the bills. I spent everything but the change in the till for supplies. Otherwise I'd send you something."

"Do you think Mom could?"

"She was just complaining last night the landlord increased her rent. She spent everything she had on the rent. You'll just have to get another job, Bobbi. You'll be alright."

"I . . . ."

"Please deposit $1.30," said the operator.

She waited a few moments, then cut us off and I pressed my head against the glass wall of the booth.

"Damn," I said, kicking the bottom panel. "Damn, damn, damn, damn, damn!"

I noticed the briefcase man standing outside the booth as I left. I could feel heat rising in my cheeks.

"Boyfriend troubles?"

"No!" I snarled.

The man shrugged and entered the booth, rattling the door shut. I tried not to droop as I walked back to the hotel. At least I had rented a room for the duration of the job.

Back in my cramped room, I flopped on the unmade bed. Could this get any worse? I felt like I was dropping down my own personal waterfall off the edge of the world, tumbling and falling.

Flat as an old shirt, I wondered how Dad could say I'd be alright. How would I get the starch back into my spine to go face nightclub managers if even my own parents couldn't (or wouldn't) help me?

It was too early to visit the clubs and I really wanted some coffee and a roll or a piece of toast—or a steak dripping blood. I pulled my remaining change out of my pocket again. I still had only thirty-two cents. Seed. Just like Olds had said. I went back to my room and drank a glass of tap water, hoping my stomach would settle.

By 12:30, back on the street, I headed for the nearest club, head high, determined to look relaxed and sure of myself. I'd never had to work so hard to keep up that pose. Waiting in the first place, I found a bowl of peanuts on the bar. Nibbling a few, trying not to gobble the whole bowl, became my entire focus for those few moments. I visited six nightclubs that afternoon, but none of the managers even gave me an audition. One had a few stale pretzels and another had peanuts for my culinary delight, but mostly, I ate nothing and tried to keep my trembling hands out of sight. That night, I forced myself to climb into bed as soon as I returned to the hotel—in order to save my strength. Cold wind whistling off the lake had burned up a lot of calories and even though the room was warm, I couldn't help shivering. As I burrowed under the blankets, I wondered whether anyone would notice if I starved to death—or froze on the street. At least I had shelter for the rest of the week. Where could I go if I didn't find work by then? Who would care if I just died?

February 11, 1942

On day three, I dragged out of bed to try the clubs in my second quadrant. Those required a longer walk on shaky legs, but I made the first one by 1:30, only to be turned down again. My friends used to talk about pancake makeup, and I felt like I'd put a pancake on my face to cover the dark pockets under my eyes. I couldn't hide the way the light in them had dulled. All afternoon, I walked on, drawing my coat tight against the bitter wind off the lake. All afternoon I wandered in and out of nightclubs, nibbling a few peanuts here or a pretzel there and looking for the one manager who would hire me. Could I complete even one set without collapsing—if I did get a job?

Finally, at seven p.m., almost too late to meet with owners or managers, I stepped into the Buckeye Club like Tom Reimer had suggested and asked for Carl Short. He was going over inventory with the bartender. As they discussed what they needed to order, I nibbled peanuts. When he finished with the liquor order, Short came over and sat next to me, leaning on the bar.

"Bring me a bourbon and water," he said before he turned to me. "What can I do for you, sweetie."

"Gene Olds sent me over. He thought you could use a singer. I'm Bobbi Bowen. I can audition if you want. I see your band is setting up."

"Olds thinks I can use a singer, huh? Wha'd you say your name was?"

"Bobbi Bowen, sir."

"Well, let's see what you can do." He walked me over to the stage. "George, this sweet thing wants to sing with us. I told her she could audition. Why don't you guys play a couple numbers with her? Bobbi, this is George. When they get done getting ready here, you can work with him. What do you want to drink?"

"Nothing, thanks."

"Suit yourself," he said and wandered off.

I sat on the edge of the stage while the band tuned up, taking note of sheet music I could see on the piano. When they were ready, George turned to me.

"What can we play for you?"

"I notice you've got *Blue Moon*. That's my theme song. Can you do it in A?"

"We'll give it a try. *Blue Moon*, guys in A."

I stepped to the middle of the stage and adjusted the mic. George turned to the band, eyeing me over his shoulder. You ready?"

I nodded.

He led the band into the first few instrumental bars. Then I stepped up and began. There I was, standin' alone, no dreams, no love. Not anymore. But, so far so good. I was still standing on my feet. My voice seemed okay. I could still project—at least with the mic. George glanced at me and grinned.

"Not bad for a kid who just walked in off the street."

When I finished the number, Short came walking out of a dark corner in the back of the club, applauding.

"Can you do anything else? How 'bout *Boogie Woogie Bugle Boy?*"

"Sure." The band struck up the first notes. I snapped my fingers and sidled up to the mic. I might get to eat tonight after all. The song wore me out, but I'd managed to put some energy into it. Short looked pleased when I finished the song. I felt certain he'd offer me a job.

"Come on back to my office and we'll talk about it," he said, leading the way through a maze of tables to an office to the right of the bar. "Maybe I can use a singer, after all."

Seated behind his desk, he brought out a bottle of bourbon and two glasses. He poured a half glass and shoved it across the desk, then poured a glass for himself.

"You seem to know your way around a mic. Where have you worked before?"

"I started out in Cleveland about four years ago, at the LakeView Jazz Club. Then I worked with the Palatino Band. WNAX ran our Saturday show live. I sang with the Jimmy Jones band around the Great Lakes and as far south as Atlanta—cut a few records."

He stood and paced the office. Too tired, worried and hungry to think about it, I sat passively.

"You seem to have the experience. You've definitely got the voice and you've got the moves, too."

He stopped right behind me, standing my hair on end.

"Let's see what other moves you might be able to make." He suddenly reached a hand over my shoulder and down the front of my blouse.

I have no idea where I got the energy, but I exploded out of my chair, bouncing off his desk as I turned to face him.

"What the *hell* do you think you're doing?"

"You want a job, don't you?" He stepped around the chair.

"Singing. I want a singing job." I detoured to the far right side of the room, heading for the door.

"Keeping me happy is part of that job."

"Not in my world."

He gave me plenty of room, so I let my guard down. I thought he realized I wasn't interested, that he would let me go. I reached for the doorknob, struggling to open it. The door was locked.

"How bad do you need a job?"

"Pretty damn bad, but not that bad. Now open this door!"

"Now, see, you have to give me something I want and then I'll give you what you want." He leered at me as he eased closer.

"I'm not giving you *anything*." I abandoned the door and lunged behind the chair. "Just unlock the door and I'll leave here quietly."

"You'll leave when I'm done with you." He sneered. "Now get over here."

I moved behind the desk.

"Sweet little sugar, aren't you?" He growled as he pushed the desk against the wall, leaving me no way around it.

Struggling to pull it out, I let him corner me. He grabbed, tearing my blouse open down the front. In desperation, I launched myself against his chest, throwing him off balance and escaping past him to the other side of the room, where I faced him, panting.

"Spitfire, aren't you? This is going to be so much fun!"

Facing him, feet braced, knees slightly bent, I waited for his next attack. When he came at me again, I stepped forward, swinging with my elbows. Apparently, I connected with his nose. I heard a dull pop and felt his blood spatter on my face. He grunted, cradling his face in both hands. He reached into his pocket for his handkerchief, holding it to his bleeding nose while he fumbled for the chair and collapsed into it.

"Give me the key."

He gestured toward his jacket pocket, fat fingers embracing his injured face. I stood looking at him, but I didn't stand there for long. I wiped the blood off my face with the front of my ruined blouse, slipped into my coat, and buttoned up tight.

"Thanks for the audition," I said as I fished the key out of his pocket, trying to keep my distance as I bent near him to get it. I fit it into the lock and stepped into the club.

Conversation around the bar stopped dead, and I noticed the bartender staring at me.

"You'd better go take care of your boss," I said as I headed for the door. Gasping when the cold wind caught me, I turned up my collar, buried trembling hands in my pockets, and trudged, head down, into the wind and darkness toward the Evergreen Hotel.

Back in my room, I sat on the edge of the bed, head up, eyes blazing. Then I began trembling all over and I couldn't stop. Prying my right shoe off with my left toes, I could almost hear my mom. "Untie them, Bobbi, you'll ruin your shoes!" Somehow ruined shoes didn't seem to matter.

Sobbing, I pounded my knee with my fist—and then made a rush to the bathroom where I emptied my already-empty stomach into the toilet, gagging and retching until I was too weak to stand. I don't know how long I lay there on the cold tiles, but I finally dragged myself to my feet and stumbled to the bed. Pulling the spread around my shoulders, I collapsed, lying on my side with my knees curled up to my chest.

As I lay staring at the wall, I remembered all the times I'd been terrified out of my mind. My odds for getting socked with another disaster oughta be just about run out. Now it's a— it's a—rapist. I'd barely escaped a rapist.

I whispered the word, "Rape." What an unspeakable word. I said it again, louder. "Rape."

Maybe I should go to the police.

Hah! Those guys in that club? They all know what he does. I could see it in their eyes. But they'd never say so. Just hang me out to dry—and I'd be hung up in a police station and I wouldn't have time to look for a job.

But all that—it's just all out there in front of you and you either survive or you don't, you know? You might not see it coming, but when it comes, you can see it. That day I faced this other thing, this creeping terror that I couldn't meet head on—like a slow-motion slide over the edge of the earth. I remembered looking out at the horizon all the times I swam by myself in Lake Erie. I remembered the rushing sound in my ears when I saw the newspaper with Jack's face on it, the evening in the apartment with my friends, listening to the latest report on the Torso Murderer, thinking I could take care of myself. I remembered the uneasy feeling I'd had from time to time, a feeling of being all alone, disconnected and sliding away into silence. My mind ran on a rickety exercise wheel.

What if I don't find anything by the end of the week? Will anybody notice if I just wander around the streets until I starve?

I folded my hands between my thighs to keep them warm, and to keep them from trembling. At least I was not in Cleveland. There was no Torso Murderer in Buffalo—at least I hoped there wasn't.

I don't remember how long I lay there before I roused myself. My hands only trembled a little when I removed the blouse and slipped into a bathrobe. I took the blouse into the bathroom and rinsed it, making it at least presentable with some extra, generic buttons in my traveling kit. While it dried over the steam heater, I tried to sleep so I would be rested for more walking next day. Surely the clubs couldn't be as bad as that last one.

February 12, 1942

By 12:30 on day four, back on the street, heading for the nearest club, I repeated the drill—head high, determined to look relaxed and sure of myself. Again, I found a few pretzels and an occasional peanut to keep me from collapsing, but I felt really weak. I could no longer maintain the brisk pace, walking from club to club. I didn't even try. I needed all the energy I could command to stand upright and look interested when I entered a club.

During the afternoon and early evening, I talked to four or five managers, but again—no auditions and no jobs. By then, my stomach growled every time I thought about food, which was almost all the time. I wondered if the managers could hear it. Maybe they were afraid my stomach would make more noise than my voice. At five o'clock I thought I could push myself one more block to the next club. If I didn't get something there, I had to return to my hotel. I wouldn't be able to keep myself upright after that. I had no idea how I would get to the nightclubs the next day.

I stepped into a place that called itself simply "The Nightclub," consciously drawing myself up and forcing a smile. "Hi," I said when I got the bartender's attention. "I'm Bobbi Bowen and I'd like to speak to your manager."

"What do you need?"

"I'm a singer and I'm looking for a job."

"He might be interested, miss, but he's out of town until tomorrow afternoon. Can you come back?"

"Of course," I said, forcing another smile. "Could you give me his name?"

"Sure," he said, wiping the bar in front of me and setting down a bowl of peanuts. "It's John Carter. Can I get you something?"

"No," I said, "I think I'll just grab a handful of these peanuts and head back to my hotel. I'll be back tomorrow, though. And thanks."

When he turned his back, I dumped all those peanuts into my handbag, hoping that would give me enough energy to return the next day. I kept my head high and my shoulders back until I cleared the door of the club, but then I could feel myself shrinking, shuffling the thirty blocks back to the hotel, nibbling peanuts one at a time. Thrilled that the hotel had an elevator, I leaned against the wall as it ground and clanked its way up to my floor. I stepped out, just enduring until I could trudge to my room, head down and shoulders sagging.

One thing about hunger—it shuts your mind off. I'd barely got my clothes off and neatly folded across a chair before I flopped on the bed and fell immediately into a dreamless sleep. I opened my eyes the following morning to pain that pulled my knees to my chest. I thought those peanuts were fermenting in there. I groaned, forced myself to straighten up, and rolled up to sit on the edge of the bed, gripping the mattress with white-knuckled fingers. I drank a full glass of water, hoping it would dilute the fire. I checked the time. Ten in the morning. Dragging around the room, I pulled on my clothes, applied makeup, leaning heavily against the sink, and tried out a weak smile on the mirror.

"That'll have to do," I said to myself and turned away. I grabbed my purse and headed back to The Nightclub.

An hour later, I sat on a bar stool and asked for John Carter. As the bartender went to find him, I ate a few peanuts, hoping I wasn't making a terrible mistake.

"I'm John Carter," said an impossibly tall man with an impossibly big smile as he stepped up and enveloped my hand. "I understand you want to see me."

"Yes, sir. My name is Bobbi Bowen and I've been singing with the Jimmy Jones orchestra around the Great Lakes and the Eastern Seaboard. I came here to sing in the Firefly Club, but it's been foreclosed so I'm looking for another job." I ran out of breath.

He grinned. "Well, Bobbi, are you willing to audition?"

"Of course," I said, hoping I could actually get through an audition.

He really looked me over. "Listen," he said. "Gene Olds called me and said you might be stopping by. Said he'd hired you, but—well, things aren't going too well for him."

"No."

"It's way too early for an audition. The band won't get here for hours, so how 'bout I buy you lunch and you can tell me all about yourself. Then if you come back at about six, we can set you up with a dressing room to change and I'll buy you dinner. I have to warn you, though, you'll be a guinea pig. Our chef is trying something new tonight—he calls it steak marchand de vin with roasted asparagus and potatoes. After dinner, the band will be ready and you can strut your stuff."

I could not believe what I was hearing. Holding my emotions in tight control, I smiled graciously—at least I hoped I looked gracious, and not wolf-like.

"That would be lovely!"

"Okay, do you feel up to walking over to the little café up the block here and chatting while you eat—about what you've done and where you've performed?"

"Sure." I hoped I could handle myself like a lady.

At the café, I ordered light—a club sandwich with chips. Making myself sick wasn't on my to-do list and I knew I couldn't eat much. The peanuts were still rumbling around and I didn't need any more trouble. So I nibbled when I wanted to gobble. By the time I'd eaten about half the sandwich, I felt full. Meanwhile Carter interviewed me and told me he was really impressed with my experience.

He winked as he paid the tab. "Olds told me I'd like you and that I ought to hire you, at least for a week. I think he's probably right. Besides, I'm looking for something special for Valentine's Day."

Flashing him a genuine smile this time, I said, "Thank you," as I wrapped up the rest of my sandwich with a napkin and dropped it into my purse.

"Okay, I'll see you at about six. Bring your appetite so Louie won't be disappointed."

At the door, he turned toward the club, and I watched him walk up the block with a long, swinging stride. I went back to the hotel, feeling stronger than I had in days. Confident that I'd have a job by nightfall, I hummed all the way back. It was about all I had the energy to do.

Back at the hotel, I rested and nibbled on the rest of the sandwich, as I began to feel a little stronger. "Just don't make yourself sick, Bobbi," I whispered as I took another bite.

By five, I'd packed up a gown and all the accessories I'd need for the night, leaving the hotel with a firm step.

At The Nightclub, Carter waited for me with a table near the kitchen. I was sure I'd died and gone to heaven.

"Alright let's just take this table here, and I'll tell Louie to bring out his experiment. Do you want the six ounce or the eight?"

"Oh, just the six. If I eat too much, I won't be able to sing."

So I soon had a succulent New York strip steak in red wine sauce in front of me. Carter kept me busy with questions so I managed to eat slowly, allowing my stomach to get used to having something in it. I remember nothing about how that steak tasted, only the feel of food in my stomach. About an hour later, with a comfortable tummy, I stepped up to the mic. I'd survived another disaster, but I'd never be the same risk taker.

PART V: CLEVELAND, OHIO

February 22, 1942

Carter gave me two weeks, then I went back to Cleveland with a little money in my pocket—a very little money. I couldn't even speak to my father. I stayed with Mom while I looked for the next job, but avoided Mowrey's. Mom wanted to know why, of course, because they could use my help, but I thought my lost savings should remain between Dad and me. I'm not sure why. Maybe I didn't want to hear Mom's "I told you so." If I'd had any money at all, I'd have gotten my own apartment and never spoken to either one of them again, I was that mad.

I guess I did a lot of brooding. Mom kept asking me what was wrong. I surely spent a lot of time thinking. Everything that had happened in Buffalo had left me scared half blind. For four years, I had worked my ass off—always learning, making myself better, selling myself, getting better gigs—so I could be safe, take care of myself. But it was all gone in a moment.

Sure I could—and surely would—manage my own money. I'd have to learn how to do that too. I'd never leave home without enough money tucked away somewhere to get home. But I had no control when the whole world went crashing into chaos.

Mom had thought I should marry Tony—back in the day. I couldn't see any safety or security in marriage, though, not when I went by

Union Station and saw all the guys in uniform kissing their wives and girlfriends goodbye. Who knew how many of them would be back? Jimmy's bass player had already gotten his draft notice and Palatino's saxophonist was in boot camp. I'd have to keep singing—I didn't know what else to do, but I no longer felt secure just because I could make my own money. For how long and would it be enough?

Jimmy Jones got a few gigs as people adjusted to being at war, but my patience had taken a fast train to China. With all my savings gone, I needed to work full time, not just a gig here and there. Unfortunately, the extent of my work had involved jamming with Carlone occasionally, after hours, and singing a few weekend gigs with the Jones orchestra. I knew people had begun going out again, but work remained sporadic.

On my way to Mileti's for tomatoes and mushrooms one afternoon, I pondered a dismal future. But then I passed the Army recruiting office—a very busy place. I stopped dead, nearly tripping several people hurrying along behind me. There in the window a bunch of bright, new posters stood out because there were *women* in them. I stepped out of the stream of foot traffic to get a good look.

Well that's a first. What's the gimmick?

"This is my war too!" read the text under a woman in uniform, backed by stars and bars. Reading the rest of the text kept me riveted for a moment, then I strode into the office.

"Where do I sign up?"

I was almost as startled at my own impulsive behavior as the officer manning the desk.

"Right here, I suppose."

"Where would I have to go?"

"Well, you would start at Fort Des Moines in Iowa for four weeks' basic training. Then you'd go wherever you're needed. Probably not outside the states—unless you want to." He looked me up and down in a familiar male gesture. "You'll have to meet some qualifications—weight and height and vision—just like the men do. You look like you'll pass, but the doctor will make that decision."

"Okay. What else?"

"Fill out one of these applications. Do you want to be an officer?"

I thought about it for a moment.

"No."

"We're only taking applications right now for officer candidate school." He hesitated. "If you want to check back."

"When?"

"I really don't know."

I started to walk out, then turned back to the recruiter.

"What kinds of things do women do in the Army?"

"You could assist officers—clerical work, issuing supplies, drilling."

I cocked my head.

"Well, you . . . There's motor pool."

"What's that?"

"You drive trucks, jeeps, cars."

"Would they teach me? I don't drive."

"Yup. There's cooks and bakers."

"Hmm," I said, "my parents have a restaurant. I work there sometimes."

He smiled. "And there's administration—filling out forms, clerical stuff."

"So when should I come back?"

"How about this? I'm taking names and addresses so I can drop a card when things get rolling for enlisted women."

I left my name and address and went on about my business. Actually, I kind of forgot about it as business began to pick up. I traveled back to Buffalo with Jimmy Jones and we actually played the job we'd been hired to do. We got another job in Philly and another in Akron. Singing and getting paid fairly regularly didn't quite put my previous desperation out of my mind. Whenever I started to relax, Carl Short came roaring back into my head.

Between shows with Jones, I sang occasionally with Palatino, headlining a weekend or two at Danceland. Each new performance gave me a little more name recognition, a few more fans, and a little extra cash to put in my own savings account—with only *my* name on the signature card. Even that couldn't erase my memory of my painful, empty stomach and those endless days and nights in Buffalo.

In mid-July, at Mom's apartment, I got a card from the recruiting office. If I were still interested, the enlisted women's applications were available.

"What do I do now?" I murmured.

Mom looked up from her dusting, across the room. "What?"

"Oh. I been thinking about joining the Women's Army Auxiliary."

"The Army?"

"Yeah. I went in and asked about it last month."

"Well, you're not goin' to do it, are you? You're making pretty good money now."

"I don't know, Mom. We have soldiers goin' all over the world. If they start gettin' killed people won't want to go out . . ." I trailed off.

"Well, that's a first."

"What's that?"

"You're gloomier than I am."

"Goin' hungry does that," I remarked, still staring at the card. I frowned, flipping it back and forth across my hand. "Things *are* goin' pretty good right now. I been thinking I could get my own apartment soon, but I don't know. I'll have to think about it."

"Wait a minute." Mom dropped the dust rag on the end table and joined me on the couch. "When did you ever go hungry?"

Damn. I let the cat out of the bag. She'll never let it go. No point in trying to be coy.

"In Buffalo," I told her, "for three days in February."

"Why didn't you have your father wire you some money from that savings account you're so proud of?"

I told her about the job that hadn't come through; and trying to get a refund; and calling Dad to wire cash; and beating the streets, eating a few peanuts and a pretzel now and then—and Carl Short. Mom didn't interrupt once, even when I told her about Dad gambling away my savings.

"How much did he lose?"

Here it comes.

"About two thousand."

"You'd saved that much?"

"I was making really good money, Mom."

"So you've got nothing left?"

"Just a few bucks I brought back after The Nightclub job and the few gigs I've had here since."

"I hope you've opened an account in your name only."

"You better believe it."

"That's why you've refused to help out at Mowrey's, isn't it?"

"I don't want to be anywhere near Dad. I don't know if I'll ever forgive him."

Mom had already surprised me by not reminding me she'd told me, but she *really* surprised me when she defended him.

"Bobbie, I don't know what it is about your father. He can't seem to help himself." She paused for a while—kind of a long while. "You remember what he was like after he broke his leg?"

"Yes. I worried about him sometimes."

"It seemed like he felt better after he'd been at the track—especially if he won a few dollars. But we couldn't afford any losses. That's why I yelled at him so much every time he lost."

"He hardly ever lost. I guess that's why—I guess I got to thinking he was invincible."

"He gets to thinking that too. He's been doing so well since he got his old job back, been too busy to go to the track—I thought maybe he'd gotten over it. It's like a sickness."

"Well, if he's over it, it's been since February. I'm just so mad at him, Mom. I could have starved over there and nobody would have ever known."

"Aw Honey!"

"I was so scared." I covered my face with my hands.

Mom reached an arm around me and held me close while I cried. Her embrace had never felt so warm.

"You understand that your father loves you, don't you?"

"If he did, how could he risk my money—my life—like that?"

"He didn't see it as a risk, and I know it still eats at him, the years you supported us."

I sniffled. "He said he thought he could pay me back—but he bet *all my savings!*"

"I don't blame you for not wanting to see him right now, but I hope you can forgive him." She released me and turned to face me. "Just don't ever trust him with your money."

"Boy, you'd better believe I won't."

"So that's why you're thinking about the Army? You want to know where the next meal's coming from?"

"That's part of it. It's just temporary, but things have slowed down for the war. It would be really great to take a break from worrying about money and men and . . . I just don't know."

We kicked around the pros and cons until Mom had to go to work, then I called Mary and we met at the beach to swim and sunbathe. We talked about my future for a couple of hours. Mary had some suggestions for me—maybe I could find some local place, wherever I got stationed, and I could sing during off-duty hours, to make a few extra bucks and keep my name out there—and to keep up with the new music. Then maybe, after the war, I could pick up where I left off.

"Or you might find a good manager who can make sure you don't get stranded."

I thought of Tony. I'll bet he'd be good at that. I giggled. "Or maybe, I'll find some rich pig farmer who'll carry me away and I won't have to worry about it."

By the end of the day, I still hadn't decided. Maybe I should join the Army to help get the war over so people would want to go out and dance again. But, with jobs starting to open, I hesitated. On the other hand, the Jones orchestra could fall apart in a hurry. Most of the members—including Jimmy—were eligible for the draft. And then I had my memory of the week alone in Buffalo. I dithered for a few days, then went in on a Monday to sign up— after a weekend with no job.

My favorite recruiter handed me a pink form and I sat down with another couple of women to fill in my name, address, phone number, height, weight, color of eyes, education, date and place of birth, as well as Mom's and Dad's places of birth—and Mom's maiden name.

Uh oh, I hope they don't find grandma in the asylum. If they find out about her, I'll probably be out before I get in.

I filled in the name. I guessed, if they found her, that would make the decision for me. I noted that I hadn't had any serious diseases, had never been in prison, and, I chuckled when I got to the last question. "Have you ever attempted to overthrow the United States Government?" No, I wrote.

There, that's done. Now I wait again.

But the wait wasn't very long at all. On Wednesday, I got another card summoning me to report for the Army General Classification Test on Friday. At the recruiting office, I learned that I needed to score 110 points to be accepted, so I sat down with the test paper and a pencil, and I sweat, thinking about the four years since I'd dropped out of high school.

The following Monday, though, I found a card in the mail requesting me to report for a personal interview on Thursday. Once again, I made the trek to the recruiting office to sit across the desk from the same male lieutenant, who proceeded through his list of questions without even lifting his eyes from the page. I had no idea whether he liked my answers or not—but I was singing again, two weeks at Danceland with Jimmy Jones, so maybe it wouldn't matter if I weren't chosen.

But I got another card—by then a familiar addition to Mom's mailbox—and swung over to the recruiting office on Wednesday, singing. I could meet the weight and height requirements, and my vision was fine. I assumed I'd soon be a WAAC.

This time, my favorite recruiter directed me upstairs to a big room with benches along the four walls. Several women already waited for the attending physician. I sat down to wait with them.

Women kept coming until twenty-five women of all shapes and sizes sat on the benches. Eventually, a woman in uniform, who introduced herself as the matron, entered the room and called role.

When everyone had answered, "Present," she said, "Good. Now get undressed. Take everything off—dress, stockings underwear, everything. I mean *everything*."

Several women looked around the room and got up to leave.

"Sit down," says the matron. "We're not done yet."

The women stood staring.

"Sit."

They sat.

"Fold up your clothes so you can carry them with you. I'll be back shortly." Then she left, closing the door.

Well, that roomful of women looked frozen. For a few moments, not a hair moved. No one spoke, hardly anyone blinked. Finally, one of the women gently laid her purse on the bench beside her, took off her hat, and laid it on her purse. Apparently, that was all she could manage on such short notice. She sat motionless, hands folded in her lap, staring at the wall across from her.

Another slipped off her shoes, pulled up her skirt, unhooked her stockings and slid them off, placing them inside her shoes. Then she stood and took off her jacket.

One by one, as if we gradually thawed, we moved, like molasses down a low hill. Without really realizing it, I began humming *The Army Goes Rolling Along.*

The woman next to me glared.

"Sorry."

When we'd all finally disrobed, we sat around the room on the benches, clothes in our laps, arms across our chests, waiting for whatever would come next. The day Carl Short ripped my blouse half off me was the closest I'd ever come to being undressed in public. Even then, I wasn't much more exposed than in some of the gowns I wore at work.

 Anyway, we didn't wait long. Ordered to form a cue, we lined up and stepped into the corridor, glancing over our shoulders and hoping no one else happened to drop in right then. One by one, we dropped out, to slip into individual examining rooms where we could relax a little bit and catch our breath.

When they were done with us, we left, silently, one by one, never catching one another's eyes as we went. Two days later, I received my orders to report for swearing in.

Well, that was quick. I guess I'm in.

On Monday, August 10, 1942, I stood, side-by-side with twenty-four other women, raised my right hand, knees shaking only a little, and swore to—well, I can't really remember what I swore to do. It all passed in a blur. I left the office wondering what the hell I'd gotten myself into. Intentionally, I allowed my imagination to linger over images burned in my brain—images of myself, wandering the streets of Buffalo alone, of fighting my way out of Carl Short's office. Couldn't be any worse, I assured myself, I headed for home to get some sleep before I had to sing. We had a gig that night.

August 12, 1942

A couple of nights later, Jones wanted to know if I could sing for a party at the LakeView on Saturday. Thinking it would make a nice last gig, I agreed. I could break the news to Jones then and try to get all my friends together afterwards. Gee, it would be good to see Fred. I figured Tony would have moved on, but if not, it would be nice to see him, too—kind of like going home.

On Friday, as I crossed the empty club. I spotted Tony. I guessed he hadn't left after all. We'd barely seen each other since I went on the road, so I swung my steps in an arc that led directly to him.

"Tony! Are you still here?"

"Not for long. I got my draft notice."

As we talked, Sammy Sansone stepped off the stage where he'd been conferring with Jones.

"Hi, Bobbi."

"Oh my gosh! Sammy. So Fred's got you here too. What's up?"

"Nothing special that I know of, but I got a call from Fred and I didn't have another gig."

"Tony, this is . . ."

"We've met," Tony said. I noticed a little tension in his voice and wondered what had him so worked up. Tony wasn't a guy who got worked up.

"Tony, we need to go talk to Jimmy about how we're going to manage this. Then I'm coming back to catch up with you."

I found Fred talking with Jones' bass player.

Fred, this is like old home night." I bussed his cheek. "How are you doing?"

"I'm doing A-OK. We had a big dip in December after Pearl, but we're doing fine now. How about you?"

"Aside from nearly starving to death in Buffalo last February, I've been doing fine."

"You're too good to starve." Fred dismissed the thought.

"Maybe." I excused myself to talk with Jones and Sansone, then I returned to Tony.

"Let's go find a table where we can talk."

We sat, head-to-head for a while, reminiscing about my run-in with that first customer way back when, and Tony's escort service.

"I really liked being your boyfriend—even if it was a game."

"For me, it wasn't a game. You were a wonderful protector, Tony— remember that night when the guy tried to grab me off the street?"

Tony nodded.

"I was so scared! You were so great to me that night!"

"You've been out of town a lot, but did you notice we haven't heard anything about the Torso Murder for a while?"

"Yeah, that's right. It was really hot and heavy for a while—every couple of months."

"I heard a rumor. Apparently the cops were questioning this guy named Sweeney. That was—must have been spring—'39, I think." He thought for a minute. "Anyway, then I heard he—Sweeney— was in an asylum somewhere."

I looked down at my finger, tracing a pattern on the table, thinking about my last night with Jack.

"Then nothing," he says.

Last one I remember, Jack was alive and we were sitting in his car, along the beach.

Gritting my teeth, I looked back at Tony.

Speaking slowly, as though he were doing some heavy-duty thinking, he looked into my eyes.

"You don't notice somethin' like that when it goes away." He hesitated. "You okay?"

"Yeah. It must have been a couple of years ago. They found those two in one night."

"Yeah. I remember that. You were still working here." Tony got a high sign from Fred. "I think Fred wants you at this big table up front here." He stood and took my arm. "He apparently has the rest of the seats saved for someone special."

"What's he got going on here?"

"Darned if I know, Bobbi. He's being real mysterious about this. He just got a call from somebody a couple of weeks ago and immediately closed the club for a special party tonight."

"I wonder what he's got up his sleeve. He's not much of a special party kind of guy."

"Don't I know it! He hired a bunch of hostesses to escort people to their tables."

"He what?" I took a closer look around. "Well, will you look at that? You'd think the Shah of Arabia was coming."

Once Fred's guests were seated, I sat all by myself looking around for the rest of the party for my table. Then I saw my mom, hauling an armload of dishes.

"Mom, what the heck are *you* doing here?"

"Hold on, Bobbi, I'll get to you."

So there I was, alone at a big table, watching my mother deliver fennel salads to guests at nearby tables, while the remainder of Fred's waiters served the others. When she was done, though, Mom sat next to me.

"I don't know what I'm doing here," she whispered. "Fred just called us and asked us to come—and cater a dinner."

"Us. Dad's here?"

"Yeah. He's in the kitchen supervising. We had orders to make sure the chef made your favorite meal just the way you like it."

"What?" My hands trembled. "I don't want to see Dad."

"I know, Honey, but I couldn't think of any way to avoid it. Apparently this is some kind of party for you. I *told* Fred it's not your birthday."

I looked around and realized Tony had slipped out while I was talking to Mom.

"Where's Tony?"

Mom glanced over her shoulder. "He's bringing in some other guests."

"But what *is* this?"

"I don't know." Mom grinned to see me caught off guard. She didn't seem to realize how explosive my meeting with Dad was likely to be.

Before the guests could start their salads, Tony came back with the missing guests, all grinning at me like a bunch of Cheshire cats. Mary Teresa, looking very pregnant, came in on Ralph's arm, giving me a big wave as soon as she spotted me, and ducking her head. Ed followed with Kate and Helen walked in on Tony's arm. Once she was seated, Tony pushed in her chair and took a seat next to me. At least I wouldn't have to sit next to Dad. Maybe I could ignore him.

"You know about this," I whispered in Mom's ear. "This is too big for you not to know."

Mom shrugged. "Eat your salad. The fennel's fresh."

As we ate the crisp, cold lettuce salad, savoring a hint of licorice from the fennel, my father came out and sat to Mom's right, spreading his napkin in his lap.

"Good evening, Bobbi," he said with a twinkle.

I glared at him. It was all I could do not to read him the riot act.

"Aw, Sweetie, I'm sorry. Your mother told me about what happened in Buffalo and I know it was my fault," he murmured. "Please forgive me."

"I don't know if I can."

"Let me make it up to you."

"How? How can you make it up? I trusted you."

"I don't know. Just give me a chance."

Everyone at the table was staring at us.

"Later. We'll talk about it later. I need to figure out what's going on."

"I don't know, Bobbie. Fred's been just like a little kid, organizing this—whatever it is."

"Eat your salad." Mom tried to divert my attention.

I didn't really want a scene, so I played along.

"Mmmmm. This *is* good. What kind of dressing did you put on this?"

"Just olive oil and lemon juice, whisked up good with a little salt and pepper."

As waiters picked up salad bowls, others brought out the entre, beef slices with rosemary, risotto with mushrooms and broiled eggplant.

"I know this meal. It's what we made for Dad's birthday the day he broke his leg," I whispered to Mom.

"Well, it's a little too early for the artichokes." Mom paused. "Bobbi. Your dad and I talked about it and we realized, what with all the pasta and potatoes all those years, we don't even know what you like."

"It's okay, Mom. I love this, but I still don't know what it's about."

"I guess we'll all find out when Fred's good and ready."

Taking a bite of my fork-tender beef, I smiled and groaned with pleasure.

"Mom, this is wonderful. What kind of wine did you use? This is not just a cooking wine."

I knew Dad would have chosen the wine and supervised all the cooking, but I wouldn't acknowledge him. It almost hurt to praise anything he'd had a hand in, but I wanted to show I was a better person then he was—so I played it up to the hilt. I glanced at my friends who looked at me, completely puzzled.

"It's a Mount Eden Cabernet Sauvignon Fred had in his cellar from before the war," Mom said, glancing at Dad. "Your father taught the chef how to deglaze the griddle. It's harder to do than deglazing a pan because your wine wants to run away."

"Tastes great! The risotto is superb as well. Dried mushrooms are a whole different animal than fresh ones," I said over the rim of my wine glass. "Who selected the wines?"

"Fred did. It's a Pomerol Merlot from the Lafleur vineyards. Good, isn't it?"

"Mmmmhmmm. Also from Fred's wine cellar? I didn't know he was such a gourmet."

"Apparently, during Prohibition and before the Germans overran France, he imported all these expensive wines. Your father bought wines from him for Mowrey's."

As his guests finished their meals, Fred called for attention.

"I have a special guest here tonight," he announced. "Mr. Ed O'Brien, owner and program director of WNAX radio wants to announce something about his new fall program. He'll be using local talent." He paused. "Well, I'll let him explain."

I shifted in my seat, glancing over at my smiling friends across the table. I looked for Tony and Fred, all smiling and looking at me. So were Jones and Sansone.

Oh my God. Is this what I think it is?

I could barely sit still.

O'Brien stood and said, "Let me make this short and sweet. I'm planning an evening show—at seven o'clock Saturday evenings so just about everybody can hear it—of big band music. I've asked Jimmy Jones and his orchestra to fill that spot." Applause interrupted. When it tapered off, he continued. "I'd like to ask Bobbi Bowen to take our radio stage as female vocalist." Again Fred's guests interrupted to show their enthusiasm. As soon as they quieted down, he said simply, "Thank you," and sat.

My excitement lasted only a moment. I'd have died for this chance two months before, but I'd already signed a contract I couldn't get out of.

"I'd like to toast Bobbi and Jimmy," Fred said raising his glass. "Jimmy, you and your orchestra have been playing together and pleasing crowds for a long time. Congratulations," he said reaching out and clinking glasses with his neighbors. Then he went on. "But Bobbi, I kind of feel you got your start performing right here." He raised his glass. "To Bobbi."

Crystal light glinted clear red through the glass he raised. I looked around the room.

Gee, even my parents were holding hands and smiling.

Helen reached across the table to get my attention.

"Now Bobbi," she said, "I can dance to your music while I'm ironing the shirts."

"Bobbi, would you come here please," Fred asked.

I pushed my chair back, holding eye contact with Helen. Then I stepped free, moving swiftly to the head table. I smiled with tears in my eyes.

"Would you say something to all your friends here," Fred asked.

"Sure." I raised my glass and looked around at the crowd.

"I'm so happy to be here and I'm really excited about this program. I hope everybody will listen to it," I paused, "but, I can't be part of it." I glanced around the room, making eye contact here and there, like I always did on stage. "I have my own announcement to make tonight. This isn't quite how I'd planned it, but here goes."

I took one of those deep breaths Greta had taught me.

"Last week, I signed up with the Women's Auxiliary Army Corps. I'm gonna be a WAAC. I leave for basic training as soon as I get my orders. I wish I'd waited a little longer, but I didn't and I can't change my mind now. I'm in for two years—or until the end of the war."

I shifted my weight and stood silently.

"A toast to your Uncle Sam," I said at last. I heard glasses tinkling as they touched. I glanced at Mom. I hadn't told her yet and she sat with both hands over her mouth. She knew how much this contract would have meant to me.

The room remained silent for a while and I felt really alone, looking out at all my friends who just sat in stunned silence. Finally, O'Brien rose.

"Come on everybody. Two years isn't long. She'll be back. Bobbi, here's what I propose. You can come on the show as a guest star any time you get home on furlough. Then when you're back for good, we'll probably be ready for a change of format, so you can step right in to give the show a new face. Sound good to you?"

"Sure, Mr. O'Brien and thanks." I turned and walked back to my seat.

"Wow," said Mom. "You really did it."

"Yes, I did."

"It'll be okay, Bobbi. You won't have to worry about making a living during the war. You heard O'Brien you'll have a job when you get back."

I couldn't believe Mom was being so, I searched for a word, kind. I couldn't remember when she'd supported my decisions like that. I stared at her for a moment, then smiled.

"Thank you."

That's when Dad decided to put his two cents in.

"See, Bobbi, you'll be alright."

I glared at him and turned to Mary. "Guess I made the wrong choice."

"Maybe not. Like your mom says, you'll have a job when you get back."

"First the Depression and now the War," Dad said to no one in particular.

I continued to ignore him.

"Well, that was a surprise," said Fred at last, standing again, "but let's get on to the dessert so we can dance to these fine musicians."

I sat smiling as the others finished their dessert. I didn't have the heart to eat mine, even though I've never met a cheesecake I didn't like. My mind just ran over with regrets.

God did I miss an opportunity. Two years is a long time in the music business. O'Brien promised, but I wonder.

Mary reached across the table. "You okay?"

"Huh? Oh sure. I was just thinking."

"What?"

"I dunno. I guess we'll see what happens when the war's over."

I didn't hear from my father for a couple of weeks and I figured he'd just decided I'd get over it on my own. He'd be wrong. It would be a long time before I forgave him, if ever. The hell I'd gone through because of him remained very clear in my mind.

Then one Monday morning, I answered the door and found him standing there.

"What do you want?"

"I know what I did is unforgivable and I want to make it up to you." He cleared his throat.

"You can't." I started to shut the door in his face.

"Wait a minute, Bobbi, please. Hear me out."

I stood considering him. "Have you ever been so hungry you were afraid you'd die?"

"No, not quite," he admitted.

"Have you ever had somebody lock you in a room and try to . . . try to . . ."

He hung his head, reaching a hand to me and letting it drop when I refused to respond. I could hear the tightness in his throat—like mine when I had to sing after I lost Jack.

"Rape you. Your mother told me—No, I haven't."

"Then you can't make it up to me."

His shoulders slumped and he seemed to shrink right before my eyes.

Good. He should have to suffer for what he did.

"The very thing I was afraid would happen to you singing in the nightclubs—I made it happen to you," he said, clearing his throat. "I'm so ashamed of what I've done and I know I can't make it so none of that happened to you."

"No. You can't."

"But would it help if I paid all your money back?"

I stood staring at him. *Another hundred-to-one bet?*

"It might," I said at last. I backed up and let him in. "How're you ever gonna do that?"

"I'm making decent money now and I'll deposit $50 in a savings account every payday."

"That'll take a while."

"I know, but I want to start today with $200."

He reached into his pocket for his wallet and brought out two crisp hundred dollar bills.

"Where'd you get this? You didn't win it at the track, did you?"

"No, Bobbi, I didn't." He hesitated a moment and I could see the muscles in his jaw clenching.

"Then where?"

He looked into my eyes.

"I sold the watch, Bobbi."

"Dad! You couldn't. That watch means so much to you. Get it back."

"I can't, Baby, it's gone. I didn't pawn it. I sold it to a jeweler." He cleared his throat. "You mean more to me than that damned watch, anyway."

I stared at him for a long moment.

"Would you consider giving me a chance to be your dad again?" he asked, holding out his arms for me.

I moved into them, laying my head on his shoulder.

"I guess," I said. I looked up into his eyes, "as long as I take care of my own money."

"Deal," he said with an explosive sigh. "It's a deal."

August 24, 1942

Shortly after the party, the Jones band went on a final tour before they started the radio show. I hung around Cleveland, singing wherever somebody could use me. At my next gig with Palatino at Danceland, Tony showed up between my second and third sets, escorting me around the club like he used to at LakeView, and hanging around until the club closed. When I was ready to leave, he followed me, touching my arm as we stepped outside.

"What'll you be doin' from now until you get orders?"

"Mostly just hangin' around. I'll sing whenever I can. Help Mom and Dad in the restaurant."

"How about dinner and dancing with me some night?"

"That sounds like fun, Tony. We didn't have much time to catch up the other night."

"How about Saturday? I got my notice, but I haven't been called up yet, so I don't know how long I'll be around either."

We made a date for Saturday and Tony picked me up right on time at Mom's apartment. He drove downtown to the Winton Hotel where we ordered dinner in the Rainbow Room. Before we finished eating, someone in the orchestra recognized me and came down during a break to ask me to sing a few numbers.

"I'm taking a night off," I said, but the people at the neighboring tables begin applauding and encouraging me to sing.

"Look, I'll be gone soon and I'd like to dance, to just enjoy *not* working."

"We heard. All the more reason to sing one last time."

"Come on, Bobbi," said a diner at the next table.

"Yeah," said his date, grinning.

I looked at Tony. He shrugged. "Maybe a couple of songs. But I want to dance—with you," he said, leaning back with a smile and folding his arms over his chest.

"Alright, but only a couple of numbers. I want to dance, too."

I sang two songs, *Blue Moon* and *Don't Sit Under the Apple Tree*, and stepped off the stage to rejoin Tony.

"I'm sorry."

"That's fine, Bobbi. I'm just happy to be with you, but let's dance before they come back."

I jumped up. "Let's," I said, catching the hand he offered.

I was panting, when we got back to our table several numbers later.

"You're even better than when we met in the neighborhood. Where'd you learn to dance like that?"

Tony grinned. "My sister and I used to go to dances together and I *did* go out with women sometimes on my days off."

"I'm sorry, Tony, I didn't mean . . ."

"It's okay, Bobbi. I didn't think of you dating outside of the club until that night at the police station."

I reached across and traced his cheek with my finger. He really was a sweet guy. "You've always been good to me, Tony. I can't thank you enough for all the babysitting."

He leaned across and kissed me. "It was my pleasure."

He seemed to be holding his breath as I gazed into his eyes. I wondered what he was thinking.

"You're . . ." I began.

Tony let the air out in a huff. "In love with you—ever since I meet you on the street that day," he blurted.

I stared in silence for a long moment. "That's not what I was going to say."

"What did you think?"

"You're a wonderful friend. That's what I was gonna say."

He took my hand. "I want to be more than that, Bobbi."

I looked down at my hand, engulfed in his.

"I hadn't thought of you that way."

Although I've sure had enough people pushing me in that direction.

"Is there someone else?"

"Nobody since Jack. At first, I couldn't think about it. He was there and then, in an instant, he was gone. It was awful, Tony. He was in college and then he was—dead."

"God, Bobbi, I never asked you how you found out."

"It was in the *Plain Dealer*—front page. I was just walkin' by the newsstand and there it was."

"Aw Bobbi, I'm sorry. Let's get out of here."

I nodded and soon we were back out in Tony's new, used Chrysler DeSoto—another dark blue one.

"Where do you want to go? It's early. Do you want to go to Danceland for a while?"

"No. Let's just drive around and listen to the radio. Is that alright?"

Tony agreed and after cruising downtown Cleveland for a while, he turned onto Lake Shore Drive. He drove out of town, turned south and ended up on a ridge of hills that overlooked the lake and the city.

"How's that for a view?"

I took a deep breath. "It's beautiful, Tony. How'd you happen to find it?"

"Just drivin' around at night."

"But you worked all night—like me."

"It's still dark at four a.m., Bobbi. By the time I got out of the club, I was usually too wound up to sleep."

"So you just drove around?"

"When I found this place, I usually came right up here. I thought maybe you could see it with me sometime."

"Aw, I'm sorry, Tony."

"I know. You don't feel the same way."

"I don't know how I feel. This is kinda new for me." I turned from the city to look at Tony. I laid a hand on his forearm. "I've spent the past four years trying to keep away from men."

"They don't make it easy, do they?"

Tony stretched his arm across the back of the seat, pulling me close. I noticed that, not only didn't I mind, but that it felt kind of good. I leaned into his embrace. He turned and kissed the top of my head. "Do you think you could ever . . ."

"I don't know, maybe, I guess it doesn't matter anyway. We're both gonna be in the Army."

He groaned. "I wish we had a little time."

"I know, Tony. But we don't."

He's never going to be rich. I could count on him, but I don't know if that's enough. I don't ever want to be hungry again.

"How about," Tony stopped to think, "how about when this damned war's over," he twirled a lock of my hair around his finger, "and we both get back home," he tipped my head up and kissed my mouth, "how about we look each other up and," he leaned in for another kiss, "how 'bout, if we're both still alive and we haven't found anybody else," he cradled the back of my head in his hand and kissed me once more, tracing my lips with his tongue, "we look each other up and just see if we could be happy together."

I pulled him down for a deep kiss, my tongue teasing.

"That's a lot of ifs," I said, finally. "I'm in for the duration. How about you?"

"I suspect it's the same for me, Bobbi. I wouldn't ask you to wait, but if we both make it."

I kissed him again. "If we both make it," I said. "Maybe . . ." I let my thought trail off, because I couldn't even imagine what could happen. I still felt too beat up to get close.

We spent as much time together as we could fit in for the next two weeks. Then Tony had to leave and I stood on the platform with my arms around his waist and his bag beside us.

"Where'd you say they're sending you?"

A train chugging into the station whistled, cars pounding together against couplers, drowning out Tony's reply.

"Washington," he shouted.

The heavy, acid smell of burning coal followed the engine as it roared past the platform along with clouds of steam.

"D.C.?"

"No Washington State, some fort out there."

More people crowded onto the platform, talking and crying, laughing and shouting, so that I had to yell. "Maybe I'll see ya when you get back."

As his train started to move, he reached down to kiss me, grabbed his bag, ran and jumped into a car.

"See ya when it's over," he yelled.

"See you," I called back, standing on my tiptoes and waving. Then he was gone, and I couldn't decide how I felt about that.

READER'S GUIDE

The Reluctant Canary Sings is a hybrid—part novel, part memoir. Ms. Colburn started with only a few facts about her mother's early life, particularly her career as a big band canary. So she took those few facts, did a lot of research and wove all of it into a work of fiction.

What do you think motivated the author to write this strange book? What are the central themes of this novel? What issues or ideas does it explore? Do Bobbi's struggles have any relevance in today's world?

Does the author succeed in revealing something about the swing era and a young woman forced by circumstance to support her family? Though minor, Bobbi's stardom allows her to make a better-than-average living for her family. Why doesn't she seem to thrive?

Aside from a broken economy, what struggles do Bobbi's parents face? What do you think about Jack—hero or villain, or just a guy trying to get along? How about Tony? What is his role in this novel?

What do you find most surprising, intriguing, or difficult to understand? Why? What specific scenes or passages captured your attention? Were they interesting, profound, amusing, disturbing, sad? What made them memorable? What did they reveal about the characters?

What have you learned from reading this book? Did you gain any new perspectives?

If you would like to have the author participate in a club meeting either in person or by phone link or Skype, you can contact Ms. Colburn at faithanncolburn@gmail.com.

AUTHOR BIO

As the first-born daughter of a big band canary, Faith A. Colburn grew up with music. Never a moment goes by when some melody doesn't pour through her head—just like it did for her mother. Often that music is those swing tunes she heard as a kid.

Award-winning journalist and author, Colburn has worked most of her adult life as a writer. With decades of living on the Great Plains, she's intimately familiar with the land and its people. Her work has appeared in numerous newspapers and magazines. She has published two memoirs and a collection of essays describing her home on the prairie. This novel is a bit of a departure, set as it is in Cleveland during the Great Depression, but a great many of the people she's met in the center of the nation come from somewhere else.

She earned Master of Arts degrees in creative writing and journalism from the University of Nebraska.

OTHER WORKS BY THIS AUTHOR

Threshold: A little boy stolen, a plainswoman married to the homliest man she ever saw, a Canadian homesteader who takes in his hired man and the whole, growing family, a husband in a hotel with a turtle in the bathtub, desperate to save a marriage—either one of them. This is a family like a prairie, woven of many strands.

From Picas to Bytes: When Joseph Claggett Seacrest arrived in Lincoln, Nebraska, on April 1, 1887, the April Fool joke was on him—the newspaper job he'd come to take did not exist. This book chronicles 100 years and four generations of Seacrest journalism—from fights to establish and defend first amendment rights, to support their communities through donating money committees, to adoption of new technologies that kept the newspaper's doors open when most mid-sized dailies had died.

Prairie Landscapes: The ramblings of one mind prowling the Great Plains, this book brings you face to face with the prairie and its creatures—a black cocker spaniel with a white necktie who befriended a runt pig—and an almost-immortal banty rooster. The landscapes stretch from the tall-grass prairies of eastern Nebraska to the grass-frozen sand sea called the Sandhills, to the Pine Ridge in the northwest corner.

See Willy See: Caught in the run up to World War II, Connor considers enlisting, expecting he will go to Europe. Maybe he can protect his sister who's in Paris with the Foreign Service. It's hard to think about leaving home and family, for another years-long exile, though. Filled with flashbacks of his travels living off the land and letters to keep him tethered to his family, Connor's story

FAITH A. COLBURN

spans two of America's most disruptive decades (The economic
Depression of the 1930s and World War II of the 1940s) in which
Connor finds his most closely held expectations thwarted.

312

SAMPLE CHAPTER: SEE WILLY SEE

June 15, 1940 – Willow Grove, Nebraska

Connor couldn't stop worrying about Nora. If someone needed help, his sister would help. That could cost her life and it would be his fault. As he worked in hard sun chopping weeds from ditches and fencerows, machete flashing, shirt soaked with sweat, he thought about his sister over there in Paris with the Nazis poised on the French border. Wheat next to the tangled fence row where he worked made a dry, rustling noise in a breeze that barely stirred its stiff beards. A lone mosquito whined around his head. He looked down the hill toward the pond, dark and muddy with not a ripple on its surface. He'd give anything to get his sister into the silly little rowboat their dad had made for them when they were kids.

Only eighteen months apart and just the two of them, Connor and Nora had spent their childhood exploring the farm together. Their dad farmed a half-section, 320 acres. They had sun-scalded short-grass pastures to roam, picking yellow coneflowers, daisy fleabane, and round, pink balls of common milkweed. They'd chased butterflies, admirals, monarchs, black velvet tiger swallowtails. They'd climbed trees and looked into birds' nests, turned over clods and watched ants fleeing in all directions. That had changed with the dust storms and Connor's high school graduation, when he headed for California seeking a job. With over twelve million people in the United States unemployed, he'd managed to get a few jobs picking fruit. But when the crop harvest had run out, he'd managed to get on with the Civilian Conservation Corps. After his two years in the Corps, he'd become a hobo, riding the rails and living on the bounty of the national park system.

While he knocked around the country from park to park, living on what he could catch, trap, or pick, the Nazis had taken over Germany and moved to take the rest of Europe. Rumors of Nazi death camps had spread throughout the country and his sister had decided to work right in the middle of it. Worse yet, Connor had goaded her into it. It drove him crazy that he remained safe at home while she worked at the edge of war. He whacked at a tough musk thistle releasing a sharp, acid odor from the severed stalk.

Still, he'd already lost his chance to go to college. He'd given up five years hopping trains, taking handouts, working the occasional odd job, and living on the land. Didn't he deserve a chance to build his future? Nora was doing what she wanted to do, anyway.

He took a savage swipe at a cocklebur. Whacking and slashing at firebush, sunflowers, burs, and hemp, he worked his way across the ridge of the hill, ignoring the dust he raised, inhaling its dry earth smell. The country still had to recover from the drought.

He could enlist, but there wasn't any point. America hadn't entered the war. No U.S. troops were headed for Europe. Maybe he could join the Canadian Army. That might get him close enough to save his sister—but he knew darned well she wouldn't leave until they closed the consulate.

I want her safe, but don't I deserve to have a life, a home?

Connor's parents, Claire and Henry, knew only what they heard on the wireless and what Nora wrote in her letters. But Connor had read the ones she wrote to their former neighbor Pauline—Nora's best friend and Connor's sweetheart. Her latest had him on the edge of panic.

> Dear Pauline (and Connor),
> Bright, clear skies and gorgeous spring in
> Paris—but the trickle of refugees I told you about

has become a torrent. Every day, we see Belgians and Dutch and people from Luxemburg. Thousands of them come into the city and fill every train car available, happy to stand if they can escape. Cars jam the streets, slowed by farm families with wagons, maybe a cow tied on behind, and some chickens in crates on top.

Remember the Mormons we read about in history? I think I know what that looked like. I see carts piled with mattresses and furniture, maybe a couple of buckets tied on the sides, a man between the shafts, and the whole family pushing.

Parisians show enormous sympathy for the poor souls, helping any way they can—a little money, some provisions, water, or advice on routes. Then they go back to their day-to-day routines and talk about how glad they are that they're safe. They're still sitting in the cafés, sipping espresso and watching the human flood. When they talk about the war at all, they say the French Army will hold the Germans at the Maginot Line just like they did during the First World War. But I look at the map. The Germans are in Belgium. Why wouldn't they go around the Maginot Line and come in from the north? I have to wonder, too, if these people have ever heard of the Luftwaffe.

Meanwhile, just to make this even more surreal, while the people enjoy their "safe" city, the newspapers go on and on about rapes and atrocities committed by the Germans during World War I. The contradictions take my breath away.

Well, I've got to get some sleep. We're overwhelmed, preparing exit visas and letters of transit, not to mention all the dispatches and the actual negotiations with French authorities who seem to be absent without leave.

Nora

Connor William Conroy agreed with his sister. The Germans would definitely go around the Maginot Line and sweep in behind.

He had worried his way through Nora's excited dispatches about seeing the Eiffel Tower, walking the Champs Elysée, and learning to read the newspapers as she improved her high school French. He couldn't share her enthusiasm when she received a promotion. He wanted her somewhere else—somewhere safe. He'd only mentioned the Foreign Service because it was the first thing off the tip of his tongue. He hadn't meant it as a suggestion—but his sister had picked it up and run with it. How could he have known when he'd goaded her into going to school that she'd end up in a war zone?

He knew the U.S. would get in it before long. He'd said so the night before at dinner. His mom had done that pushing thing with her hands that she did when she didn't want to talk about something. He'd turned to his dad.

"Look Pop, Roosevelt's declared a national emergency. The car companies are making tanks; Congress approved munitions sales to the Allies and we're shipping tons of stuff to England."

Henry took a scoop of mashed potatoes and ladled gravy onto them. "I know son, but I hope we can send enough support to the British and French so they can stop it there."

"I doubt it."

"Well, there's no draft yet, so I think Roosevelt's hopeful."

"It's just a matter of time, Pop. I know I'll get dragged into it eventually. Maybe if I take the initiative now, I can be out before it all goes to hell. Maybe if I get over there, I can talk some sense into Nora."

His mother gave him a sharp look. "Isn't it bad enough Nora's over there getting bombed? You want to get into it too?"

"I don't necessarily want to, but maybe I can get in and get out."

His mother's hands pushed.

Nora had written reassuring letters to the family about the safe bomb shelters under the consulate. They'd received one that

morning, full of Nora's busyness and all the papers she had to type
and how they had to go to the shelters sometimes at night for an
hour or two—a minor annoyance, she'd written. Good thing, too,
because they'd begun hearing on the radio that the Germans were
bombing Paris, but Connor wondered how reassured his parents
were. Now he knew. He hoped Pauline would have another letter
when he picked her up for their date that night. But first he had a
fencerow to clear.

In the drainage ditch still worrying about Nora, he swiped at a
clump of blooming hemlock, releasing a cloud of pollen that made
him sneeze.

"Aw Hell," he said.

He finished circumventing the wheat and returned to the farmyard
where he helped his father with chores, pumped a kettle of water
at the pitcher pump, set it on the stove to heat, and ate supper
with his parents. By the time the dishes were done, Connor's water
had boiled, so he dragged in the copper washtub and bathed.
Cleaned up and dressed, he headed for Hastings and a Saturday
evening with Pauline. When he knocked, she waited for him with a
letter in her hand.

"Come in and sit. I'll get us some lemonade."

He took the letter and did as she told him, beginning to read and
feeling his way back into an overstuffed chair.

> Dear Pauline,
> The Germans are coming, and the Parisians
> seem utterly shocked! The authorities have
> burned petroleum reserves outside the city, so
> the air is full of soot. It stinks! You know how
> you spilled oil on the car engine that time? Ten
> times worse. My eyes water all the time. It gets
> on everything. I have to wash my hair every
> night and it's greasy by noon. It settles on every
> document I type so there are fingerprints and
> smudges on them. There's just nothing I can do
> about it.

We have a good bunker under the consulate, but those huge blasts roar and thump overhead, shaking dirt and bits of concrete from the ceiling. The car factory took the first hit. Almost 300 people died that first night, most of them civilians. I'm sure Mom and Pop have heard about the bombing, so I'll try to call them and tell them I'm okay. Mom will worry anyway but it's the best I can do. The authorities have restricted phone service, so I hope I can get through. (She hadn't yet.)

I'm simply amazed at how Paris has turned on the refugees in only a few days. Rumors fly now that they're some kind of German Fifth Column—a spy network. So, the Parisians shut them out, refusing them any help at all.

It's the kids, Pauline. In that stream of refugees, I see little children who have gotten separated from their parents. In Paris, even though the bombing has gone on for only three days, we already have orphans—kids whose parents died in collapsed houses or in the streets—wandering around, bloody and confused. I wasn't supposed to, but one morning before dawn, I went into one of the bombed-out areas. I saw a little guy, he couldn't have been more than two or three, tearing along the side of the street, through the rubble. You know how babies like that run, all stiff-legged? I started to grab him, but one of the gendarmes managed to catch him first and take him somewhere. I don't know where. Nothing I could have done for him, I guess.

Now, in addition to Belgians and Dutch, we have people coming from northern France. Parisians too, are starting to leave—the ones who have money. The poor sots who have to work for a living continue to go to the factories every day because they're dependent on their paychecks. The French authorities can't seem to figure out what to do or how to defend the city.

It's chaos here and nobody seems to know what
to do about it.

Nora

Connor looked up, the letter trembling in his hand.

"I got her into this, you know."

Pauline took the paper and laid it on an end table, sat across from him, and took his hands.

"How do you figure? To me, she looked pretty excited to go."

"One night, we were sittin' around the house and Nora fussed about how she wanted to see some of the world like I had."

"That sounds like Nora. So how are *you* responsible?"

Head in his hands, he started talking, remembering the evening and filling in the details for Pauline.

I'd just retired from being a hobo and come back to the farm, you know, settled into the routine. I helped Pop prepare for winter, making repairs on sheds and equipment. During lengthening nights, we all talked about where I'd been and about riding the rails and people I'd met.

"You know, Connor, I really envy you," Nora said one night when we sat alone by the heater stove, looking again at pictures.

"Why's that, sis?" I asked.

Nora reminded him of all the places he'd been and the people he'd met. He could almost see her lower lip coming out in a pout when she'd reminded him she'd barely left the farm in all that time.

"What're you gonna do about it, Nora?"

"I don't know. What *can* a woman do with just a high school diploma?"

"What do you want to do?"

"I want to go places—cities like Chicago, New York, and Paris."

"Okay, then think about how you could do that."

"I don't *know* Connor!"

He'd kept on pushing her. He couldn't be sure any more how he felt about the results—glad that she got to do something she really wanted, but scared for her safety, maybe a little responsible for getting her into danger.

"What do women do in those places? What kind of jobs do they have?"

"Just secretaries, Connor, and store clerks, and nurses—but I don't want to be a nurse. Anyway, all those things are *boring*."

"What could make it less boring?"

"I DON'T KNOW!" Nora glared at him.

"WELL THINK!"

"What are you two hollering about?" Claire asked, bustling into the front room.

"Oh nothing." He gave her one of his broad, toothy grins. "I'm just trying to get Nora to solve a puzzle."

"Connor, you and your puzzles." She sat down and picked up her book. "Where's your dad?"

"I think he's out checkin' things, makin' sure the doors are all latched. We're s'posed to get a blow tonight."

 When Henry came back to the house, the family set a couple of kerosene lanterns on the table and settled down with their books, occasionally reading a particularly interesting passage aloud. After an hour or so, Claire went to the kitchen to make popcorn, stoking up the cook stove with just the right number of cobs. Henry headed for the cellar with a lantern to retrieve some apples. Nora looked up from her novel.

"If I could do it in Istanbul."

"What?"

"You asked me what could make secretarial work less boring."

"Oh. Istanbul?"

"Or Paris, or New York City, or Hong Kong."

"Okay. That's good. So how do you get a job being a secretary in those places?"

"I don't know."

"That again. Are you willing to flounder in ignorance all your life?"

"Damn it, Connor."

"What're you gonna do? Stumble around and be miserable?"

"What *can* I do?" she demanded, blue eyes flashing.

"You just told me you could be a secretary in any city in the world. So where are you gonna start?"

"Not Willow Grove, Nebraska."

"What's not in Willow Grove?" Henry asked, setting a bowl of apples on the table.

"Jobs. For me."

Claire set the popcorn on the table as Nora grabbed an apple. She crunched off a big bite, glared at Connor, then looked back at her book. Connor sat staring at her, munching a handful of popcorn as she tried to chew. When she peeked up at him, he grinned.

"Nora wants to go to secretarial school."

That remark started everything.

Connor looked up at Pauline. "See? I *am* responsible."

"I don't see that at all. Anyway, how did she go from being bored to Paris?"

"Well, I'd brought up secretarial school. Pop looked from one of us to the other, just chewing a handful of popcorn with that thoughtful look he gets. He glanced at Mom. She widened her eyes and shrugged. You know how she does. Pop swallowed. 'I wonder how we'll manage that.'"

"You know Nora. 'Well, we don't,' she mumbled, and I grinned at her. She'd taken a really big bite of that apple and could barely chew. She kept glaring at me, trying to keep from drooling."

"She kept arguing, like she does even when she's getting what she wants. She said she didn't have any money for school. If I couldn't go, then she couldn't. That's when I put my big foot in it.

"CCC sent most of my money home. I had no expenses when I worked in the Grand Canyon. I'd sent most of that money home, too. I told her I had a grub stake. I'd help her out.

"She argued some more, so I said she'd have to pay me back with interest, when she got a fancy job with the Foreign Service."

"See, Pauline, not only did I goad her into going back to school and provide a way for her to do it, I'm the one who suggested the Foreign Service. I said the first thing that came into my mind."

"So what, Connor? She could have got a regular job. I offered to get her on here at Dutton Lainson."

"You did? Really?"

"Yes, I did. But she had bigger fish to fry."

"Boy, that's the truth! When I said Foreign Service, she got that dreamy look she gets sometimes. You've seen it."

"Yeah, I've seen it and once she gets it there's no point in discussing reality."

"She does get focused. Anyway, Pop wanted to know what the heck we were talking about, especially what the Foreign Service had to do with anything.

"Nora wants to see the world," I said.

"Mom stared at her, 'Nora?' "

"'Well yes,' said Nora, 'I do. I love you and I love this place, but I want to know what's going on in the world. I'm sorry Mom, Pop, but I don't want to be a farmer's wife.'"

Connor looked up at Pauline. "We all crunched and munched for a while. You know Pop usually takes a while before he speaks. Finally, He asked why Nora hadn't said what she wanted, and Nora said she didn't want to hurt anybody's feelings."

"That sounds like Nora."

"Mom wanted to know why Nora thought she'd be hurt and that's when Nora finally admitted she doesn't want to be like Mom and Pop."

"Well, Mom never hesitated for a second. 'But you *are* like me and your father. You love your family, and you cherish the land. Did you think we had no curiosity about the rest of the world?'"

"Nora and I just stared at them. We'd never thought of them that way. 'But you seem so contented here,' Nora said finally."

"'Yes, and I suspect you'll find that kind of contentment some time. But the time for contentment is rarely when you're young,'

"Pop, of course, got right back to the issue at hand. He suggested we go to town and hunt up the typing teacher; see if he could help us find a school. Said Nora would probably have to work part time.

"So that's what we did. I took Nora into town the next day to see the typing teacher, and also Everett at the Post Office. He told us what he knew about getting federal jobs—Civil Service exams and the like. And then things just happened and now Nora's in France."

When he finished, Connor looked up at Pauline. "It's my fault she's over there with bombs falling on her."

"Connor, that's just plain nonsense. Nora's doing what she's always wanted to do—seeing the world and helping people. What could be more Nora than that?"

"But she'll take risks—and get hurt."

"I admire her for that."

"Me too, Pauline, but I'm scared to death for her."

"Well, my dear," she said, taking his hands and pulling him to his feet, "Nothing we can do about it, so let's go dancing."

He rose and followed her out the door, still thinking about how Nora had lost those five years he complained about too, working like a dog and hardly ever leaving the farm. At least he'd seen some really magnificent country.

He settled Pauline in the car and walked around.

"What're you all slumped over about?"

"Me?"

"Yeah. You walked around there like you'd kicked the dog and killed the baby."

"I dunno."

He started the car and headed for the dancehall.

www.ingramcontent.com/pod-product-compliance
Lightning Source LLC
Chambersburg PA
CBHW060941120726
47910CB00002B/426